ADVANCE PRAISE FOR LUCKY

"A wild and deeply satisfying rollercoaster ride through the world of a con artist with a heart of gold. Propulsive and affecting, *Lucky* is the most fun I've had reading a book in quite a while."

Taylor Jenkins Reid, *New York Times* bestselling author of *Daisy Jones & the Six*

"Stapley's gorgeous writing cuts to the bone, and her grifter heroine, both vulnerable and fierce, is driven by a genius premise. With equally compelling alternate timelines, Stapley takes readers on a gripping, heart-wrenching journey of resilience, hope, and redemption. A stunning read!"

Samantha M. Bailey, #1 bestselling author of *Woman on the Edge*

"Meet Lucky Armstrong, an unconventional heroine who is on the run from her past with a winning lottery ticket that could change her future. A story of survival, redemption, and forgiveness, *Lucky* explores the power of second chances. A riveting caper full of heart, I loved this book!"

Karma Brown, bestselling author of *Recipe for a Perfect Wife*

"A grifter on the run who wins the lottery is only the opening gambit of this high-fueled twisty tale through the life of Lucky, daughter of a con artist who seemed doomed to make her father's mistakes. Will the money save her and provide her with redemption or lead her down darker paths? You'll want to put this on your to-read list immediately."

Catherine McKenzie, *USA Today* bestselling author of *I'll Never Tell*

"With an original premise, a gutsy-yet-vulnerable heroine, dodgy villains, and bad choices galore, Marissa Stapley's highly entertaining *Lucky* is sure to wow readers. Fast-paced, skillfully crafted, and beautifully written, this book had me stay up late and get up early to find out what would happen to that winning lottery ticket. I loved it!"

Hannah Mary McKinnon, bestselling author of *Sister Dear*

"This fun romp, with deeper themes of identity, family ties, and the meaning of truth in a life built on lies, kept me greedily turning pages late into the night. Perfect for book clubs—or anyone looking for their next unputdownable read."

Colleen Oakley, *USA Today* bestselling author of *You Were There Too*

"Stapley has created a complicated woman just as magnetic and compelling for her readers as she is for the people she fleeces—and luckily, readers will only get richer by being swept away with her story of curious fortunes."

Kerry Clare, author of *Waiting for a Star to Fall*

"Stapley's novels are always filled with strong, intriguing women and *Lucky* is no exception. Lucky Armstrong is the flawed, fascinating character at the heart of this gripping novel, and as we follow the twists and turns of her adventures, we're not sure where she's going to take us—but it's a hell of a fun ride."

Elizabeth Renzetti, bestselling author of *Based on a True Story* and *Shrewed*

PRAISE FOR *THE LAST RESORT*

"Harnesses women's anger.... The story's emotional core is wrapped in a taut thriller."

Toronto Star

"Fast-paced, expertly plotted, and highly entertaining, this novel is perfect for fans of Liane Moriarty!"

Karma Brown, bestselling author of
Recipe for a Perfect Wife

"An impossible-to-put-down thrill ride of a read ... It will fascinate you, enlighten you, break your heart and mend it again."

Jennifer Robson, bestselling author of *The Gown*

"Gripping.... Stapley shows a real knack for suspense."

Publishers Weekly

"An exciting addition to the psych thriller world—with an emotionally complex twist."

Roz Nay, bestselling author of
Hurry Home and Our Little Secret

"Stapley pulls off a tale that's both spine-chilling and heartwarming."

Christina Dalcher, bestselling author of *Vox*

"Couples with secrets, people who tell lies—nothing is as it seems.... Fans of Agatha Christie will surely love this modern whodunit from the first to the very last page."

Hannah Mary McKinnon, author of *Sister Dear*

"Stapley's writing is fast-paced while still cutting deep. . . . *The Last Resort* is all of these things: a nail-biter, a page-turner, a thoughtful, powerful exploration into who we are in relationships and on our own."

Laurie Petrou, author of *Sister of Mine*

"An excellent beach read for anyone who loves romantic suspense."

Booklist

"Deeply addictive and simmering with tension, *The Last Resort* had me breathlessly turning the pages all the way through to its explosive conclusion."

Lucy Clarke, author of *The Blue*

"Stapley delivers a twisty, expertly written mystery you can sink your teeth into."

Karen Katchur, author of *River Bodies*

LUCKY

Marissa Stapley

HODDER

First published in Great Britain in 2021 by Hodder & Stoughton
An Hachette UK company

1

A CIP catalogue record for this title is available from the British Library

Paperback ISBN 978 1 399 70381 9
Trade Paperback ISBN 978 1 399 70434 2
eBook ISBN 978 1 399 70382 6

Printed and bound in Great Britain by Clays Ltd, Elcograf S.p.A.

Hodder & Stoughton policy is to use papers that are natural, renewable
and recyclable products and made from wood grown in sustainable
forests. The logging and manufacturing processes are expected to
conform to the environmental regulations of the country of origin.

Hodder & Stoughton Ltd
Carmelite House
50 Victoria Embankment
London EC4Y 0DZ

www.hodder.co.uk

This book is for my mother,
Valerie (1951–2020),
who taught me to be brave and resilient.
But not how to grift; that,
I had to research.

The world is full of trickery. But let this not blind you to what virtue there is; many persons strive for high ideals, and everywhere life is full of heroism.

—Max Ehrmann, "Desiderata"

February 1982
NEW YORK CITY

S omeone had left a baby outside the nunnery. And it was
Margaret Jean's night to listen for the door. The rest of the
sisters had their earplugs in and couldn't hear the wails that pierced
the air. But still, she stayed motionless in her bed, hoping someone
else would wake and relieve her of the drama. Sister Francine, for example, who loved to be busy. Sister Danielle, who had a solution for
everything. The baby's cries grew louder, and still no one else woke.

Margaret Jean touched the gold crucifix around her neck. She had
been at the nunnery only a few months; she was still undergoing her
aspirancy. The nuns were supposed to decide the following week if
she could become one of their order. This was the first night she had
been left in charge—a test.

She wasn't really Catholic. She had forged a baptismal certificate.
It had seemed like a brilliant con, her best one yet, to pose as a young
woman seeking to pledge her life to the church. No one would ever
look for her here; she would be safe. Except—she was expected to be
a saint. And she wasn't one.

The crying continued. It was freezing out there. The child could
die. She forced herself to stand, pull on a cardigan, and move off down
the hall, a flashlight in hand.

She pushed hard against the wind to open the front door. A little
bundle rested on the middle stair. Pink blankets. A tiny fist, curled

and shaking. *Dear God, if only this could be someone else's problem,* Margaret Jean found herself praying. This habit was as new as the one she had borrowed to wear tonight. It felt like a costume.

There was a man walking along the sidewalk toward the cathedral. He stopped and stood at the base of the steps, listening, then walked up them while Margaret Jean stood still, watching. He knelt. He said something to the baby, but Margaret Jean couldn't hear what because of the wind and the crying. He lifted the baby into his arms, and she stopped her wailing.

Margaret Jean remained as still as possible. The man looked up at her. He placed his hand on his heart. "Sister," he said. The wind died down. The habit fell back around her face and shoulders. The man moved up the stairs with the baby in his arms.

"Sister," he repeated.

She nodded. "Hello." The man was too handsome, like Cary Grant or Rock Hudson. She had met this kind of man before, had the kind of intimate knowledge of men like this that nuns were not supposed to have. The elbows of his jacket were threadbare, but his shoes were mirror-shiny. His hair was gelled so it barely moved in the wind.

"I'm John," he said. "I'm sorry you were awakened by my child."
"Your child?"

"Yes. And"—here, he raised his eyes heavenward—"thank God I found her. My wife, Gloria, has been struggling with . . . well, you know. The baby blues." There was a faint hint of an Irish lilt in his rounded vowels. "Tonight, I went out to work and when I returned she was beside herself. She told me she'd gone and left the baby somewhere. A church. I've been walking around the city all night, trying to find which. And now here she is, thank God."

"Why didn't you call the police?"

"And get my own wife arrested?" He was staring into her eyes, searching for something. She knew he wouldn't find it. "Instead, I prayed. For a miracle. And here it is! I found my child. You can go back to bed now, Sister."

Margaret Jean looked down at the baby. "Your wife should seek help," she said.

"Of course. I promise she will. But my wife deserves another chance. Don't all God's children deserve another chance, Sister?"

The way he was speaking to her, it was as if he knew her—as if he knew all about the second chances she did or did not deserve. She felt a wave of compassion for him, coming upon her as quickly as the bread delivery truck now barreling down the street, about to begin its early-morning rounds.

"I hope," she began, trying to think of the right thing to say, "that you and your family are blessed with good fortune."

The man was looking at the gold crucifix around her neck. "We could use a little help," he said. "I could sell that gold. Is there any way you could spare it, Sister . . . ?"

"Margaret Jean," she supplied.

"So we could pay for groceries," he continued. "And for formula, since my wife's in such a state her milk has dried up."

The necklace was just a prop. Real gold, but a prop nonetheless. She took it off and placed it on the baby. "It's fourteen-karat." It felt good to do good, she realized. To give rather than take.

She peered down at the baby.

"What's her name?"

A brief hesitation, but "Luciana," he said. "We named her after my mother."

Margaret Jean chose to believe him. She placed her fingers on Luciana's brow and made the sign of the cross, just as the priest had done to her hours before, during the Ash Wednesday service. "Your sins are forgiven," she said, raising her eyes to the man's.

The problem with reading the Bible too often, day after day, the way an aspiring nun was required to, was that you started to believe miracles could happen anywhere. Even in Queens. Margaret Jean imagined that she really had blessed the child, and the man. That she was protecting them and would see them both again someday. That she had done the right thing.

She bolted the door behind her and returned to her monastic cell, where she prayed for the baby and the man, prayed that they would be blessed, that they would be lucky.

PART
ONE

CHAPTER ONE

Luciana Armstrong stood in the bathroom of a gas station in Idaho, close to the Nevada border. She was wearing a white blouse, navy blazer, matching skirt, and low heels. Her hair was tied back in a neat bun. "Goodbye, Alaina," she said to her reflection—and tried to ignore the sadness. She had been sure Alaina was going to stick around.

She took off her clothes and shoved them in her handbag. Then she pulled out a minidress and a pair of stilettos. She snaked the dress over her body, smoothed down the gold-beaded material, felt a twinge of sadness as her hands passed over her flat stomach, shook out her hair. A stranger was reflected back at her now.

"Hello, Lucky," she said.

In the gas station convenience store, she roamed the aisles. A man buying cigarettes whistled at her as she tried to decide between cheese puffs or pretzels. She grabbed both and approached the register, skimming the newspaper headlines as she waited: DAY OF RECKONING ON WALL STREET; ANALYSTS PREDICT 2008 MARKET CRASH WILL BE WORST OF ALL TIME. Then a cardboard stand on the counter caught her attention: MULTI MILLIONS LOTTERY, it said. Reading it, she was ten years old again, hurtling down the I-90 to who-knows-where–next with her father. "You're the luckiest girl in the world," he had always told her. And he had always bought a lottery ticket when they stopped at a gas station rest stop like this one. "We'll never win, but we can hope," he often said. "The lottery is the greatest con of all time, kiddo. Proves our government is just like us, tricking people into thinking any dream can come true." When he said things like that it made Lucky feel better about who they were, and the things they did.

She reached the cash register. Impulsively, Lucky grabbed a lottery playslip from the stand and filled out her numbers, the same ones she had used just for fun when she was a kid: Eleven, because that was how old she had been when she had thought to have lucky numbers. Eighteen, because that was the age she couldn't wait to be at the time, thinking adulthood was going to unleash some sort of magic into her life. Forty-two, because that was how old her dad had been when she had come up with the numbers. Ninety-five, because that was the highway they were driving on that day. And seventy-seven, just because.

She handed the paper to the cashier. He printed off her lottery ticket and handed it back. "You should sign your name on that," he said. "People forget, and then their ticket gets stolen or lost. It's a big jackpot this time, three hundred and ninety million."

"I have a higher chance of being struck by lightning, *twice*, than I do of winning that jackpot," Lucky said. "It's just a dream, that's all." Then she turned, ducked her head as she walked past the security cameras and out into the parking lot. She put the ticket in her wallet and imagined herself in a beach house in Dominica, taking the ticket out once in a while and remembering her dad—before he had landed in prison.

Outside, her boyfriend, Cary, had finished filling their silver Audi's gas tank. He saw her, grinned, and mouthed the word *Damn*. She blew a kiss at him and walked toward the car, letting her hips sway. But a voice made her turn.

"Could you spare any change?"

A woman was sitting with her back against the concrete wall of the station, holding a sign that said UNEMPLOYED, BROKE, ANY-THING HELPS. Lucky took out her wallet. She emptied it of several hundred—then paused and pulled the blouse, skirt, blazer, and shoes from her bag.

"Take these," Lucky said.

"Where would I ever wear them?"

"Sell them on consignment. Or . . ." Lucky leaned down. "Use them to pretend to be someone else."

The woman blinked at her, confused. "*What?*"

"Never mind. Just . . . take care, okay?"

Cary was grinning as she walked toward him again. She got in the car and he grabbed her chin, turned her face to his, kissed her mouth. "You're looking damn hot, Mrs. . . . what did we register at the hotel as, Anderson? I think it's great that you went in there looking like an investment banker and came out looking like the girl I used to know. You never dress like this anymore. I *like*. And now I see why you wanted to go to Vegas so badly." He let go and she felt something shift between them. "But it's funny that you're always thinking you can, I don't know, redeem yourself or something by giving money out to people like her. Soon you won't feel that need anymore. Soon you'll forget all about it."

She felt suddenly irritated. "People 'like her'? And I'm not trying to redeem myself. I'm trying to help people who need help."

"Why?"

Out the window, the woman had her hand lifted in a wave, but Lucky looked away.

"Make up for the money we've stolen by acting like Robin Hood?" Cary went on. "Steal from the rich, give to the poor? It's cute, I guess." He started the car and pulled out. "But it's never going to work. We are who we are, Lucky." He had a way of digging straight down to the painful secret spots in a person's psyche. And, not for the first time recently, she felt a niggling sense of worry about this. They were moving to a remote island together. It was just going to be the two of them. They would never be able to leave.

Cary merged with the traffic on the highway and turned up the stereo. A thumping techno beat filled the car. He glanced at her and smiled, and she smiled back.

"This is going to be fun," she said to him, hoping to convince them both.

"Sure. It is. We need some fun. Blaze of glory, right?"

She opened a bag of pretzels and tilted it toward him. They were just a regular couple on a road trip, nothing to fear. "What will it be like, in Dominica, do you think? What kind of house will we live in?" It had been like a game, back when they had first met, to dream of the life they were going to build, construct a future in their minds. They hadn't had much time to dream about this next incarnation of their lives, given that they were leaving in such a rush. "Oceanfront, obviously—but, what do you think, pool or no pool?"

"Mmm?" Cary reached into the bag and grabbed a handful of pretzels, then glanced in the rearview mirror again.

"No pool," Lucky decided. "Who needs it when you have the ocean, right? And we'll get a dog—a rescue, like Betty was, and go for long walks with her on the beach every day." The words dried up as soon as she mentioned Betty. The LOST DOG signs were still posted on poles around their neighborhood in Boise. The loss of Betty was yet another ache inside her empty body.

"Do you think someone found her?" Lucky said. "Someone good?" Cary glanced at her now, before turning his attention back to the highway.

"Found who?"

"Betty." There was a lump in her throat.

"Sure. Bet she's being well taken care of right now. Don't you worry about her. Betty will land on her feet." Cary took one hand off the steering wheel and reached for Lucky's. "I know it's hard. But everything is going to be fine." His hand was clammy. He was scared, she could tell.

The truth? So was she.

September 1992

THE ADIRONDACKS, NEW YORK

Lucky worked with her father, and this meant she'd been traveling around the country for as long as she could remember. She was only ten—going on thirty, her dad would say. She'd seen a lot of the world. She knew things.

For example, Lucky already knew that money didn't just come to you; you had to chase it. Which was often exhausting. "Some people have to hustle harder than others," her father would say. "You come by your name honestly, though. You're luckier than most when it comes to money. But you still have to hone that luck. Make sure it never leaves your side. That's going to be a hard job."

For the first time, they were going to have an honest-to-goodness vacation, though. They'd recently had a run of good luck, and her father was feeling flush. He was taking her to a fancy hotel in the Adirondacks. "No work for a whole week. Just reading, relaxing, swimming, doing whatever you want."

Lucky pressed her face to the car window, then touched the gold crucifix she always wore around her neck. It had been hers since she was a baby, a gift from her long-lost mother, one of the few possessions she carried with her when they traveled, the only thing she had that was really hers.

Lucky was in the back seat, surrounded by books that had been "borrowed" from the library in the town before last. Stealing library books made Lucky feel guiltier than almost anything else, but her dad would say it was the government that paid for those books—and that the government owed them. Besides, they needed the books because she was homeschooled—"road schooled," he called it.

They sped past a sign that said WELCOME TO NEW YORK, THE EMPIRE STATE. "Hey, isn't this where I was born?" he called it.

"You were born in New York City," her father said. "Not out here in the mountains."

"But isn't this where my mother is from, though? Around here somewhere? Didn't you say that? That Gloria Devereaux was from here?"

"Did I?"

Lucky put aside the book she had been reading, *The Elegant Universe*. She didn't know that other ten-year-olds were reading Goosebumps stories, not books about string theory. She didn't know any other ten-year-olds. "Yes. You did. You came home one night from a poker game and I asked you where Gloria was from, and you said 'Adirondacks.'"

"You shouldn't ask me questions when I've been drinking too much, which I probably was after that poker game. Say, what's in that book you're reading?"

"Tell me a story about my mother," Lucky pressed. "Tell me about Gloria."

"I need to focus on the road." This was a lie; her father could drive on a freeway blindfolded.

"Come on," Lucky said. "Just tell me one tiny thing."

"I came home one night from buying you formula, and, poof, she was gone" was all her father had ever said about her mother's departure. He made it sound final, like Lucky's mother had completely disappeared—but she had to exist somewhere out there, didn't she?

When Lucky got like this, when she prodded for more information, her father's reaction was almost never good. Sometimes he got mad and told her to stop poking at old wounds. Sometimes he said it was cruel of her to bring up things that made him feel so sad. But every once in a while he'd relent and throw her a crumb.

"Why was this necklace so special to her? Why did she leave it behind for me to have? If she didn't want anything to do with me, why did she leave *anything* behind for me at all?"

Lucky thought he might not answer. But then, "She attended St. Monica's Parish," her father allowed. "That necklace was a gift from a nun who lived there."

"Parish?" Lucky repeated.

"Yeah, like a church."

Lucky had never been inside a church. "What happens?" she asked. "At church?"

More silence. Then, "There's a lot of talk about what it means to be a good person. About what God might do to you if you're bad. Where he might send you. About hell."

"Oh." Lucky frowned. She'd heard of hell but hadn't given the idea much thought. People sometimes told her father to go to hell.

She touched the necklace and gazed out the window again at the velvety-looking Adirondack Mountains coming into focus. As little as she knew about religion, about what made you good and what made you bad, she worried that she and her father were definitely bad. They lied, they stole, they snuck around. She had read enough books about heroes and villains to know which side they were on.

There were a dozen more questions she wanted to ask her father now, but perhaps she didn't really want the answers. She picked up her book again as her father tuned the car radio to the Yankees game.

"Another hour or so, kiddo. Sit back and relax. We're going to have a great week."

Eventually they approached the elegant hotel, which sat on an island attached to the mainland by a short bridge. The island was surrounded by the glittery water of Lake George.

"Nixon stayed here," her father said as they approached the Sagamore. This prompted a short lecture studded with facts. "Nixon actually did some *good things*," he concluded as he pulled the car around a circular driveway and landed it in front of a stately white building. "But it got lost in all the bad. That's usually what happens."

Lucky admired the turrets and balconies and stained-glass windows of the hotel, then turned her focused attention on the people milling about.

"Between this and all your book reading, that's school done for the day, kiddo."

Lucky barely heard him. It was a long shot, she knew, but she was still looking for her mother, searching the faces of the guests and staff. She had another clue now: Her mother had gone to church. She'd had a friend who was a nun.

A valet approached. She unrolled the window and stuck her head out. The air was fresh. This was going to be a perfect week. Lucky could feel it.

Upstairs, inside their hotel room—which had a large window with a view of the mountains, lake, and resort grounds—Lucky's father put down his battered suitcase, which was covered in stickers from all the places they'd been. He flopped down onto the bed closest to the window without taking off his shiny shoes, put his hands behind his head, sighed happily, and closed his eyes. Lucky put her smaller suitcase on the second bed, unzipped it, and began to unpack. She lifted out a yellow bathing suit and glanced at him.

"Can I go to the pool?"

"You're on vacation, Lucky. You can do whatever the hell you want to."

"What if kids my age aren't allowed at the pool by themselves?"

Her father's eyes were closed. "Then just lie about your age," he said.

Outside, Lucky wandered the hotel grounds for a while. She by-passed the crowded pool and walked down to the edge of the lake—but when she stepped in to swim, a lifeguard blew his whistle at her and shouted, "You can't swim there!"

Lucky turned and squinted. "Why not?"

The lifeguard pointed down the beach to a small area marked out by buoys. "That's the swimming area!"

Lucky walked toward the swimming area. It was crowded. She stood by the water for a moment, surveying the writhing mass of bodies, the shouting adults and shrieking children. Then she turned and headed back toward the pool. There, she sat at the edge with her legs dangling in the water, in the quietest corner she could find—which wasn't very quiet at all—and surveyed the children swimming, splashing, spitting, dunking. She watched one young boy swim to the edge and clutch the concrete, closing his eyes, rapt. A yellowish cloud bloomed in the water below him and she looked away, repulsed.

Then someone sat down beside her. It was a girl about her age with chestnut-brown hair that was as smooth and shiny as Lucky's was coarse and corkscrew wild. The girl slid her legs into the water, too, and Lucky looked down at her feet. The girl had a toe ring and it glinted in the sun.

"Isn't it ridiculous?" she said.

Lucky was startled. "Yes," she managed to reply, wanting to agree with whatever it was this girl said.

"I mean, there's this whole beautiful lake, and they expect us to swim in there." She pointed toward the beach and the tiny swimming area, then turned back to Lucky and the pool. "Or in here. No *thank you.*"

Lucky tried to size the girl up, but she wasn't used to sizing kids up. She got the sense that what you saw was what you got. "Yeah," she said. "No *thank you*. That kid over there, I think he just peed."

The girl hooted with laughter and pulled her legs out of the water. "Ew!"

Lucky pulled her legs out, too, and hugged them against herself.

"Wanna go for a walk?" the girl said. "Around the corner, the lifeguard can't see us and you can go for a proper swim." She stood and Lucky scrambled to her feet, too. "I'm Steph, by the way."

Lucky loved that name; it was on her list of favorites. "I'm Andrea," she said, which was the alias she and her father had agreed upon for this trip. "Most people call me Andi." She'd made this part up on the spot and was glad she had because Steph smiled.

"Andi. I like that," she said. "Come on. Let's go."

Steph and "Andi" stayed out until the sun started to set over the water and the mountains went from gray-green to purple-blue. "My mom will be worried," Steph said eventually. "I should get back."

"Yeah, my dad will be, too," Lucky said, even though that likely wasn't true.

"It's just you and your dad?"

Lucky nodded.

"It's just me and my mom," Steph said. She'd started to stand but she flopped back down on the sand and Lucky waited to see what she would do next. The sky above them was turning a heavy blue now.

"My dad died," Steph said.

"I'm sorry."

"Thanks. I miss him."

"How did he die?"

"Heart attack. He was really healthy—but I guess he had stress from work, or something. My mom always says if he hadn't worked so hard, he'd still be here. She cries about the money we have. She gives it away to charity, says she wishes we were poor and that he were still alive. And sometimes I forget he's dead and I look for him. Sorry. You probably don't get it."

"I do get it," Lucky said. And then she added her lie, like a matching earring. "My mom died, too." The made-up story flowed easily from her lips. She didn't even feel guilty for it, because she wanted this so badly. When she was done talking, Steph reached for her hand and squeezed. The sun was almost down now. In the sky, a star flickered on, then held. Lucky squeezed Steph's hand back; a tear slid down her cheek. She wasn't crying because she was sad, and she wasn't crying for her mother. For once, she was crying because she was happy. She had made a friend.

"All right, so let me get this straight," her father said the next night. "I'm still Virgil, but you're Andi for short. We're from Lansing. Drove here for an end-of-summer treat. Came up through Toronto for fun, went to the top of the CN Tower. Your mother died last year. A rare blood disorder. It's brilliant, Lucky. Really, it is."

"I wasn't trying to be brilliant. I was just telling you in case you talked to her. I didn't want you to mess up my story. She's my fr—"

"I was chatting with her mother earlier. Name's Darla. I arranged that the four of us are going to have dinner. Guess we're not on vacation anymore, kiddo. We've got a job now. These people are loaded. Darla was wearing a tennis bracelet at the pool, for God's sake. Still wearing her ring but, thanks to you, I know she's a widow. Anyway, we're meeting them in half an hour and we have a little more of our story to get straight. We're going to tell them you're sick, too, with the same rare hereditary blood disorder that killed your mother. That I can't afford the treatments, that coming here was a wish you had and I wanted to grant it because—well, I just don't know how long you'll live."

"Dad. Please, do we have to? Isn't the one lie enough?"

He was fixing his tie in the mirror, but now he turned to her, perplexed.

"But we're only here for the week. Then we'll move on, as we always do, and you'll never see her again. She's not your friend. This is our job! Remember, we might be flush now, but our luck is always changing. And money doesn't last forever. I spent a hell of a lot of it on this week."

Lucky hung her head. "You said we were on vacation! You said that's all it was!"

Her father sighed and sat down beside her on her bed. "When an opportunity presents itself, you have to take it, kiddo. Or someone else will. I thought I taught you that. You can't let your guard down, ever. Not even when you're having fun—*especially* when you're having fun. Now come on, get moving. Fix your hair and dry your face. We're due downstairs."

The next morning, Lucky sat at the edge of the pool and dipped her toes in. The concrete scraped at her thighs. Steph plopped down beside her and Lucky turned to look at her, trying to memorize her so she'd never forget this. Steph's hair cascaded down her shoulders. She had freckles on her nose, a crooked grin—but she wasn't smiling now.

"It's school next week," Steph said, glum, as she put her feet in the water beside Lucky's. "Summer's almost over. I can't believe it."

Lucky searched for a response, but then Steph realized something and frowned. "Sorry. You don't get to go to school. You're homeschooled. Because you're—"

In that moment, Lucky really felt it: sick. She felt ill at the idea of pretending to be sick to this person she was supposed to see as a "mark" but who she wanted to actually be able to call a friend. A real one. She felt sick all through her body, like she really did have the same rare blood disorder she had lied and said had killed the mother she had never actually met.

"I'm not sick," Lucky said. The words burned out of her throat. Was she really about to betray her father, to go against his story? They'd have to leave the hotel. Right away. She'd never see Steph again. But still. Soon she was never going to see her again anyway—and, worse, her supposed friend was going to remember Lucky, remember *this*, for the rest of her life.

"My dad just says that," Lucky continued, staring up, directly at the sun, willing it to burn her eyes blind. "I'm not sick. I'm fine. Perfectly healthy. Nothing is wrong with me."

Steph turned. She reached forward and put her hand on top of Lucky's. "Really?" she asked.

"Really," Lucky answered.

Steph paused for a moment, considering. Then she said, "It's okay."

"It's not," Lucky said, and now she was crying. "It's *not okay.*"

"I get it. You want to pretend you're fine so that you will be fine. I heard my mom on the phone with her bank. It's supposed to be a surprise, but she's going to give your dad the money he needs for those procedures. You're going to get better. Isn't that *great?*"

Lucky was seeing black spots now. "Your mom shouldn't do that—"

"Oh, Andi. It's okay, we have *lots* of money. You'll be able to go to school now. Maybe." Lucky felt tears streaming down her cheeks to her jawbone, *plop, plop,* onto her collarbones. "Maybe you'll move closer to *me,* maybe you'll move to Bellevue and we'll live near each other. I know my mom would like that. She really wants to see your dad again. And we'll go to the same school, and it will be just perfect. And maybe"—she was grasping Lucky's arm now—"our parents will get married. And we'll be *sisters.* Come on, imagine it!"

Lucky looked away from the sun, blinked over and over until

the world came back into focus, stared into the pool water, at their toes beneath it, side by side. Steph had given her a toe ring too; their matching rings glinted in the waves. Sister feet.

"I guess you never know," Lucky said, lifting her hand away from Steph's to rub at her cheeks until they were dry. But Steph reached up and grabbed her hand again.

"I know," she said. "I know you're going to be just fine. One day, it's going to be as if this rare disease you have just . . . disappeared."

"Yes, one day," Lucky said. "That's exactly what it's going to be like."

CHAPTER TWO

Deep inside the Bellagio, Lucky sought out Cary; he was leaning against a distant bar, watching. She winked at him, then looked back down at her cards. The opponent to her left, a guy so young he had pimples on his chin, called the bet in their game of Texas Hold'em.

"Two hundred."

She pretended to be thinking hard. The sounds of the casino rose around her: music, clinking glassware, laughter, a shout.

"I raise to three hundred," she replied. The pimply kid barely suppressed a laugh.

"Ma'am, that's an illegal raise," the dealer said. "You have to double the bet."

"Right. Silly me! So I double it, then."

"Four hundred to you, ma'am?"

"That's right."

The dealer turned to the nondescript middle-aged man on Lucky's right. He was wearing a wedding ring but had been ogling her since she sat down, making no secret of it. He raised, too, then tried to get a glimpse down the neckline of her dress. Lucky pretended to be so dim she didn't notice. The fourth player, a man in a too-baggy suit, folded. So did the pimply kid.

"I fold, too, I guess," Lucky said, tossing her red curls over her shoulder. She could feel Cary still watching from across the room. She allowed herself to meet his eyes again; one corner of her mouth rose in a secret smile. When she had her new cards she nestled them against her cleavage, blocking the view of the middle-aged man beside her. Cary laughed. This felt good. She hoped Cary felt it, too. It was why she had wanted to come here: so they could both find a way back to each other before they took off.

"Ma'am? Cards on the table, please."

"Oops. Sorry. Forgot that rule, too." Lucky laid her cards flat and smiled at the man.

The man with the baggy suit called pre-flop. In the past hour he'd raised only once. It meant he had a big card—not that it changed anything. When it was her turn, she raised to six hundred, then nodded, as if proud of herself for finally getting the hang of things.

"Twenty-five hundred," said the pimply kid.

The middle-aged man called the pimply kid's bet, and so did the man in the baggy suit.

"I'm all in," Lucky said, looking over at Cary. But he was talking to a man at the bar, their heads bent together, their expressions intense. A tingling of fear, a whisper in her ear. *Who is that?*

"Excuse me? Hello?" The pimply kid was leaning in, eyes narrowed. "Are you bluffing?"

She stared back at him wide-eyed, her hands clasped in front of her. "I can't answer that, of course."

He shrugged. "I fold," he said. The other two players folded, too. The dealer nodded at Lucky and slid the chips—nine thousand dollars' worth—toward her. The pot was hers. Cary was alone again, leaning against the bar, staring off into the distance.

"All right," said the pimply kid. "Show us your aces, then, if you weren't bluffing."

"I never said I wasn't bluffing." Lucky stood, flipping her cards as she did. They were terrible: a five of spades, a ten of diamonds. She looked down at her winnings, then shoved half toward the dealer as a tip—while he blinked in disbelief—and the rest over to the pimply kid. "Have fun. That was great. Thanks, y'all." The players stared, astonished, as she turned and made her way toward the bar.

"Hey, you should have kept those chips," Cary said when she arrived at his side. "Looks like you won a lot."

"But why? We're leaving tomorrow. We have enough money in our Dominica account. I'd have to show ID to cash these in. Plus, it was just for fun. The looks on their faces! Totally worth it."

His expression was hard to read. It was, she realized with a sinking feeling, his poker face.

"Are you okay?" she said. "Who was that you were talking to?"

"Oh, just some guy wanting to know where the bathroom was," Cary said. He stepped closer. Now he was looking at her the way he had when they had first met, back when his gaze had made her feel like she was one of the wonders of the world. "I love you so much, you know that? You make everything fun. Come on." He pulled her toward the bar. "You're right. We're rich. And we need to celebrate. Celebrate life. Bottle of '85 Dom, please," he said to the bartender.

"Cary, no, it's getting late, and we have an early flight—"

"So we won't go to bed, then," Cary said with a laugh. "You said you wanted to have the best night of your life before we left, and the night is still young." He reached for the bottle while she reached for him.

"I just meant I don't think we'll finish it. We have to wake up so early to get to the airport. I thought we'd just go back up to the room and . . ." She kissed him and he turned his attention away from the bar.

"We have plenty of time for that, Lu. Tomorrow, we run away. Tonight, it's a party. Like it's our last night on earth." He planted one more kiss on her lips. As the bartender popped the champagne cork, Cary said to her, "Repeat after me: I just want to party all night."

She accepted her glass. "I just want to party."

"All night."

"All night," she repeated dutifully.

He grabbed the bottle and strode across the casino. They reached the exit and the security guard called out, "Hey, you can't take that bottle—" but Cary handed him a hundred-dollar bill without breaking stride. Lucky took off her stilettos and dangled them from her fingers as she ran to catch up with him at the elevator bank.

He pulled a card out of his pocket. It said STAFF ONLY. When they got on the elevator, he used it to access a restricted floor.

"Where did you . . . Oh, never mind."

"That's right, babe. You don't need to know."

He took her hand as the elevator doors opened, pulled her down a hallway, to a door. It led to a rooftop with a staggering view of the city below.

Cary walked to the edge and raised his arms, the bottle in one hand, his glass in the other.

"Be careful," she said.

Gently, Lucky tried pulling him back, but he held his body rigid.

Finally he stepped back, took her in his arms.

"Are you ready to have an unforgettable night with me?"

"It's already been pretty unforgettable. I mean, I bluffed out all those guys—"

He refilled her glass. "I want you to forget about everything else and just *be* with me. Fall in love with me again, Lucky. Tell me you love me, and will love me, no matter what."

"Of course."

"Always? No matter what?"

"Cary, what's going on with you?"

"Nothing. I'm okay. This is just . . . I can't believe we're doing this."

"But we are. There's no going back."

He lifted his glass and tapped it against hers. "No going back," he said.

They turned and faced the skyline. Far below, the lights of Las Vegas spilled out across the ground like jewels from an upended box, the glitter ending abruptly at the dark edge of the desert. She looked down at it and breathed deep; her fear became excitement. Something stirred inside her that felt like hope—the kind of hope a lottery ticket held just before you checked its numbers. Cary took her hand and led her down into the dark and steaming Las Vegas night that was suddenly just beginning.

I t was done. Lucky and her father left the Sagamore Hotel a day before they had said they were going to, and didn't say goodbye to Steph or her mother. The money order was in John's shirt pocket. Lucky could see it. She tucked her nose back into her copy of *The Elegant Universe* so she wouldn't have to talk to him, so she could pretend she lived in a different world, maybe even a different galaxy. They pulled up outside a bank. He went inside, and when he came out, he had a spring in his step and a thick envelope of cash in his hand. He locked the envelope in the glove compartment.

"We're really rolling in it now, kiddo," he said.

She didn't respond.

"Aw, come on. You're still sulking?"

More silence.

"All right. Well, I have something that might cheer you up."

He drove an hour before pulling to the side of the road. She could see water glimmering behind a line of trees.

"Behold, Chapel Pond," he said when they got out of the car. But it didn't look like any pond she had ever seen. It looked more like a lake, and was surrounded by cliffs that were dotted with climbers. Lucky peered up at them. How could you be that brave? The climbers moved ant-like up the rock slabs while falcons and hawks dove and swept around them.

"You can swim here," her father said, drawing her attention back to the water. "It's cold and fresh and perfect. And see? None of them bobbles you hate."

"Buoys," Lucky said, miserable, angry with him, and yet—he was right. It was perfect here. Her father was taking off his shirt, revealing his lanky frame. Women thought he was handsome, like a movie star. Steph's mom had felt that way, which was why he had been able to charm her so easily and take her money.

"This is today's classroom," her father said now. "You couldn't ask for anything better, Luciana." He didn't often call her that.

"She'll hardly miss the money," he had muttered the night before as they fell asleep, talking to her or to himself, she wasn't sure. "Stephanie's dad had money, and there was quite the life insurance plan, too." But the money wasn't the point. Her father had pretended to give Steph's mother something: he had pretended to give her love. She *was* going to miss *that*. Lucky knew it.

He pointed up at the climbers. "Some of the world's greatest have climbed those slabs," he said, drawing from a pool of random knowledge deeper than the glacial pond itself. It always amazed Lucky, all the things he knew. Even then, as sad and angry as she was, she drew toward him to listen.

"There was a fire here once," her father said. "A poet described it as 'Dante's Inferno.' I read that somewhere. The fire was so hot it made the rocks break off and fall into the pond. Picture it. Sizzling and steaming as they hit the water. A lake of fire."

Lucky looked up at the climbers and imagined the fire, centuries ago, turning those cool-looking rocks into lava.

"And now, look at it," her father was saying. "All right again. Like the fire never happened. The world's like that. What matters in one moment, it doesn't matter the next. Things that fall apart eventually come back together again. Everything passes. You can be sure of that."

"Maybe we could be like that, too," Lucky said. "Maybe we could change. What if we put a down payment on a house, settled down a bit, with all the money Steph's mom gave us?"

"Maybe, kiddo."

The water was clear at the sandy shore and black as a chalkboard in the depths. It was mirrorlike around the far edges, and Lucky knew she wanted to swim out there and sit on a rock she could see poking above the surface of the pond like a high table. She could sun herself like a turtle and try to forget.

"Ready?" her father said. She nodded and followed him as he bounded down the beach, past a bleached-out tree skeleton that had toppled sideways in the sand. She plunged in; the water was the perfect kind of cold. She swam the way she had wanted to all week at the Sagamore. She swam toward the rock, going underwater for as long as she could stand, then surfacing and pulling in big gasps of air before diving back down. When she reached the rock, she found it was steeper than it had looked from afar. With determination, she pulled herself up to the top of it, her arms shaking with the effort.

Her father was already waiting for her there. He offered her a hand up at the last possible moment. "Good job, Lucky," he said. "Excellent work. I'm proud of you."

"Don't," she said, suddenly ashamed all over again. She moved away from him, preparing to dive into the water again and swim to shore, but he held her back.

"I'm sorry," he said. "I know it wasn't easy for you to give up something you really wanted, for us. I'm sorry it hurt you. I wish the world were a different place, but it isn't. The odds are stacked against us and we have to grab what we can, *when* we can—even if it doesn't always feel like the right thing to do. This was a real break for us, kid. Money like this means we can indeed start chasing after some of our dreams and not worry about small-time stuff for a while. And it was all because you sacrificed for it. That's why I'm proud of you—not because you're a good con artist, but because you did a hard thing. I love you, kiddo."

She was looking up as she listened to him speak, watching a climber reach the top of a ledge. Once he had made it, he stood on the edge and surveyed his surroundings. When he looked down into that pond, what did he see? Just a normal father and daughter, that was what. Two people who might soon swim to shore, get into their car, and head to their normal house and their normal life.

"I'm doing the best I can on my own," her father was saying.

"Oh, Dad. I know you are. It's okay." She turned to him.

"You're all I've got, you know."

"You're all I've got, too. Don't be sad. I'm sorry."

He reached for her and they hugged, and she tried not to think about how *she* was the one apologizing to him. Somehow, the tables were always turning.

"You're tough, Lucky. You can handle anything."

He was right: she was tough. The odds couldn't stay stacked against her forever. And when they changed, she'd truly be the luckiest girl in the world.

CHAPTER THREE

Lucky stretched across the king-size bed and ran her hands over its silky sheets, searching for Cary's warm skin. She lifted her chin and arched her back. "Morning, babe . . ."

No answer.

She opened her eyes. She was alone in the bed. She caught her reflection in the mirror on the wall: her hair was down her face. Last night's mascara was making its way down her face. She didn't look like a person who belonged in a suite at the Bellagio; she looked like she'd crawled out of a dumpster. A wave of nausea hit. Way too much champagne last night.

"Cary?"

Silence.

They had set their phone alarms for four o'clock in the morning so they could be at the airport by five. Hadn't they? Lucky rubbed her forehead, then her eyes. When they'd returned to the hotel after their night out, there had been a man in the lobby, the same one who had been talking to Cary at the bar in the casino.

"Who *is* that?" Lucky had slurred. Had Cary said something about the man being his new friend? If he had, in her champagne-buzzed state, nothing had seemed unusual about that.

"Go upstairs," she hazily remembered him whispering in her ear. "Now. And only open the door if it's me. Get our bags ready to go, then close your eyes for a few minutes. I'll be back soon, I swear."

She had passed out on the bed, expecting he would wake her when he came back up.

Now there was sunshine pouring through the crack between the curtains. The clock on the nightstand said it was 10:23. She was supposed to be on a plane right now. Where was he?

"Hello?"

She listened for the shower: nothing.

Maybe their flight was delayed. Maybe he was getting coffee and breakfast. She walked into the sitting room. His suitcase was still there beside hers by the door. She picked up her phone to try his number.

His phone went straight to voicemail.

Her stomach roiled again. She retched as she ran to the bathroom, barely making it before she was sick. What was in that champagne? Had Cary—

No. He wouldn't. Not Cary. Not to her. This was just a hangover.

Eventually she lifted herself from the cool marble floor. She tried his phone again but it was still off. She turned on the television and switched it to the news channel so she could double-check the time: 10:45 now.

". . . David Ferguson and Alaina Cadence," the newscaster was saying, using the names they had gone by in Idaho. "Wanted for bilking dozens of senior citizens living in Boise out of savings, and laundering money. They were posing as an accountant and a restaurateur and are suspected to have already moved large sums to overseas bank accounts before fleeing. Retirement funds have been emptied out, lives have been ruined—and now the police have announced there are suspected connections to organized crime . . ."

She turned. Her face was on the television. Cary's face was there, too. WANTED FOR FRAUD, EMBEZZLEMENT, RACKETEERING, the news banner below their faces read.

Her panic rose as she listened to the newscasters speak. Video footage showed news vans outside their house in Boise. She stepped closer. Why were they talking so much about seniors? It was a lie. It had only been the affluent, not the elderly. That's what she and Cary had agreed on. That was what her father had always taught her: steal from the rich, give to the poor—yes, fine, a little like Robin Hood. What was so bad about taking from people who had so much more than they needed? The anchor on-screen kept talking, describing it all wrong. Lucky hadn't done those things—at least, not all of them. Not racketeering, either.

Cary. What did you do?

Lucky turned the television off. She walked to the safe and peered inside. He hadn't taken his passport, which meant he'd had another alias lined up, other forms of identification she'd never be able to guess. It meant he had been planning this for months, had never had any intention of escaping to Dominica with her, had always planned to leave her to atone for all this by herself.

"No!"

Her voice in the empty room was a bitter, lonely sound. She sank onto the bed and put her face in her hands. She was just as bad as all the marks her father had told her to keep an eye out for over the years. The ones who were easy to scam because if offered love, or friendship, or a good sob story, they willfully blinded themselves, they chose to trust. "Blind trust makes the world go 'round, kid," her father would say. "And when it comes around to you, you grab that brass ring. Take what you can."

Apparently Cary had been given that same advice. And she shouldn't have been as surprised as she was.

You have to run, Lucky. You can't just sit here, waiting to be caught.

She stood and went to her suitcase, opened it, dug down, searched until her hand found the zippered pouch: inside it was her cache of fake IDs, a box of hair dye, and a pair of scissors.

The lottery ticket was there, too, the one she had bought the day before, what felt like a lifetime ago. As she held the ticket up, the hope of it bubbled inside her for just a second. *What if?*

But that was just a dream. Nothing could get her out of this. She tossed it on the floor and went into the bathroom with the dye and scissors, where she began to hack away at her distinctive red curls, forcing her mind to go blank so she could fill it with the information she would need to develop a new identity and start running.

"Bonnie Skinner," she said to the mirror. The name was from a byline she'd seen in *Gambling Insider*, one of the magazines that had been fanned across the bar when she and Cary had arrived in their suite the day before. "Bonnie," she repeated, heading out to the bar to check the masthead. It was printed in Phoenix, which was where she was now from. Bonnie was a freelance writer, here on a thrilling business trip that was a far cry from her ordinary life as a mother of two.

She shoved her shorn curls into a pillowcase and applied the dye to her remaining locks. After she rinsed it, her now-brown hair dried in curls close to her head, like an older woman's style. Perfect. She moved through the room, throwing clothes in a backpack and gathering other items: bills, change, the lottery ticket she had abandoned on the floor. She put those in her wallet, and searched the room for any more bills and change she could find. She put their passports and her phone into the pillowcase with her cut hair and tied it shut, then grabbed her backpack and headed for the door.

Never look back, her father used to say when they would leave a place behind. But she couldn't help herself: she turned, she looked. It was a disaster. Dye-stained towels, a broken glass, empty bottles on the floor. She thought of the maid who was going to have to deal with this mess, maybe even lose wages while being interviewed by police. She took a few twentys out of her wallet and left them on top of a pillow. The door slammed behind her, and Lucky was gone.

Haircut time," Lucky's father said, waking her in the middle of the night. He was holding the scissors from their sewing kit, the one that had belonged to his mother, he had told her, with its rattan exterior and the red and white roses woven over the surface.

"What?" Lucky mumbled, turning her face away from him and burying it in the musty-smelling pillow. They were staying in a rooming house, a ramshackle log cabin at the edge of the North Maine Woods.

"You've got to cut your hair off," he said matter-of-factly. "And then we have to get out of here. Come on." She sat up and faced him. She could smell whiskey and cigar smoke on him. Her heart plummeted.

"Why? I thought we were staying here for a while."

"Yeah, well, we can't. I faked a wire transfer to pay for this place and I have a feeling the jig is about to be up. And also . . . I played a game of blackjack tonight with the wrong people."

"Dad."

His hangdog expression was so familiar. "Lost the rest of the money, and then some," he said, as if she didn't already know that. "We have to leave before they come looking for what I owe."

"I told you not to—"

"And I told you there was no other choice. I had to try to earn back some of what we lost after we were robbed. But I failed."

This was the unfortunate reality for people like them: You had to carry cash, you couldn't have a bank account; and when you traveled with cash, you had to decide whether to carry it all with you or leave it in your room. Sometimes you trusted the wrong person, or sometimes, someone figured you out and the next thing you knew, your money was gone. Or sometimes, it was just a fluke. They'd been robbed before, but never this much. Mostly because they'd never had this much.

"I don't want to cut my hair. I just want to sleep!"

"Please don't give me a hard time about this," he said. "I'm just as upset as you are."

She squeezed her eyes shut. "No, you aren't. No one is asking you to cut off your hair."

"It's just *hair*."

A mother would understand that it was not just hair. A mother would understand that Lucky was getting to the age where she looked at herself a little longer in the mirror, where she saw the styles the other girls were putting their hair into and tried to do the same.

"Come on. You're a little young still for preteen histrionics."

She tossed the covers to the floor and glared at him. "Am I? Because when you always tell me I'm basically a grown-up! Seems to me I should be able to act however the hell I want!"

He sighed and looked at her sadly, and this just made her angrier.

"We simply have no choice. We have to go back in."

"Back in" meant away from the border towns. Back to the major cities, where the money was a little easier to come by. They always got so close. "Once we get to Canada, we'll lead an honest life," he would tell her. But he didn't know what honest meant.

Lucky wanted to scream; she wanted to cry. Lately she'd been feeling this way more and more. Like the world didn't make sense—like *her* world didn't make sense. No other kids lived like this. She knew it. And she was done.

She tried all her tricks to get the tears to stop threatening, but nothing worked. One trickled down her left cheek. And while she was distracted by that, her father grabbed a hank of her long, curly, waving flag of hair, and *snip*—it was lying there like a dead animal on the floor. "Was that so bad? Easy-peasy."

She jumped from the bed. "How dare you?" she shouted, and he flinched.

"Keep it down, for heaven's sake! I told you, we're in trouble."

"We're always in trouble. Always, always, always!"

He shrugged, because there was nothing to say to that. They were always in trouble because they *were* trouble.

She glanced at the door then. There was a tingling in her fingers and in her bare toes, and there was that word singing through her head. *Run*. She thought of the vast forest that started just behind the rooming house, how cool and green the mossy floor of the woods would feel on her feet. She could eat berries and bark to survive. She could hide in a tree, and he'd never find her.

Run, run, run. She turned, she opened the door, and she ran before her father realized what she was doing. She would do it all by herself. She would go to Canada. She didn't need anyone. Least of all him.

CHAPTER FOUR

Lucky took the stairs, all twenty flights down, and exited the Bellagio through a back door into the heat of the Las Vegas morning. She found a dumpster and disposed of the bag containing her hair and cell phone, and the passports. She had flushed her SIM card down the toilet upstairs.

She pressed her large sunglasses against her face, hitched up her backpack, and walked out onto the sidewalk, into the teeming mass of tourists on the Vegas strip. She ducked into a shop and browsed the T-shirts, found a pink one that said *Welcome to Fabulous Las Vegas* and a matching baseball cap.

"Do you have a changing room I could use?"

She closed the door, ripped the tags off a hot pink belt bag, and put it in her backpack.

Next, she went to a Duane Reade, bought rust-brown lipstick, the wrong shade of foundation, and mouse-gray eye shadow.

Then she found a coffee shop bathroom, where she layered the makeup on, smudging a little lipstick on her teeth. After, as she walked down the strip again, she felt her body tighten and her muscles coil defensively. She couldn't help but brace herself. For someone to start shouting her other name. For a firm hand to clamp down on her shoulder and tell her she was under arrest.

Eventually, she reached her destination: she was at the Bellagio again. As she walked through the ornate front doors and toward the casino's security, as the sounds of the slot machines grew louder and the air grew still and cool instead of desert dry, as she thought of the young pimply poker player from the night before and the new strategy she would employ to connive him, she felt her fear give way to anticipation. It rose through her body like fizz in a champagne flute and curdled her stomach.

She headed over to the bar, where she ordered a diet cola on the rocks with lime. "No rum, no rye, no vodka?" the bartender asked, one eyebrow raised.

"No, thank you," Bonnie Skinner said. "I abstain from liquor. I'm just parched, though, from this desert heat, except too much soda gives me the—" She patted her belly and grimaced; the bartender looked away. "So I like it in the little glasses." The bartender started polishing snifters, and she smiled down at the bar top. She'd done it; she'd managed to turn herself into a woman people barely noticed.

Lucky wandered away from the bar and through the slots area, her drink in hand, listening to the endless barrage of money going in and money coming out. The house always won; she knew that. But it wasn't the house she was interested in.

She kept moving, pursing her lips and squinting at different machines as if trying to decide on the right one for her, but not landing on one. The sound of the slot machines was an endless, swirling *ka-ching*. She walked toward the green-clad tables for blackjack, roulette, craps, baccarat, and finally poker, where she'd been the night before. She stopped when she reached that last table. There was a rail around it, a table in the middle, penned in. She leaned against the rail. Four men were playing the game. As she approached, one of them stood, shook his head in frustration, and left. Two of the remaining men—one late-middle-aged, the other one younger, with greasy black hair in a ponytail—were hunched over their cards as if their lives depended on it.

The third player was the person Lucky was looking for—the pimply kid from the night before, still wearing the same clothes. She'd expected she might have to wait around for him for a while, but here he was, looking like he hadn't slept yet. He sat in the same relaxed position she remembered, hands folded over his cards. He leaned forward and raised. The two men at the table met his bet. The black-haired man raised, the middle-aged man folded, and the pimply young man smiled. Then he touched a medallion around his neck. She did something she had noticed the night before, too: he touched a medallion around his neck. She peered at it, but from this distance she was unable to tell what was engraved on it.

"All in," he said.

Players fell in and out over the next hour. The kid won every time. Lucky leaned against the rail, pretending to be rapt.

Eventually the kid checked his watch. "Time for my afternoon siesta," he said to the dealer, sliding chips across the table as a tip. Lucky counted them: seven.

"Thank you, sir," the dealer said, putting his tip under the table.

As the young man walked away, Lucky caught up, then fell into step beside him. He didn't seem to notice her at first, or perhaps he was trying to ignore her. "Well, *that* was fun," she said. "It's on my bucket list, you know: to play a few hands of poker at the Bellagio with one of the greats. And you—you're *great* at the game. But, alas, I was too nervous to buy in. I'm still learning. Researchin'."

Now he was looking directly at her, and she could see a flash of boyish pride in his eyes. What she did not see was any hint that he recognized her. Good.

"You been playing long?"

"A while," he said.

"Like, maybe since birth?"

He turned toward the exit. "Uh, yeah, something like that," he said. "Anyway, thanks. And bye."

He was speeding away from her, but she caught up. "I'm a writer," she said. "A reporter for *Gambling Insider*."

This made him stop walking. "Oh?"

"I'm writing an article about the new up-and-comers in the game. People like you. The young, exciting, fresh faces of this country's gambling scene. I'd love to interview you, Mr. . . . ?"

"Gibson," he said. "Jeremy."

"Yes, I was just going to say that! Of course I already know who you are. Everybody does. Am I ever glad I got to watch you play. The thing is, I'm on the red-eye out of here tonight. So if I'm going to interview you for the feature, it has to be now . . ."

"Okay. Sure," he said, taking his hands out of his pockets. "Why not?"

"Great. Do you want to get a coffee?"

"Nah. Let's go up to my suite. I have a postgame routine and I always have to stick to it." He veered off toward the elevator and she kept up, the feeling of being right about a mark ferrying her along in its triumphant current. From the moment she'd seen him the day before, she'd known what an easy mark he could be. It wasn't money he wanted, not exactly. It was praise and recognition for being able to do something no one else could do. What he didn't realize was that people did what he did all the time.

"Wow," she said when they walked through the door—on the seventh floor, suite 717. It was the exact same type of suite she had vacated just that morning but she still said, "I mean, *wow, wow, and holy moly*."

She grabbed the branded notebook and pen sitting on the little writing desk near the front door. "Okay, so let's start at the beginning. How does everyone in your family feel about being related to a poker star?"

But he wasn't paying attention to her. He had clicked on the television to CNN. It was a replay of Hillary Clinton standing on a stage, hands held high in victory after winning the Kentucky primary. "She'll never be president," Jeremy said. "No one wants a chick as president during a financial crisis. What do women know about money?"

"Well, it's 2008. Women these days——"

He talked over her. "And look at that one. That woman DA, in Manhattan. She's always on TV. The media freaking loves her, and why? Because she's a *chick*?" Lucky caught a glimpse of the woman he was disparaging, saw red hair and an earnest expression. She looked familiar. Lucky must have seen her on TV before. Jeremy was still talking and she had to focus. "What did you ask me before? About my parents? They hate this, what I do. They don't understand it. My father thinks I should be back home in New York, getting all set up to run the family business, but that's not the life for me. You know?"

She swallowed and smiled sweetly. "My parents wanted me to be a nurse, but I always wanted to be a writer, so I went for it. You want something extraordinary, I get it. Because you *are* extraordinary. When you sit at a poker table, it's like magic. I saw it. *Everyone* saw it."

"Yeah," Jeremy said, nodding along to the story she was weaving. He walked over to the bar and ran his hand along it. "Want anything? A cocktail? Anything at all?"

"You go ahead."

He opened the bar fridge and took out a Coke, cracked the can open, and chugged half of it. Then he extended his arm as if he were a king displaying his domain. "You're lucky you ran into me," he said. He put the can down on the bar top. The newscasters had now started talking about the Multi Millions lottery jackpot, about how the winner hadn't yet come forward, but he clicked it off. "I'm going to make this the most interesting article your magazine has ever published. Hey, you have to see this bathroom. Come on." He walked ahead of her, still talking loudly, his words echoing off the marble walls of a bathroom she already knew well. As she followed him, she passed the bar, where he had emptied his pockets when they entered the room. There were a few bills, coins, errant poker chips—and his key card. In one fluid movement, she switched her suite key with his and continued into the next room.

"It really is incredible," she said. "Look at this place. Wow! This bathroom alone is the size of my room! I've never seen anything like it." They were standing in the middle of the bathroom; their faces were reflected in dozens of mirrors, an endless line of Bonnie Skinners and Jeremy Gibsons.

"There's something familiar about you," Jeremy said out of nowhere. He was watching her many reflections in the mirror, too. Her heart seemed to seize in her chest for a moment, but she kept smiling. Her cheeks were starting to hurt; she had been smiling so hard, but she kept doing it. "Your eyes . . ." he said, and she wished she'd been able to find somewhere to buy colored contacts to disguise her distinctive light green eyes. She'd do that as soon as she got out of here.

"Oh, I get that all the time," she said. "I have one of those faces. Familiar like."

"Yeah, I guess," he said, and wandered out of the bathroom again while she stood and stared at her many reflections, waiting for her heart to start beating at a normal pace again.

Then she came back out, her notepad and pen at the ready. "Tell me more," she said. "I'm fascinated. I could listen to you talk about your life all day. Now, you mentioned your postgame ritual. Tell me more about that. What are the things you absolutely must do to guarantee you have a great game?"

Jeremy sat on the couch and crossed his legs. "Interesting question," he said as she settled down in a chair across from him and began to scribble down his answers.

He talked about himself for hours, while "Bonnie" dutifully

transcribed. On the note paper, she revealed him slowly, like a sketch. He was superstitious, never played a game without his Saint Cajetan medal around his neck—Cajetan, he told her, was the patron saint of good fortune, and the luckiest day of all. Plus, his feast day was on the seventh of August. "I know it sounds cheesy, the whole 'lucky number seven' thing, but I have to tell you, it's worked for me. I always stay on the seventh floor, you see, and my room number always has to have at least one number seven in it. And they accommodate me, of course, because I spend so much money here. I can have whatever I want."

Finally, he yawned and rubbed his eyes, which were bleary and red. "I really need a nap," he said. "I always sleep a few hours during the day, and then I'm back at it again."

"How many hours do you sleep, usually? For the rest of the afternoon, into the evening, or . . . ?"

"No way. An hour or two is all I need. I'm a really deep sleeper. Then a Red Bull, and I'm off."

"I need to get back to my room and pack for the trip home, anyway. Thank you, so much, for your time. I'll mail you copies of the magazine, here, to your attention, when it's printed next month."

Instead of heading to the elevators, she ducked into the ice room down the hall and waited. Twenty-five minutes later, she returned to his room. She had her story ready, in case he woke up: that they'd accidentally switched room keys, and she was just trying to return his to him without disturbing a genius who needed his rest.

She could hear him snoring in the bedroom. There were still bills and chips scattered carelessly on the bar. She took a few of them, but made sure it wasn't too many. She didn't want him to notice anything amiss. Then she moved into the bedroom and opened the closet. Another loud snore, and then his breathing became quiet and even again. The safe had a four-digit code, and she got it on her first try: 7777. Jeremy was a predictable guy.

There was at least twenty grand in the safe. She could take it all, but he'd call the police and describe her. She didn't need that. So she only took a thousand. He might notice that, but she doubted it.

She was back out in the front room again. She switched the key cards and left. The door barely made a sound as she closed it.

October 1992
NORTH MAINE WOODS

Lucky ran as fast as she could, down the stairs and out the front door of the rooming house. She ran through the yard, hopped the fence, and crashed through the woods behind it. The rooming house smelled of onions and lard; the woods smelled like moss and pine. She inhaled it all in gasping breaths. *Run, run.* She didn't stop, not even when her feet felt like they were being shredded on the forest floor and her chest felt like it was going to explode. She kept going until she couldn't anymore.

Then she fell to her knees, stayed on all fours looking down at the carpet of moss, sticks, rocks, and pine needles, then up at the darkness through the tops of the stately trees that crowded around her. There was a stump a few feet ahead. She crawled to that and sat. As her heartbeat returned to normal, other sounds crept in: the *chirp-chirp-chirp* of a nearby cricket, the *hooo-oo-ooh* of an owl, the flutter of wings, a rustle in the greenery that made her turn, wary, but then a vole emerged and looked at her quizzically before darting back into the brush. She relaxed again, put her elbow on her knee and her chin on her palm. "What now, Lucky?" she said.

It was cold. Her feet, which had at first stung from the flight across the forest floor, now stung from the cold of the fall night, and she wasn't wearing anything but a nightgown. What had she been think-ing? The truth was, she hadn't been thinking at all. She lifted a hand to touch her hair, the hair that had caused so much trouble with her father, and the beginnings of panic stirred in her stomach and chest. Should she just head back the way she had come? Which way, exactly, had she come, though? She remembered taking a few twists and turns, doing just about anything to lose him. And now she had. But in the process, had she lost herself, too?

She closed her eyes and then opened them a few seconds later. Something was in front of her. It had skulked out from the brush.

Lucky gasped.

A cat, and a big one. It crouched and emitted a low hiss. She wanted to scream and run. Instead, she leveled her eyes at it and forced herself to stare it down. She searched her mind for a solution and remembered camping out with her father once near the Rocky Mountains. In the morning they'd taken their garbage to the dump and there had been bears, brown and hulking, down in the pit. Lucky had been terrified, but her father had assured her the bears weren't going to hurt them as long as they held hands and made themselves look as big as possible as they walked backward away from the pit.

On shaky legs, Lucky stood atop the stump and drew herself up to her not-very-considerable full height. "Listen," she said to the lynx—for that was what it was, although she didn't know it. "I am *bad news.* If you eat me, you are going to drop dead immediately. Do you know who I am? I am Luciana Armstrong. You see this hair?" She lifted a red lock. "Redheads are deadly to all animals. Especially cats."

The lynx didn't move.

Lucky stepped off the stump and backed away, still admonishing the animal in her firmest, surest voice. "You just . . . you just watch out, okay?" The lynx watched her for another moment, then turned and disappeared into the brush. She kept backing up, afraid to turn. When she bumped up against a warm, moving thing, she screamed.

"It's just me! It's just your dad! Lucky, thank goodness! I ran as fast as I could, but I couldn't find you."

She'd never heard her father sound scared. She'd been livid with him before, but now she pressed her face into his chest and smelled his familiar scent: those vanilla cigarillos he liked to smoke, and a subtle spicy aftershave, and the onions from the rooming house, and just him, the familiar scent of the only parent she had ever known. She stayed that way, with her head bowed into his chest, for a long moment before looking up at him. How could she ever have believed she'd be fine on her own?

"There's something out there," she began, her voice wavering now. "A big, scary cat."

"I know that, kiddo. I saw you, standing on that stump, giving that lynx what-for. And then—well, you saw it! That big cat just took right off. And do you know why?"

Lucky's head was still swimming with panic, so she didn't know how to answer.

"Because it's like I always said. You're more than lucky. You're not like other kids at all, not like other people. You have special powers. You're magic. You know that, right?" Her father crouched down and lifted her onto his shoulders. "Nothing can hurt us, Lucky! Not as long as we're together. You understand that? But we have to stay together."

She felt relief as the edge of the woods came into her line of vision, and the trees began to thin out. Soon they were back on the path she had taken into the woods in the first place, and the log-cabin-style rooming house was near.

Her father set her down just outside the back gate, which was swinging open, blowing gently in the night breeze. "We need to stick together. You understand? Just because you're special doesn't mean you're ready to go off on your own. You still have a lot to learn."

"I understand, Dad."

"And besides, we're all we've got. You and me. I'm the only person you can trust." He walked ahead of her, through the gate and into the house. She ran to keep up so she wouldn't be left alone outside.

"Wash the dirt from your feet and warm up. I'll make us something to eat," he said when they were back inside.

Later, she came out of the bath, her hair wet and combed down her back. She picked the scissors up from the table and cut the rest of her hair off herself.

CHAPTER FIVE

The tour bus rumbled down the Nevada desert highway and Lucky hummed to herself as she looked out the window. She had recently read an article about how singing and humming helped with anxiety, but it wasn't helping hers.

She lifted her sunglasses and rubbed her eyes, which were bleary from staying up all night haunting the northern strip. She had gone to an internet café and made a few attempts to access the offshore account she and Cary had opened. But it had disappeared. She had no access to the money. When her time had run out, she left the café and walked up and down the strip, waiting for dawn, when the bus tour she was planning to take to the Grand Canyon would be leaving. Going on a bus tour was the last thing Lucky wanted to do. But she was still pretending to be Bonnie Skinner. And Bonnie sure was excited to be heading off to see one of the wonders of the world.

She had checked the news: their car had been found in the underground lot of the Bellagio, so the police knew she and Cary—or, rather, David Ferguson and Alaina Cadence had come to Las Vegas. They were looking for a couple, though, not a woman alone. And they wouldn't be checking tour buses. Wanted criminals didn't generally go on sightseeing tours.

She stopped humming when a man sat down in the aisle seat beside her. She had seen him when they were getting on the bus.

Middle-aged, forgettable face, wearing shorts and a T-shirt. She had thought he seemed familiar, but then he had passed her seat and disappeared to the back of the bus. Now here he was. Why had he moved to sit beside her? *Not everyone is a threat*, she told herself. *Maybe his seat mate wouldn't stop talking to him. Maybe sitting at the back of the bus made him carsick.* She kept taking small glances at him, small sips she hoped he wouldn't notice. Brown hair, brown eyes, wedding ring. She had seen him somewhere, she knew it. But where? At the casino? In one of the shops she'd been to? Or did he just have one of those faces everyone thought they had seen before?

The man caught her staring and she smiled tightly. He didn't smile back. She started humming again and folded her hands protectively over her belt pack.

"Isn't it so exciting?" she said to him, thinking if she got too chatty maybe he'd move again. "Going to see the Grand Canyon? Definite bucket-list item."

"Sure, real exciting," the man said.

"Could you please excuse me? I just need to use the little girls' room." He didn't stand for her, or even move his legs, so she had to squeeze past, feeling herself recoil as her leg rubbed against his. *Run. Run.* But there was nowhere to go.

In the tiny washroom, she checked her makeup. There was no need to reapply. Her skin was now sallow-looking all on its own, her eyes red and tired. She looked away from her reflection and unzipped the belt bag, slid the bills out and counted them, then began to distribute them among her bra, her pockets, a few extra bills in her shoes. Soon, all that was left in her wallet was her lottery ticket. She pulled it out, looked down at it for a moment and wondered when the draw was, then put it back. She clipped the bag around her waist again and left the bathroom.

The bus was starting to slow. It turned, and she could see the canyon off in the distance.

Soon, she walked off the bus along with everyone else; the strangely familiar man was up ahead, and soon she lost sight of him and felt relief. There was no crisis, nothing to worry about; he was just some guy. She moved slowly along behind everyone else, pretending to organize her things. Then, when no one was looking at her—and no one had really been looking at her anyway—she turned and headed in the opposite direction.

For about half a mile, she walked along the side of the road without seeing more than a few trucks. She followed the signs for Tusayan. It was steaming hot and she was rationing her water, but eventually she decided it was time for a break and a long drink: perhaps she'd walk faster if she stopped thinking about how thirsty she was. She slid the backpack off her shoulders, then bent over and searched for the large water bottle she had purchased before getting on the bus.

She was just lifting the bottle to her lips when someone hit her from behind. The bottle flew from her fingers and onto the dirt in front of her, lidless, hemorrhaging its contents. She felt a hand clamping down on her forearm like a vise.

Cold metal against her neck. A switchblade. She looked into the eyes of the man from the bus, and realized in an instant that she had seen him before—twice. He had been in the poker game with her two nights before, and in the poker game she had been watching yesterday, while scoping out the kid.

With the hand that was not holding the knife he ripped the belt bag from her waist. "Hello again."

"Hello," she said politely, trying to maintain her Bonnie Skinner the Tourist veneer. "Could you please let me go? You're hurting me."

He laughed an ugly laugh. "You can drop the act," he said. "I know who you are."

Lucky noticed a truck way off in the distance, hurtling toward them.

"It is you, isn't it? I thought so, yeah. Those eyes aren't forgettable. Neither are your tits, even under that big T-shirt." She remembered him ogling her when she'd been playing poker two days before. He had seemed a harmless annoyance. She didn't normally underestimate people like this. "Saw you hanging around at the poker table yesterday, and there was something about you. I realized you were the same broad who had bluffed us all out. Takes a scammer to know one, right? *Then* I realized I'd seen a face just like yours on television." He was moving the blade slowly along her neck, stopping at each freckle, a slow and dangerous pause. "I never forget a face," he said. "It's my talent." His knife snagged on the chain around her neck. He tugged. "What's this?" he asked, touching the gold cross.

"Costume jewelry." He tugged again, but the chain held. He dumped out the belt pack and the lottery ticket blew away. Instinctively, she snagged it with her foot and stood on it.

"Where is it? All that money you stole from that kid? All that money you stole from those folks they were talking about on the TV?" He dumped her backpack now. "Where ya hidin' it? Come on." He pulled her by the arm down an embankment and she was forced to stumble forward and lift her foot. The lottery ticket blew into some sagebrush. She lost sight of it as he dragged her behind a line of trees. The road disappeared from view, too.

She considered her options. She could raise her knee, hit him hard between the legs, then start to run and hopefully make it to the roadside by the time the truck passed by. But what if her timing was off, or what if the driver didn't stop, or what if the driver also recognized her and called the police? Or what if she didn't hit the man hard enough and he stabbed her? There were too many variables.

And she had waited too long. She heard the truck pass. The man pressed the knife into her neck so hard it stung. "We can do this the hard way," he said, and he was so close she could smell his oily hair and his rank breath. "Or the easy way." He pulled at her T-shirt, and it ripped at her collarbone. "I know you have more than what you're telling me."

Lucky held up a hand, palm out, in front of herself, feeble protection. "Okay, okay. Just hang on. Let me get it. The money, I'm getting it." She reached into her bra while he watched too closely. She pulled out the first wad of cash from her bra, then the second one from her pockets. She handed both to him and he lowered the knife and counted the money.

"Bullshit," he said when he was done counting. "That's not all of it."

"I only took what I needed from the kid. I spent some of it on a bus ticket and—"

"*Bullshit*. You know what? Take off your clothes. Everything. Take it all off, show me what you're hiding."

"Listen, I swear, that's all the money I have. My partner ran off with the money from the Boise scam."

"Take. Off. Your. Clothes."

Lucky had grown up knowing there were some things you just had to do, like swallowing medicine or jumping off a high diving board into deep water or stealing from people you wanted to love.

But this was not one of them.

She straightened to her full height, which was about an inch taller than the man. She swept her gaze over him. He was nothing; he was no one. "You have it all there," Lucky said, her voice stern and commanding. "All my money. Everything. And what's there, that's not bad for a day's work. But I *can* give you something else—"

"Oh, yeah, I bet you can—"

"You have to promise you'll let me go. And then I'll give it to you."

"What?"

"I'll tell you about luck. About making money come to *you*. About changing your life so you don't have to play small the way you do, holding women up with a cheap knife at the side of a highway."

"What the hell would I—"

"You want to be more, don't you? You want to be the guy they're giving a suite at the Bellagio, you want to be the guy who's getting all the respect. Right? Beautiful women falling all over you, wads of cash in your pockets, *and* in the bank . . ."

He didn't say anything, but he let his hand fall to his side as she spoke. With the knife no longer pointed in her direction she felt even more in command of the situation. "Promise you're going to let me go," she said. "And I'll tell you more of what I know."

He cleared his throat. He squinted at her.

"You're not going to come across someone like me again," Lucky said. "I am one of a kind."

"All right, I promise," he said, his voice husky now.

She breathed in deep, but the air was hot and dry and caught in her lungs. "If you want to be a successful con artist like me, you've got to listen to your hunches. Follow those hunches as far as they'll take you. You need to figure out what your instincts are, and listen to them. The second thing is, you have to believe, really believe, that you will get where you want to go. You have to speak, dress, become the person you want to be. Pretend you already are that person." She dropped her hand to her side, until it was parallel with the knife that still dangled in his. "And when you walk up to a poker table?" He was nodding now, nodding along with her words, waiting for some crumb that would change his life. She grabbed the knife, and it cut into her palm as she wrested it away from him and held it up, an inch from his eye. *"Never, ever underestimate anyone. Especially not me."*

She stepped back, still pointing the knife at him, still shaking. "Walk that way," she said, indicating the road. She thought about demanding the return the money he had just stolen from her—she needed it, desperately. But she also needed him gone. If she made him angry, he might try to get the knife back from her. She wasn't sure she could overpower him. This had to end, and fast. "Walk that way, and I won't kill you."

"Fucking bitch," he said, but he didn't move closer.

"I'm not a bitch. You're lucky you met me, asshole. Now, go.

I don't ever want to see you again, got it?" She commanded, "Start walking. That way." She followed him up to the road and pointed back toward the canyon, still holding the blade aloft. He snarled at her once, animal-like, but then he turned and started to walk. She could feel blood dripping from the palm of her hand into the dust at the side of the highway. Sweat dripped down her back and legs, too. When the man was a dot on the horizon, she turned and went down the embankment to retrieve her backpack and water bottle from the dirt. She dripped what was left of the water onto her tongue, and started to shake.

She raised her hand to her chain and cross pendant, and the shaking stopped. It was always in moments like this one, the bad, lonely moments, when she wished the hardest for the mother she had never managed to find.

Lucky leaned down and took the few bills she had left from her shoe. A flash of yellow paper in the brush nearby caught her eye. Lucky walked forward, bent, and scooped up her lottery ticket, caught on a tiny branch.

She crumpled the ticket in her hand. She didn't want to think about her father right now, locked up in prison, unable to help her, either. It just made her feel even more alone. The piece of paper she held was worth nothing, and she knew it, but she still shoved it into her pocket and felt the effervescence of hope as she did, for just a second. It was enough to keep her moving forward.

"**H**appy birthday, kiddo," her father said. "It's a lucky year for you. You're eleven years old. And eleven is a lucky number. This is going to be your best year yet."

He handed her a small box, then sneezed. He'd been battling a cold that week. She opened the box to reveal a pair of dainty earrings, rose gold with glinting diamonds. "Those are real diamond chips," her father said while Lucky gazed at them.

"They're pretty," Lucky said. "But . . . my ears aren't pierced."

"Oh. Right." He blew his nose. "They were the only thing I was able to palm in the jewelry store."

She could tell she'd hurt his feelings.

"Well, I guess I better go out there to earn a bit more for someone's birthday cake and birthday dinner," he said, standing and starting to get ready to leave for the day.

Lucky felt her stomach curdle. "I'm sorry," she said. "I didn't mean I didn't like the earrings. Just maybe . . ." But she didn't finish the sentence, because the material things she wanted—a Discman; a brand of shirt she'd seen other kids wearing when she went to the mall— she could acquire on her own easily enough. What she really desired, though, was to actually *be* one of those normal kids, a dream that felt more impossible by the day. She watched her father carefully in the morning light streaming through the curtainless window on the main floor of the house they were renting in Novi. Then she shut the lid of the earring box.

"Maybe I should work alone today, Dad. Instead of you."

"Ah, no, it's all right."

"I think I'm ready. People don't always trust *you*, but I'm a kid."

Now he was nodding, looking at her in a new way. "People always want to trust a kid. Okay, birthday girl. You're on."

———

She decided on a watermelon drop. It was a con she'd helped her father with a few times, but she'd never tried it alone. She got a drinking glass from their kitchen, which she placed in a thick plastic bag and smashed with a hammer in the sink. At the sound of the breaking glass, her father looked up from the newspaper he was reading on the couch but didn't say anything.

She found a shoebox and poured the broken glass into it, then wrapped the whole thing in brown paper. Using a pink marker, she wrote *To Mom* on the paper. She added a heart, then a flower, then decided that was enough.

"See you later, Dad," she said as she walked out the front door. "I'm going to the mall."

"That's my girl," he replied. "Good luck."

As she walked, she held the package in her hands with reverence, as if it contained a Fabergé egg or a valuable jewel.

Her father's age-old advice rang in her head: *You have to believe it yourself or it won't work.* And she did. She did believe it.

At the shopping mall, she stayed in the parking lot, positioning herself at the edge of the curb. Shoppers rushed past her and she watched them all carefully, examining their faces. *No. No. She won't do. Not him. Aha. Yes. Her.*

She stepped down from the curb and into the path of a mother rushing along with her sullen teenage daughter a few paces behind her. It was the daughter who had attracted Lucky's attention first. This woman would long for the days when her daughter used to draw her pictures, carefully wrap her gifts, desperate for her mother's approval. Not so anymore . . .

Lucky knew all of this in an instant, and the knowledge made her feel like she was floating. The woman was looking back at her daughter, asking her to *hurry up* while the teenager rolled her eyes and moved even slower. Lucky didn't like that girl, because that girl had no idea how fortunate she was. It wasn't fair.

Lucky got into position. The woman slammed into Lucky, and Lucky hit the ground. She'd have a bruise on her backside for sure, but there was always a price to be paid. Her dad had taught her that, too.

The package hit the concrete, and the glass inside made a shattering sound.

The woman turned to see Lucky sprawled on the sidewalk in front of the mall. "Oh my goodness, I'm so sorry," she exclaimed. "Are you okay?" She bent down to help Lucky up. But Lucky stayed where she was and thought of the saddest thing she could imagine: her own mother, Gloria, being absent from her life. How that teenage girl didn't have a clue. Her eyes filled with bitter, angry, heartbroken tears. Lucky sat up, took her head in her hands, and started to rock back and forth on the concrete.

"My mother," she sobbed. "That gift is for her birthday. I spent all my money, I'd been saving for months. It was a surprise for my mom. She's sick, oh, oh, oh, what am I going to do now?" Another gasping sob. She slowly got onto her hands and knees and reached for the box a few feet away. "Listen," she said, shaking it. "It's broken. It's ruined!"

The mother was in a state of despair. She looked from Lucky to her daughter to Lucky again. The daughter just rolled her eyes and muttered something about her mother being so clumsy and embarrassing, which made Lucky cry harder.

"Hush, hush," the mother said as she took a packet of tissues out of her handbag and gave one to Lucky.

"Thank you," Lucky said, and wiped her face with it. The woman looked at the box in Lucky's hands, took in the heart, the flower, *To Mom.*

"What was it?" she asked in a soft voice, while her sullen daughter stood with her arms crossed a few paces away.

"Mom," the teen said, "I'll meet you at the food court in an hour, okay?" She walked away without waiting for an answer.

"What was the gift?" the woman again asked Lucky.

"A f-f-figurine. R-r-royal D-d-doulton. The one of Princess Diana. My mother is a b-big fan. I saved all year. Oh no, oh no no no."

"Did you buy it here? At this mall?"

"N-no. I just came here for a card. I got the figurine at a special antiques dealer downtown. He said they're very hard to find." Another sob. "I can't believe this. I have the worst luck, the very worst. I just wanted to make my mommy happy."

The woman reached out and touched Lucky's arm. Perfect. It was working.

"How much did the figurine cost?" she asked.

"A hundred and forty-five dollars." Lucky's heart was pounding in her ears. "I sh-should get home. Mom's waiting for me."

"Come with me," the woman said. "It's going to be all right." Lucky followed the woman through the front doors of the mall and to an ATM, where the woman took out $160 and gave it all to Lucky.

"A little extra," she said. "So you can get her a nice card. And maybe a little treat for yourself. You're such a sweet little girl. Your mother must be so, so proud of you."

Lucky knew the woman was thinking of her sullen daughter, mourning the past that would never be again. The sticky hugs and kisses. The unconditional love. How could you not love your mother, if you were lucky enough to have one?

"Thank you," Lucky said as she pocketed the money. Then she turned and walked away fast, hoping the woman would think she was eager to get home to her mother.

Once she left the mall, the soda bubbles that had been coursing through her went flat. The bills were safely stowed in her pocket, but Lucky felt terrible. She had started to suspect after the Sagamore, after Steph and her mom, that every mark was going to leave its mark on her—but she hadn't wanted it to be true. Today proved it. She had swindled that woman, and the woman hadn't deserved it. She didn't deserve the shoddy way her daughter treated her, either. She didn't deserve any of it.

Lucky was crying when she got home, tears that were true and real, that came from that dark and lonely place inside her that just seemed to get bigger every day.

When she walked in the door, her father jumped up from the couch. "Lucky, my God. You were gone a long time. What happened?"

She handed him the money. "I did it," she said. She climbed onto the couch and pulled a threadbare blanket around herself. Then she kept crying while her father stood by, mystified and helpless.

"Where is my mother?" she asked when she could finally speak.

"Can we try to find her? Like really try, not just say we're trying?"

Her father looked at her for a long moment, then sat down beside her. "You want a mother," he said. She nodded. "And a life that isn't like this one. Something different. Something more . . . conventional. It's all you really want, isn't it?"

She wiped her nose and nodded again.

"And you're still upset about that friend of yours, that girl, Steph, and her mother, Darla. You wish we hadn't done that." Should it have bothered her, the way her father was reading her in the same fashion he read his marks? Maybe. But it didn't. She felt relieved she didn't have to explain herself to him.

He was silent for a moment, watching her carefully. Was there anything else he would see, anything about her that she herself didn't know? "Pack your bags" was all he said. "Pack up everything."

"Why? Where are we going now?"

"Bellevue, Washington. We'll go see Steph, and Darla. You're right. I need to give you a proper birthday present. The one thing you really want."

"But they're not going to want to see us," Lucky said. "Not after we stole from them."

"They have no idea we stole anything. And they're going to be thrilled to see us, trust me. I should have thought of this a long time ago."

CHAPTER SIX

Lucky was in a twenty-four-hour diner in Tusayan, sitting at a corner table, nursing yet another coffee refill. Her feet still ached from walking to the Arizona town she was now in, all the way from the Grand Canyon. It had taken two hours. Her hand was stinging from where the man's blade had cut into it, but it had stopped bleeding, at least.

Outside the grimy diner windows, it was the golden hour. Even the dust on the street looked special—but Lucky knew it wasn't, that it was just plain old desert dust, the same that now coated her skin and her clothes after her long walk.

"More coffee?" The waitress was beside Lucky's table, one hand on a skinny hip, coffeepot in the other. She wasn't looking at Lucky; she had her eyes on the row of televisions behind the diner counter. Each of them was tuned to a different news station. There was that woman again, the Manhattan DA Lucky had seen in the Vegas hotel room with Jeremy. Lucky wanted to stand, get a closer look at the woman, who strangely felt like someone she knew, but she couldn't do that. She had to look away from the televisions, stay inconspicuous as her face and Cary's appeared on one of them, above the words GRIFTING BONNIE AND CLYDE COUPLE STILL ON RUN.

"Yes, thank you. And I'll have the all-day breakfast. Over easy. Wheat toast."

"Alrighty." The waitress poured the coffee, eyes still on the television. When she was gone, Lucky stared down at the table, wishing she had a book, anything to keep her hands and her mind busy. A woman's voice at the table beside her cut through her thoughts.

"Hear about that young couple taking money from all those old folks? What is this damn world coming to? Young people today just take, take, take. They don't want to have to do the actual work."

Lucky scowled. *All those old folks.* It had hardly been *all* old folks. Yes, okay, some of her clients had been seniors. She had been going over it in her mind. There had been Harry and Faye Alpert, who were in their eighties, and Burt Martinson, an elderly widower—and yes, recalling this fact, and how little it had mattered to her at the time, made her feel guilty and ashamed. But what about the other clients, the young, wealthy ones with far more money than they needed, than *anyone* needed? What about the people who probably weren't going to miss the money, ever?

A different voice now: "Did you hear that one man had to cancel heart surgery because he can't afford it anymore? *All* his money is gone. Apparently they're having a benefit to try to help him out. Poor man. I plan to donate."

Lucky chewed her lip and glanced at the screens again, but her face was gone. *Heart surgery?* Which client had been sick? *All his money was gone?* Had they really taken all of it? She had never seen it that way, like cleaning someone out. All her clients had to be at a certain income and asset level. These were the kind of people with an endless supply of family money. They would all be fine, no matter what. Wouldn't they?

"Hope they catch them soon."

Lucky had nothing to say to that. Her eggs arrived. She swirled the yolks around with her fork, too galled by a combination of shame and indignation to eat anything now.

"Hey," said the female customer's voice she had heard talking a moment before. "Look at that. The Multi Millions jackpot ticket got sold. Three hundred and ninety mil, holy geez."

"Where, here in Arizona?"

"Nope. Idaho."

Indeed, on two of the screens, Lucky could see the interior of a gas station convenience store, where a man stood holding one of those big novelty checks. She squinted at the screen, but it looked like any convenience store. Still, she kept watching. Her heartbeat quickened. Did the store look familiar? Was it the Idaho store she'd been in, where she'd bought her lottery ticket? That was the beauty of it. That, right there, was the grift itself: that moment of hope, that quickening of pulse, the *what if, what if it's me, what if it's my ticket, what would I do with all that money, who would I become?*

Lucky took the lottery ticket out of her wallet and smoothed it on the greasy table. Her numbers stared up at her.

"You all good here?"

She covered the ticket with her hand. "Just the bill, please," she said to the waitress. A moment later, the waitress dropped it on the table. Lucky put the ticket back in her wallet, counted out enough money to cover what she owed and a tip, and stood, feeling dazed, like a person abruptly awakened from a dream.

Outside, the golden hour was over; the specks of dust had lost the light and gone back to being the dirt Lucky had always known them to be. She walked slowly. Her plan had been to go to the bus station after she ate, where a bus to Williams—which had a train station, and could get her wherever she decided to go next faster than a bus—was scheduled to leave in half an hour. But now, all she could think about was checking her lottery ticket.

She saw a sign ahead for the Daisy Mart convenience store and picked up her pace.

"Can I get a printout of the winning lottery numbers for this week's Multi Millions draw?" she asked when she was inside, at the front of the line.

"Sure thing." The cashier picked up a sheet beside the register. "Lots of people have been asking. I printed a bunch out. Here you go."

Lucky glanced at the sheet, then looked up. 11-18-42-95-77. She knew those numbers. Those were *her* lucky numbers.

"Are you sure these are the right ones? For this week's draw?"

"Positive, lady."

Lucky rushed from the store and out onto the street. She stood, heart racing, palms sweating. She needed to go somewhere private and check the ticket against the printout, needed to see for herself that the numbers did indeed match.

There was a McDonald's up ahead. Inside, she caught a glimpse of a television in the seating area, tuned to CNN. $390 MILLION LOTTERY TICKET SOLD IN IDAHO CONVENIENCE STORE STILL UN-CLAIMED read the banner on the screen.

Lucky made her way to the restroom at the back of the restaurant. She closed and locked the door behind her and leaned against it, her breathing ragged, her body shaking.

She took the lottery ticket out of her wallet. There it was, an artifact from a world she had believed to be long dead, staring her in the face. *You're special. You're lucky. There's no one like you.*

11-18-42-95-77.

She took the printout from the Daisy Mart out of her pocket and compared them.

11-18-42-95-77.

She had the winning ticket.

Lucky wanted to scream—but not in the way a person who had just discovered they had won the lottery normally would. If she came forward, she would be arrested. What good would the lottery ticket be then?

She folded the ticket and put it inside her shoe. Then she stood, staring at herself in the mirror in that familiar stance, the one that meant she had to think of something: a new identity, a new plan, a new path toward this glittering dream, something, anything.

Think of a name. Think of a story. Think.

But all she could do was stare at her own face. "Lucky." She spat it at the mirror. She walked out of the restaurant and back onto the dark street, trying to move as if she had purpose—even though she felt more lost than she ever had before.

March 20, 1993
BELLEVUE, WASHINGTON

Her father's Buick backfired as it pulled up in front of Steph's house. It was a roomy split-level ranch-style home with a manicured lawn and a long driveway, exactly how Lucky had pictured it. There were mountain peaks in the background; the sky was a watery blue, fading into dusk. The streetlights flickered to life and the kids who'd been playing catch or throwing sticks to dogs began to make their way inside—but a few of them stopped to look at the Buick, wary of its size, its rust, its rattles and booms. When it backfired again before her father turned it off, Lucky wanted to crawl under the back seat and hide forever—except crawling under the back seat would mean missing this: the way the setting sun reflected off clean windows; the way the butterflies meandered toward bushes, then rocketed back as if that were the last thing they had intended to do; the good cooking smells in the air, not onions and lard like the rooming houses she had lived in, but instead the scent of steaks on the grill and pies in the oven.

"All right, Andi," her father said, cocking an eyebrow. "You ready?"

Lucky got out of the car. The front door had opened and she could see Darla, Steph's mom, outlined in the doorway. There was the sound of a dog's bark, and then a golden retriever was bounding down the driveway toward her. This had to be Blossom, the dog Steph had said her mom bought after her dad had his heart attack, to make them both feel better. And it had helped a bit, Steph had admitted. A puppy helped with everything. Blossom stopped barking and nuzzled Lucky's hand.

"*Virgil?*"

"Darla," her father said, his voice full of emotion even Lucky almost believed was true. "I'm so sorry. Can you forgive me for taking off on you like that? I got scared. I fell so hard for you, so fast, and it didn't feel right. So I ran away. I didn't know what else to do. I'm even more in love with you than I was last summer. I've thought of you every moment of every day since."

"Oh, Virgil. Me too. I never stopped believing I'd see you again. And now here you are."

Lucky felt sick. Her father was lying to Darla, again, and Darla was falling for it. Why wasn't she suspicious? Why wasn't she staying mad, at least for a little while, and questioning a man who had taken off in the night and not said goodbye? No, instead, Lucky could hear the sloppy, gross sounds of the adults kissing as she knelt down and buried her head in the dog's fur so she wouldn't have to listen anymore.

"*Andi?*"

She looked up. Suddenly it was all worth it.

"Oh my God, I seriously thought I was never going to see you again!" Steph exclaimed, running down the driveway toward her. "Did they work? Did you get them? The treatments?"

Lucky took a deep breath. "Yes," she said. "I'm one hundred percent better. They said it was a miracle."

Steph grinned, then whooped. "Really? That's amazing! And now you're . . ."

"Here," Lucky said. "Now we're here." The parents had walked away together, around the side of the house, where they could continue their reunion in private. Steph rolled her eyes, but then looked at Lucky and grinned again. Blossom still stood at Lucky's side, wagging her tail.

"She likes you," Steph said. Blossom was even more beautiful than Steph had described her, her flaxen coat shining under the now-lit streetlamps, her gentle tail wagging in slow motion, her great panting mouth appearing to arrange itself into a welcoming grin as she looked up at Lucky. It was all too good to be true, and yet it was true. Darla had welcomed her father with open arms. John had told Lucky that if Darla didn't get too angry when she saw him, that meant they were going to be able to stay.

Darla and "Virgil" came back out from the side of the house. Darla was smiling. Her lipstick was a bit smeared. "Andi!" she said. "Let me get a good look at you. Is it true, you're all better?"

"Sure is," her dad said, his eyes on Lucky. It was barely noticeable, and yet so poignant, the way he lifted a hand and dashed away a non-existent tear with a knuckle. "The transfusions worked. Look at her! She's completely healthy. Thanks to *you*, Darla. I hope you can forgive me for what I did."

"Oh, stop, Virgil, I told you I forgave you already. I forgave you the moment you pulled up in front of the house."

The next thing Lucky knew, just like in a movie, Darla was in his arms again, this time embracing him with even more abandon.

"Come on," Steph said, and Lucky followed her into the house, the dog on their heels. She had wanted this, exactly this—but it didn't feel right. If she could just forget that they were lying, if she could just believe that what they were saying was true, everything would be okay.

The problem: It was impossible to forget. She felt the lies across her shoulders like a yoke as she walked into the house she had dreamed of, with the friend she had dreamed of—and understood for the first time that not everyone had to be careful what they wished for, but she did.

Two months passed. Lucky tried, every day, to be happy. But all she could think about was this being over someday. She and her father had never talked about how long they would stay, but Lucky knew it was temporary. Everything with them was temporary. Still, she could tell when she looked at him that her father was happy, that he was enjoying this—who wouldn't? Darla treated him like a god. "I'm so happy to have a man to cook for again," she'd say. "No, no, put up your feet, relax." Darla had even found John a job working as a salesman at a furniture store owned by a family friend. When he came home, Darla would have a drink waiting, and a home-cooked meal.

"It's bizarre," Steph would whisper to Lucky. "Like it's 1952, not 1993." Still, Lucky knew Steph liked that her mom was happy and not laser-focused on Steph alone, which apparently she had been before Lucky and her father had shown up. Before, Steph had had all sorts of rules—and her mother would worry like crazy if she came home even thirty seconds after the streetlamps turned on. But now in the evenings, Steph and Lucky could run through the meadow with the other neighborhood kids, catching salamanders in their hands and then setting them free. Once the gloaming shifted into night and they were due back home, they'd walk back slowly, chatting—and Darla was never mad when they were late.

It was almost summer, when the nights would stretch even longer. And for the first time in her life, the change of seasons meant something different to Lucky, because of school. Lucky had been enrolled at the private school Steph went to, using the faked documents her father had brought with him. "They hardly checked them," her father had whispered to her the evening he and Darla had returned from the school registrar. "All they wanted was a big fat tuition check." It went without saying that Darla had paid for it. Darla paid for everything, and it didn't seem to bother John, but this gave Lucky a sick feeling that was constant, like when you ate too much sugar even though you knew it was a bad idea. It made her lose her appetite, but if she ever said she wasn't hungry, Darla's eyes would widen with concern. She'd put her hand to Lucky's brow and hold it there, featherlight. Lucky would have to sit still, pretending this sort of maternal gesture was something she was familiar with, something her own mother had done, too, back when she was alive. It always brought tears to her eyes, but she never let them out.

As for school, Lucky adored it. At school, she felt real: she truly was Andrea "Andi" Templeton, a fifth-grade student. Steph was a grade above, and that made Lucky nervous at first, but in the end it was a good thing because it meant Lucky could focus on her studies—and she quickly shot to the top of the class, especially in math.

As soon as the bell rang, at recess, lunch, or the end of the day, Steph was there. Lucky was never alone, had none of the problems a kid who had started at a school very close to the end of the year would normally have. She already had a best friend. Not just a best friend; they were practically sisters. "We *are* sisters," Stephanie would whisper.

"Sometimes I forget you're only eleven," the teacher, Mrs. Gadsby, said to her one golden afternoon. "You're someone special, Andi. You're going to do amazing things."

"Thanks, Mrs. Gadsby. I've never had a teacher like you before."

This wasn't a lie, at least. And Lucky tried so hard, every day, to say as many true things as she possibly could.

CHAPTER SEVEN

Lucky was in Williams, Arizona, now. The lottery ticket was tucked into her bra, where she could keep it close. She kept waiting for the moment of elation about discovering she was the winner—but it didn't come. The ticket was an impossible dream. And she had no viable plan for its redemption. Nor her own, not yet.

The only thing she had managed to decide was that California would be her next destination. But to get there would take more than the little money she had left. She exited the bus station and stopped by a store for some fabric tape, hair gel, and a stale sandwich from a cooler by the cash register. She ate the sandwich as she walked toward the large hotel in the center of town, the one with the conference center. She walked confidently through the lobby until she found a sign with the information she was looking for: there was a salon professional and beauticians' trade show in one conference hall, she discovered, and a small business sales summit in the other.

In a restroom, she made herself up: cat-eye liner and dark brows to match her new darker hair, which she slicked back with gel so that the short haircut looked at least somewhat stylish and sleek. She couldn't wear a bra with her backless cocktail dress, so she used the tape she'd bought earlier to secure her lottery ticket by taping it carefully to the inside of the skirt. "Lisa," she said into the mirror. Lisa was a hairdresser from Minnesota with big dreams. She was here for the trade show, selling a deep conditioner and her own patented technique for administering it.

Transformed, Lucky walked out into the hall, her backpack held casually over her arm. She stood out—but she also blended in.

She checked the hotel layout, then took the elevator to the fifth floor, and the hotel's bar. Perched on a stool, she passed the afternoon drinking club soda and pretending to pore over the trade show program, which she had found discarded on a bench. Eventually the bar started to fill with salespeople and hairdressers, done for the day. Lucky ordered a vodka martini and nursed it for an hour while she watched and waited. A man sat down beside her, glanced at her appreciatively once, twice. He was pleasant-looking but not too handsome; he had on a drab gray shirt with a butter-yellow tie. He wasn't wearing a wedding ring, but the puff of pale skin was there, telltale. He had probably left it up in his room.

"Can I buy you a drink?" he asked, just like she thought he would. "Oh—well . . ." She stared down into her empty glass as her stomach swirled, surprised by what she was experiencing: grief, sudden and insistent. The idea of what was supposed to come next, of flirting, smiling, potentially touching and kissing someone other than Cary . . . she couldn't. And it made her so angry. Cary had abandoned her. Their relationship had been one very long con—but he was still the only man she had ever loved. The only man she had ever been with.

"No, thank you," she managed to say.

The man shrugged. He paid his bill and he was gone.

Lucky considered her options. *It's either this, or you sleep in a bus shelter. And then you could get picked up by the police and brought in and that will be it. All over.*

Soon enough there was another man, sitting on her left. She watched him as he settled himself onto the stool and ordered a beer, asking first if the bar had the specific craft brew he was looking for on tap. She detected a New York accent. She looked over at him again and smiled shyly when they made eye contact. He returned her smile, polite, then looked down at his phone. Like the man before him, he was middle-aged. He had a pleasant face, a receding hairline, a glinting gold band on his left ring finger. His eyes looked tired, smudged underneath as if he had been up late the night before—another lackluster sales conference in yet another lackluster town. He took a book out of his briefcase. Dale Carnegie. *How to Win Friends and Influence People.*

"I loved that book," she said—which was somewhat true. Her father had read it to her when she was ten; many of the concepts had been integral to their cons over the years. She could still remember the "six ways to make people like you": *Act like you're interested in them. Smile. Remember names. Encourage people to talk about themselves. Talk about their interests. Make people feel important.* Carnegie had intended all these things to come from a genuine place. Her father had not.

She put her hand over her mouth. "*Sorry.* Here I am, bugging you when you're trying to read. Ignore me."

"Oh," said the man, looking surprised she was speaking to him at all. "It's okay. It's an interesting book."

"Here for a conference?"

"Yes. Small business expo. You?"

"Salon professional and beauticians' conference."

His phone was beside his hand on the bar. On the lock screen, Lucky could see an image of a wide-hipped blond woman in sunglasses, standing on a beach, holding two kids by the hands, smiling. She could picture his life all at once: When he came home from his business trips, he was tired, but the wife was exhausted. Tapped out from taking care of the kids, when *he* was tapped out from trying to make a living. They argued. He felt unappreciated. She did, too. Both of them had probably fantasized about a moment like this, in a hotel bar with a stranger. No consequences, because no one would ever find out.

"It's my first work trip," she said. "I've never really been anywhere. And . . ." She blinked quickly, then reached up and dabbed at the skin under her eyes. "Never mind. Sorry. This is so embarrassing, crying in front of a stranger."

"No, it's okay," he said, leaning in. "What's wrong?"

"Just, it's not going well. It's—" She drew a shaky breath, then signaled to the bartender. "Can we get two shots of tequila?" She gazed at the man again. "You'll have one with me, right? I so badly need a little perk-up, and tequila always does the trick."

The bartender plunked the shots and a saltshaker in front of them. The man hesitated, but said, "Oh, why not," and they both tilted them back. "Now, what is it that has you so upset?"

"You probably wouldn't find it very interesting."

"Try me."

"Well—what's your name?"

"Tim."

"Tim, I'm Lisa. I sell beauty supplies to salons. Boring, right?"

"I'm sure there's *something* interesting about it."

"Okay, fine. There is, actually." She leaned close. "You see, there's this whole technique to using the deep conditioners. A special head massage technique. And honestly? If you do it right, not only does it feel great for the client, and they only *ever* want to have you as their hairstylist, but it helps the product penetrate better, meaning your hair actually *is* softer and healthier, and less resistant to styling, more resistant to damage . . ." She trailed off. "Sounds like I'm giving you the sales pitch here," she said, gazing into his eyes.

"This might be the tequila talking, but I *love* a good head massage, Lisa," he said.

"Well, Tim." She inched a little closer. "If you love a good head massage, I'm your girl."

By the third tequila shot and the second head massage, she had his wedding ring, watch, and wallet. No kissing required.

"This is the most fun I've had in a long time," Tim said, growing serious, unaware that anything was missing yet, clueless and happy.

"Thanks," she said.

His hand was close to hers, and she let her pinky rub against his.

"Where did you come from, Lisa?" His voice was husky.

"Wisconsin," she replied. "I'm just a regular old girl from Wisconsin."

"You are *no* regular girl."

They gazed into each other's eyes. "Come to my room," she said. "Give me a five-minute head start so I can . . . slip into something more comfortable." She giggled. "Sorry, cheesy, but true—and then meet me at room five-oh-five. I'll leave the door open for you."

"I can't wait, Lisa. And I can't believe my luck."

She stood, grabbed her backpack, and sashayed from the bar, shooting one last come-hither look at his besotted face.

She took the elevator down to the lobby. In the restroom, she slid off her stilettos and dress, carefully peeled the lottery ticket from the inside of the skirt and put it back inside her bra, pulled a T-shirt over her head, and put on jeans and her baseball cap.

Outside the hotel, she could see the lights of the city bus. She put her head down and ran for it. She deposited her fare and sat down in a seat close to the back, her face turned away from the window, just in case.

The bus started moving. After a few blocks, she felt safe. She reached into the front pouch of the backpack and felt the cool metal there: his watch, wallet, and wedding ring. What was he going to tell his wife had happened to his stuff? Perhaps he'd tell her he'd been robbed. And he would never make this mistake again—and probably wouldn't feel too guilty about it, either, because he had already paid for it. He had done something bad, or wanted to, at least—and something bad had happened to him in return.

He'd get over it.

The city bus traveled along the route she had checked earlier, until she could see the bright lights of the EZ Pawn. She walked in and laid the watch and the wedding band on the counter. The woman behind the register picked them up without a word and took them into a back room. She emerged a moment later. "We pay $23.50 per gram of 14K, $22 if you want cash on the spot. And this ring is six grams, so $141, or $132. And the watch you can put on consignment, and we'll split $200 fifty/fifty with you. If you want cash for it now, we'll give you $50. And hey, what about that necklace you're wearing? That looks like it might be worth something."

Lucky hesitated, then reached up to the back of her neck and unfastened the gold crucifix. She put it down on the counter. The woman took it to the back and returned a moment later. "Same deal, fifty/fifty on $200, or $50 here and now."

Lucky snatched the necklace back. "I can't", she said. "But I'll take cash for the others."

The woman shrugged. "Okay. So, that's $182 total," she said, counting out cash. With the two hundred from the man's wallet, and the hundred dollars she had managed to keep hidden from the man who had robbed her, Lucky now had almost five hundred dollars.

She walked outside and stood in front of the pawn shop, refastening the necklace that had belonged to her mother. Finding her mother someday wasn't a dream she was giving up on, she realized. Especially not now, when she needed the family she didn't have more than ever. Lucky had no idea where to begin looking for her, she never had—but she was not going to allow the hope that she might find her someday die.

Lucky started walking, headed back toward the train station. If her timing was right, she would reach San Quentin by morning, and walk straight into the last place she wanted to be.

W hen Lucky and Steph returned home one evening, after a Saturday spent playing with their friends, John and Darla were in the backyard arguing. Lucky froze. What if Darla had found out the truth? "Maybe we should go back," Lucky said. "Give them a minute . . ."

"No way. It's pitch dark now. I'll be grounded."

"Yeah," Lucky said, still hesitating at the gate. "But—"

Her father's voice rose up in the darkness. "She's my daughter, and I'll decide which doctor she goes to. She has her regular appointment in two weeks' time, and I'm taking her, and, Darla, you don't need to worry—"

"I'm not *worried* about you going on a road trip, Virgil, I'm worried about Andi! She needs to be observed more frequently than once every few months, by a doctor in a different state. I'm telling *you* I'll pay for it. You don't have to worry about money. You're here now—I want to take care of you, of *both* of you. Why won't you let me?"

Silence. The sound of crickets. A door slamming, which Lucky realized was Steph's back door. Her father was done talking, apparently. In the darkness, Darla sat alone on the deck, head bowed.

"He can be such a jerk," Lucky told Steph, holding on to the gate as if letting go would cause her to fall backward. She could already feel it all slipping through her fingers. She thought that maybe they would leave that night, that her father would wake her and they would steal away. She had tears in her eyes when she looked at Steph. "I'm sorry," she said.

"For what? You haven't done anything wrong," Steph said, reaching for Lucky's arm. "I know your dad *says* it's all fine, but you must be so scared some days, scared that it's all just going to . . ."

"Fall apart," Lucky whispered. "Yes. I'm scared of that. I'm scared there'll be nothing I can do to stop it."

"You need to let us take care of you. We're family now. It's kismet that we met, don't you think?" That was Steph's favorite word right now, *kismet*. But no, it had not been kismet. It had been bad luck. Lucky knew this and Steph didn't, and it had driven a wedge between them, all at once, as thick as one of the pickets in the fence. "My mom wants you to see my pediatrician," Steph said. "She told me to try to talk to you about it, but I hadn't yet. Just to make sure you're okay. Maybe bring it up with your dad, okay?"

"I will," Lucky said, decisive. "I'm going to talk to him right now."

She left Steph standing there and walked into the yard, passing Darla, who was still sitting alone in the dark, without saying a word. But then she paused for a moment and looked back. She saw Darla watching her, her expression expectant and open. She didn't know anything, didn't suspect.

"You all right, Andi? Want to talk? Come sit here with me."

"I need to go talk to my dad," Lucky said, and turned away from Darla.

She found him in the master bedroom, sitting on his side of the bed. "Listen, kiddo, I wanted to stay here longer, I wanted to do that for you, but things are getting a little—"

"Just send me to the pediatrician. He'll look me over and find me in perfect health, no sign of any illness—which is exactly right, and true, and miraculous. They'll be so happy. And then we can stay. Maybe forever. Please, Dad? I really want this."

"You don't understand," he said in a low voice. "It's not that easy. No matter what, we couldn't be happy here. Not forever."

"Why not?"

"Because it's not human nature to be satisfied. Your happiness would unravel eventually—even if it weren't already at risk of unraveling because of all the lies we told to be here." We. Complicity. Partners in crime.

"I'm just a kid," she said, but the words didn't ring true. She had never had the chance to be just a kid. That's why she wanted to stay here. To be a kid who maybe, just maybe, could grow into a regular person. A person like everyone else. Not a thief, not an eleven-year-old con artist.

"You love her a little bit, don't you?" she asked. "Darla? The way she loves you?"

He looked sad when he said, "No. I can't. You get it, don't you, the way it feels with a mark?" Lucky refused to nod. "I feel disdain for her. For being so trusting. When a person falls for something like this, hook, line, and sinker—well, I could never, ever love someone like that. You get it, Lucky."

"No."

Except she did. She felt the same way about Darla and sometimes, in dark, upsetting moments, she even felt that way about Steph, wanted to shake her and say, Hello, aren't you paying attention? Why are you just buying all this?

"You could go, and I could stay," she whispered. "You could just . . . take off."

He switched on a lamp, and she could see his face. He looked sad, and she felt guilty for suggesting they part ways. "Kiddo. I understand how badly you want this. But do you really think she would treat you the same if I just took off? She'd look at you and think of me."

"Never mind. Forget it."

"You and me, we need each other. You know that."

Lucky swallowed hard. But the lump in her throat now felt permanent. What if lies wedged themselves inside you and turned into something ugly? What if she really did get sick? "I do know that," she said. "But I just want a year. One whole year in a single place, being Andi. And then we can go."

"The longer we stay, the harder it will be."

"I don't care," Lucky said. "I don't see how it could be any harder than it already is. Every day, I wonder if you're going to tell me it's time. I need an end date, and I need it to be a long enough time that I at least feel . . . that I at least feel like this really happened."

During his long silence, she was sure he was thinking of a million different excuses, all of the explanations airtight and impossible to argue with. But instead he said, "All right, leave it with me. I'll do my best."

"Thank you," Lucky said, and she turned and left the room feeling, for the first time in her life, like she'd won the lottery—and it wasn't going to be enough to sustain her.

CHAPTER EIGHT

Lucky stood still, arms out, as the guard patted her down just inside the tall barbed-wire gate of San Quentin State Prison. The lottery ticket was tucked into her wallet, perfectly innocent.

"All right, that way," the guard said when he was done, and Lucky moved forward with the rest of the crowd. She followed the gravel path inside and was soon in a reception area where she was to present her ID for a second time. She was Sarah Armstrong, John Armstrong's niece. She lived in San Francisco, worked at a bank. She had been using this ID to visit her father for the past decade. He had served less than half his sentence so far.

The guard glanced at the driver's license, then back up at Lucky. "Haircut?" she asked. Lucky nodded. "He has another visitor. She's just gone in. So you'll have to wait in the area outside the visiting room until it's your turn."

Lucky sat down in a cracked plastic chair. Who was visiting her father? She clenched her jaw with frustration as the minutes ticked past.

Nearly an hour later, a woman emerged from the visiting room. It had been nine years since Lucky had last seen her. Her dark brown hair was pulled back in a low, stubby ponytail, shaved underneath. She was wearing loose jeans and a tank top, and work boots with scuffed toes. Marisol Reyes. One of her father's former "business partners" from the grift that had landed him in prison.

"Lucky?"

She stood. "What's up? Recruiting John for another risky job, if he ever gets out? Are you even allowed to be here, Reyes?"

"My parole doesn't restrict prison visits. And no, of course I'm not recruiting him." She was reaching into her pocket.

The guard stepped forward and said, "Hey," as she held up a rectangle of cardstock.

"Just giving her my business card," Reyes said. The guard approached and examined it before handing it to Lucky and returning to the other side of the room. *Marisol Reyes*, it read. *Driver. San Diego Third-Strikers Foundation.*

"What is this?"

"It's the organization I work for now. A nonprofit—"

"Are you serious, Reyes?"

At least Reyes had the good grace to flush and look away. "This is legit. It's a group of lawyers who help third-strikers—like your dad—get released from prison. I'm a driver, like the card says. I pick people up if the lawyers are successful in getting them out, help get them identification, clothes, a meal, leads on places to live—"

"And maybe recruit them? For your so-called charity? Maybe pawn them off on Priscilla? You should be ashamed—"

"I don't work for Priscilla anymore. You know how badly I always wanted to get away from her. But listen, we don't have time to discuss any of that. Your dad is struggling." Reyes glanced at the clock behind them. "You should get in there."

"Struggling how?"

"Forgetting things. A lot of things. Just call me, okay? To talk about your dad, but . . ." She stepped closer and lowered her voice. "I saw you on TV. And I promised your dad I'd always look out for you. *Call me.*"

Then Reyes was gone, out the waiting room door, while Lucky moved forward into the visiting room, which resembled a cafeteria. She spotted her father, sitting alone at a table in the corner, staring vacantly ahead. He looked smaller.

He started to stand when he saw her, then sat back down. The guilt she had managed to keep at bay swarmed around her like bees.

"Hi, Uncle John," she said, sitting down at the table.

"How've you been, Lucky?"

"You're not supposed to call me that," she said, voice low.

"Sorry. It was . . . ?"

"Sarah."

"Right." He smiled, embarrassed. "Sorry, it's been a while. Sarah Armstrong. My niece."

"Reyes mentioned you haven't been feeling well."

He frowned. "Did she? You saw her out there? Well, I'm not *that* bad."

"Ten minutes left!" the guard nearest the door called out.

Snippets of other conversations rose around them. "I miss you so much . . ." "We're having some troubles . . ." "Ramen noodles would be nice, maybe some chocolate . . ." "Baby Katie did the funniest thing last night . . ."

"I'm in trouble," Lucky finally said. But she smiled so it would just seem like they were having a normal conversation, and her father did the same, his smile wobbly. "Cary. He—"

"He turned up again, after all these years?"

"This is hard. I didn't tell you, but we were together. For the last decade." She couldn't tell if he was surprised. He looked hurt, more than anything. "I'm sorry, okay? I don't have time to explain it all now—but he took off on me."

"Ah, well, good riddance. I didn't tell *you*, but I always knew he was—"

"You don't get it. We were . . . working." She looked at her father steadily, hoping he would understand. "We went too far. A lot of money was involved. Not ours."

"I see," her father said. "I know what *working* means."

"We had a plan. To go to Dominica. But instead, he took off. The day before yesterday. Now they're looking for me. I'm in trouble." She saw the hurt in his eyes and it was a hard thing to witness: the pain she had been planning to cause him by taking off.

"Truth is, I don't know how I can help you," he said sadly. "Not from in here. I'm so sorry, kiddo. I never wanted this to happen to you."

"I have something that could help, though—something big." She glanced at the guard nearest their table, but he wasn't paying attention to them. "Remember you and me, our road trips when I was a kid, how you'd always let me buy a lottery ticket and play my lucky numbers? Do you remember?"

"Sure," he said. "Of course I do."

"I bought a ticket to remember you by."

"Like I was dead or something? Gone from your life, that was going to be it, after everything—"

"I won."

He stopped talking. He blinked a few times. "How much?"

"All of it."

"Don't joke."

"I won three hundred and ninety million dollars."

He hooted out a laugh. "Did I hear you right? Are you sure you're not putting me on?"

"Why would I come all the way here, under my current circumstances, to tell you a joke about a winning lottery ticket?"

He was silent. Then, "Well, what are you going to do about it?"

"That's what I was hoping you could help me with."

"Have you done the math?" he asked.

"What math?"

"On how many years, if you got brought in. Any idea?"

"It would be a lot," she said over a frightened lump in her throat.

"More than you. Probably thirty."

Reyes's card was still in Lucky's hand. She had been fiddling with it, hands nervous in her lap, but now she lifted them onto the table and her father looked at it.

"No—what you should *not* do is ask Reyes for help. She's on probation. She's doing so well. Couldn't be associating herself with someone who was—well, you know, trouble. Did she tell you when you saw her in the waiting area, about her job?"

Lucky shoved Reyes's card in her pocket. "I won't call her," she said. "Don't worry. You'll get out, with your precious Reyes helping you." The bitter jealousy in her voice made her feel seventeen again. "And I—" In the silence between them that followed, Lucky was aware of the seconds ticking past, seconds that had seemed so precious before but were now worthless. "Who knows what I'll do? Not your problem, I guess."

"Five minutes!" a guard shouted.

He started wringing his hands, a nervous habit she was not familiar with. "You know," he said, unclasping his hands and putting them on the table, "you truly are the luckiest girl in the world. I've always told you—"

"Stop. Please. Not now. I'm *not*."

"Sure, it's complicated. But you'll find a way with this ticket. You just have to have faith."

That word. The idea of having faith, of being good. Lucky reached up and touched the crucifix hanging from her neck.

"What about Gloria?" she found herself saying, the gold of the cross warm against her fingers.

That confused expression was back on her father's face.

"Gloria? I haven't thought about her in years."

"Where is she now, do you know?"

"She'd be outside of Cooperstown, of course, still running the Devereaux family fishing camp, which she ran off from the city to do after she left me high and dry—unless she's dead, which I doubt; she's too young, younger than me, of course, and we're still technically married so you'd think someone would have told me. But why would you ask—" A slow dawning; he realized he had said too much, and Lucky realized she was missing something—but what? "Oh. Shit," her father said.

"What if I did it, went to that camp you just mentioned and found her? Wouldn't having a winning lottery ticket be attractive to her, to anyone? Wouldn't it help her want to know me? Finally? Millions and millions of dollars?"

"Oh, God, kiddo. Really? You've never even met her, and you're going to show up in the situation you're in? It's not just about the ticket, or the money. Gloria is—"

"Four minutes!" shouted the guard.

"You used to act like I never had a mother," she said. "Like I dropped onto this planet fully formed. Like I don't need her and never have! But you know where she is—"

"This is why you really came. To grill me for information about your mother. You don't visit for a year, and now you come for this."

It was a familiar game, this quick attempt to turn the tables. At least he was up to it, at least his mind was working well enough to play it. Cold comfort.

"No. I came to ask you for help."

"All right, then. I'll help. You have this ticket, and all you need is someone to cash it in for you. Someone you can trust." His eyes lit up. "I have an idea. Darla, Steph! They were like family, once."

"No, they weren't. We were just pretending."

"You could go to them, tell them I ended up in jail, and you, you never had anything to do with any of my cons. Steph loved you like a sister, you can't deny that. Go to them, appeal to their emotions. It's brilliant, actually, because we know the things they'll do for love. Tell them they're all you have, even to this day, and now you're in trouble, and could they cash in the ticket for you. It's perfect."

"I don't understand why you think I have a better chance with Darla, with Steph, than I do with someone who has an actual blood connection to me. I need a sure thing here."

"Priscilla, then. That woman can make anything happen."

Lucky felt any hope she had held out when she had decided to come here fly away from her, out the barred windows. "No way."

"She'll help you. You'll have to give her a cut, of course—"

"That woman is a snake."

"I wouldn't go that far. She's changed. She's rehabilitated. Jail either makes you worse or it makes you better. Now she's running a women's shelter in Fresno—"

"She was barely in four years—"

"Plus, she'd be interested in knowing where her precious Cary got off to, don't you think?"

"I have no idea where he is."

"But you can make her think you do."

"One minute!" called the guard.

"What if I call Priscilla tomorrow, let her know to expect you?"

"Please, don't do that. And don't tell anyone about this ticket. Promise me that. This has to be mine alone."

"Come on, old man." A guard was at their table now. Her father flinched at the sight of him.

"Okay," she said, pushing her chair back. But her father was leaning forward, gripping her arm.

"Reyes told you he was no good," he whispered. "You think I didn't know who he really was and that you had something going with him, but I did. I should have made you stay away from him."

She stepped back.

"Uncle John," she said, keeping her tone even, trying to keep smiling, "he's exactly like you."

Her father's smile faded. "I would never abandon someone the way he's done to you."

"Now!" The guard snarled. He had a grip on her father's forearm.

"All right, all right, no need to get testy. Not so tight. I'll go, I'll go." He looked at her again. "See you later, kiddo," he said, as if nothing had just happened, as if they were just a regular uncle and niece, bidding each other farewell until next time.

The split-level ranch house was lit up inside and out. Darla hosted a Christmas Eve open house every year and neighbors had been in and out all afternoon and evening. Blossom had a red bow on in place of a collar, and as the party wound down the girls took her upstairs to the bedroom they shared, where they had been instructed to change into their Christmas pajamas, get in bed, and read their new books. New pajamas and a new book were a household tradition on Christmas Eve in the Dixon house, apparently. Lucky hadn't known what to say when Darla asked her what types of books she liked. The last book she'd read was *Les Misérables*; she'd left it behind in Novi without ever finding out what had become of the wretched Jean Valjean and the tragic Fantine. But she knew Darla would think it strange for a girl her age to ask for that book. So she asked for the latest Goosebumps story. Stephanie had asked for a V. C. Andrews novel, and squealed as she read, vowing to lend it to "Andi" after she was finished.

Eventually, Steph put her book down. "I can't concentrate," she announced. "I'm too excited." She scratched her dog's ears. "Blossom, if you hear Santa's reindeer tonight, you have to bark real loud and wake me up, okay?" Even though she was a year older than Lucky, Steph still believed in Santa Claus, and fervently. Lucky didn't have the heart to tell her there was no such thing. Her father had never bothered to hide the truth from her, and he'd mentioned in an aside to her the other day that he had been tasked by Darla with finding hiding places for all the "Santa gifts." He'd also casually suggested that Lucky ask for jewelry, and perhaps gold. "Maybe a locket or something. Something we could have melted down when we——"

He'd seen her face and stopped talking. "You never think about anything but money," Lucky had said. This was the first time in her life she'd really felt how magical Christmas could be, and he was ruining it.

"You don't understand what it takes to survive," he replied.

"We're surviving fine. We can just stay here and we don't have to *steal* anything——"

Darla arrived home then, arms laden with shopping bags, and the conversation ended.

"Hellooo," Steph was saying now. "Zone out much?"

"Sorry, I'm really excited, too. So excited I can't think about anything else."

"You're going to *love* Christmas here. Family tradition is a pile of presents for each person, like a *huge* pile." Steph's eyes were dancing with anticipation. "But first you have to open your stocking." She pursed her lips. "I have something for you that's really special. I don't want it to get lost in all the chaos." She leaped from her bed and started rummaging in her closet until she unearthed a very small box, which she handed to Lucky.

"What's this?" Lucky asked, staring down at it. She'd gotten Stephanie something, too, a peasant top she had admired at a store at the mall. But looking down at this small box, she realized there was something special inside. Something more special than a peasant top.

"You shouldn't have," she began, just as Steph said, "I bought it with my chore money." Now Lucky felt even more ashamed. Steph's mom had paid for the top. Lucky had used her chore money to buy a sterling silver tie clip for her dad. She had wanted this Christmas to be as special for him as she could make it, hoping that seeing how they could live, how happy they could all be, would make him want to stay beyond the year, he had promised her—which was rapidly running out. Three more months.

Stephanie came over to sit on Lucky's bed, and the Goosebumps book thumped to the floor.

"Girls!" Darla called from downstairs. "Almost time for lights-out!"

"Just a few more minutes, Mom," Steph called back, then turned to Lucky again. "Come on, open it."

"All right, all right!" Lucky said. She carefully parted the tape from the paper without ripping it at all.

It was a pale blue jewelry box. She flipped it open. Nestled inside was a golden charm bracelet. There were two charms: one was a heart with the word *Sisters* engraved on it, and the other was in the shape of a dog that looked just like Blossom. "I thought the gold would match the necklace from your mom," Steph said. "I'm going to add one on your birthday, and one again next Christmas. Forever, for the rest of your life, I'll get you charms."

Lucky started to cry. "I can't," she said. "I can't accept this."

Steph was aghast. "Don't you like it? I'm sorry, I thought—"

"No, no. It's not that I don't like it. It's just that—it's too much. Nothing is right about any of this." She swallowed back a gasping sob. Any day now, Steph and her mom would find out about all the lies she and her father had told. Any day now, it would all fall apart.

Lucky put the bracelet back in the box and squeezed her eyes shut. A fat tear rolled out and down her cheek.

"I don't understand why you're so sad," Steph said. "Does it . . . does it make you think of your mom, is that why?"

Lucky opened her eyes. Steph had given her an answer. She wiped her cheeks. "Yes," she lied. "I don't want to wear any jewelry other than my necklace. It feels disloyal, somehow . . ." Lucky covered her face with her hand. "I'm sorry," she said through her fingers. "I really, really am."

"I'm the one who should be sorry."

There was a noise at the door and the girls looked up. Darla and John were standing in the doorframe.

"Everything okay in here, girls?" Darla asked. Lucky wiped her tears away with her fists. She took a deep breath.

"Can I talk to my dad?" Lucky said. "Privately?"

In the old Buick later, Lucky could still see her breath. There hadn't been time to warm up the car, of course. After Steph had finally fallen asleep, Lucky had gathered a few things, whatever clothes and books she could find in the dark, and shoved them in her school bag. She had taken the bracelet and charms, knowing her father would scold her later if she didn't.

"You could take a few," her father had whispered as they had tiptoed through the living room, Blossom on their heels, her tail wagging. Lucky had ignored the suggestion, bypassed all the presents, and carefully opened the front door while her father held the dog, one of the many things she was going to have to forget about this place.

Perhaps Steph thought the sounds of them leaving the house were the sounds of Santa and his reindeer, or perhaps she just slept right through it. It didn't matter now. They were on the highway, miles away. They were never going to see Steph or Darla again.

Lucky exhaled in a big white puff as her father sped up on the empty road; no one was out on Christmas Eve; everyone who was coming home for the holidays had already arrived. It was only people like them who would be out on a night like this. The drifters. The rolling stones.

"Anything I can do to make it feel better, kiddo? It's Christmas, after all."

"No," Lucky said.

"This is for the best," her father eventually said, after the miles between them and Bellevue had increased even more. He took one hand off the steering wheel and placed it on top of hers. "We won't involve people anymore. It's too easy to get hurt—both us and them—when you've got to worry about people and their feelings."

"What if we just don't do this at all anymore? What if we just moved somewhere, and settled down, and you got a job, like other dads do? And I went to school. You always told me I was smart. I could go to school, and then high school, and then a really good college. I could get a job and take care of you. It doesn't have to be like this."

He turned on the radio, but it was Christmas carols so he turned it off. "I know you wish you were like other kids, but what you maybe don't realize is that what you're really wishing is for me to be like other dads," he said. "And I'm not. I don't know any life but this one. I don't know how I'd go about changing that. What sort of job could I even get?"

"You could do anything you put your mind to. I've seen you."

But he went silent again, and they were getting close to the border between Washington and Oregon when she realized the conversation was over.

"Get out the map, Lucky. Atta girl. Let's figure out our next stop."

CHAPTER NINE

Lucky stared out the window of the bus, sifting slowly in her mind through bad option after bad option. When she arrived at the bus station in San Francisco, she was still undecided. She looked at the schedule, considered buying a ticket to Fresno—but she wasn't ready to see Priscilla yet, if ever.

Only, what if Priscilla knew where Cary was? Did that matter to her? Lucky pushed the thought aside. She had to keep moving forward, beyond the heartache of being abandoned by Cary, beyond all the other things that had hurt her in her past.

But names she had tried to suppress for years still came to mind as she stared down at the bus schedule in her hand. *Darla. Steph.* She had tried so hard not to think of them, ever, after she and her father had driven away from their house. How could her father think any good could come from contacting them now? Hadn't they hurt them enough?

She kept poring over the bus schedule, moving her finger over the destinations, rejecting them all. Finally, she just closed her eyes and pointed. She opened her eyes. Baker City, Oregon, it was.

Before boarding, she picked up a copy of the *San Francisco Chronicle.* There was only one article of interest:

YOUNG BONNIE AND CLYDE COUPLE
WHO FLED BOISE STILL ON LAM

An Idaho Supreme Court judge has issued a warrant for the arrests of Alaina Cadence, 26, and David Ferguson, 30, in connection with investment fraud and money-laundering charges.

The FBI is also now involved, with an investigation launched into the couple's alleged connections to organized crime and racketeering. District attorneys' offices in several states, including New York and California, are joining the investigation . . .

Lucky stared at the black-and-white words until they blurred. She could still hear Cary's voice from that day at the gas station, cutting, dismissive, telling her how funny he found it that she was always trying to redeem herself—when meanwhile, only he had known she was beyond redemption. *I'm not trying to redeem myself. I'm trying to help people who need help,* Lucky had said that day, what felt like a lifetime ago. Was that it, though? Did she truly, in her heart, want to *help* people? She had a strange way of showing it, if so.

She flipped through the paper again. There was also a small article about the lottery ticket. MASSIVE MULTI MILLIONS LOTTERY TICKET WINNINGS STILL UNCLAIMED, read the headline. *The winner still has several months to collect the winnings before they will be returned to the lottery pot . . .*

Lucky put the paper away and took the lottery ticket out of her wallet, slowly, carefully. It was frayed at the edges, ripped on one side, and she knew she needed to find a place to keep it where it wouldn't get so beaten up—but that was a hard thing to do when you were constantly on the move.

Three hundred and ninety million dollars.

She allowed herself to consider claiming the money. She rummaged in her backpack and took out a pad of paper and a pen, both pilfered from Jeremy's room at the Bellagio. She could start by repaying the people she and Cary had stolen money from in Idaho. She began to make a list. There were twenty clients, and she owed a few million between them. She would find a way to secretly pay it back, if she ever got that lottery money. She would make it right.

She tapped the pen against the page.

Steph. Darla, she wrote. She would find them again. Someday, somehow, she would pay them back for all the lies she and her father had told.

She paused, then wrote, *Gloria.*

Her mother wasn't one of the people she owed money to—but she owed it to herself to find her. And she was determined to. Not today, but someday she would.

When she was finally the kind of person any mother would love.

———

Lucky decided to get off the bus before it reached Baker City, in a tiny town called Little Spring that wasn't much more than a general store, two churches, a smattering of houses, and a motel and truck-stop diner, joined together, in the midst of a bunch of trees with a view of mountains in the distance.

She headed to the diner, noting the HELP WANTED sign in the window as she walked in, her body stiff from sitting in one position on the bus for so long. In the bathroom, she splashed water on her face and brushed her teeth. She attempted to fix her hair, then looked away from her tired reflection. She would decide who she was later on. She checked on the lottery ticket, which was now in an envelope in the front pocket of her jeans.

She ordered the breakfast special, and nursed her coffee long after she was finished eating. The owners of the diner were an elderly couple named Benson and Arlene; Lucky knew this because everyone who walked in the restaurant called them by their names. Lucky seemed to be the only stranger in there that day. Even the truckers who passed through were on a first-name basis with the friendly proprietors.

The breakfast rush ended. Benson and Arlene stopped refilling her coffee and were shooting her anxious glances. She stared down at the table until a story came to her. She approached the counter with her head lowered. It wasn't hard for her to pretend to be nervous, out of place, a little scared. She was all these things. "I'm Ruby," she said. "Ruby Cullen. I saw the sign. In the window?"

"That sign's been up for years," Benson replied. "We're getting too old to do all the work ourselves. But no one has ever applied. Not enough people in this town."

"I'm backpacking across the country, and I've run out of money. I've got lots of restaurant experience." It spilled out easily; not all of it was a lie. "I have references . . . although they're all in California."

"Wouldn't waste money calling anyone long distance," the old man said, looking deep into her eyes while Lucky worried he might suddenly realize he'd seen that green before, the exact green of a spearmint-leaf candy, an unusual eye color. But his expression didn't change. If anything, it grew warmer. "Well, now, why don't you just have a go at it and we'll see how you do during lunch?" He smiled reassuringly and she smiled back. She donned the yellowed apron he handed her, rolled up her sleeves, and got to work.

The lunch rush turned out to consist of only twenty customers over the course of two hours. Still, Lucky had to work hard to keep up. It had been a while since she'd worked in a restaurant, and she'd never waited tables before. But she quickly got into a rhythm and started to have fun. She would stand at a table and size up her customers, make a game of guessing what they were going to order. She was right almost every time. "Ain't you gonna write that down?" one trucker asked her after reciting a particularly complicated order.

"I have a good memory," Lucky said. She took two more orders before crossing the room and calling them out to Benson, each one word perfect.

"You really are a pro," he said. "Why don't you try the dinner hour next?"

During the frequent lulls, the elderly couple asked her questions about herself. "So, what made you decide to go—how did ya put it—backpacking around the country?"

"I was married. But he turned out to be a real asshole. Oops, pardon my language, Arlene. He wasn't a good man. I needed to get away." Lucky paused here and let those words hang in the air, but had to look away from their trusting faces, how aghast they were at the idea of her facing the abuse she was hinting at, at the idea of her running away because she was scared, maybe. If she was trying to be a better person, she was off to a questionable start. "I had the idea I'd go for a long hike, I guess. Try to clear my head."

"A young woman like you should not be going off hiking or hitch-hiking alone. It isn't safe," said Benson.

Arlene was frowning, too. "You'd best not be doing that anymore, hitchhiking, at least. You'll stay here for a while, all right? Stay here, work a bit, and have a think about deciding on a proper destination, rather than wandering around. There must be a family member or a friend you could go visit. Someone who would notice if you didn't show up."

"I do have a few friends," Lucky lied, her heart aching at this one.

"But . . . I'd need a computer to look them up."

"We don't have our own, but you'll find one or two at the library," Arlene said. "You can use my library card or Benson's to get the internet access. Go tomorrow morning, between breakfast and lunch."

At that point it was eight o'clock, and the stream of suppertime customers had trickled to almost nothing. Lucky's feet were sore as she stood at the counter, counting her tips. The townspeople didn't exactly tip generously, but at least they tipped a little. She had twenty-six dollars to her name now, plus whatever hourly wage the elderly couple was going to give her.

"You did a good job, young lady," said Benson. He put down the newspaper he was reading. She caught a headline: MULTI MILLIONS LOTTERY TICKET—BIGGEST PAYOUT IN U.S. HISTORY—BOUGHT IN IDAHO STILL UNCLAIMED. Then he handed her a room key. "You'll stay in room one-oh-six," he said. "Has the nicest view—of the trees, not the parking lot. And we won't hear of accepting any payment. You can stay as long as you need to."

Lucky decided then and there that she wasn't going to take anything from these strangers, nothing more than their kindness. It would be easy—and it would be wrong. And nothing from their customers, either, even though memorizing and recording the credit card numbers of truckers who passed through had crossed her mind many times that day.

"Thank you," she said, accepting the key. It was cool in her hand. It was the very thing she had wanted: a room to herself, somewhere safe to sleep. And she hadn't had to do anything she hated herself for to get it.

"Happy to do it, Ruby. See you in the morning."

Days passed, and the routine at the diner became pleasant. Lucky now knew everything about the business, from the safe combination, to the passwords for the bank accounts, to where Arlene and Benson set their wallets down during the day. And the only thing this made her feel was important.

She went to the library most afternoons. She created a fake social media profile and typed in names. Marisol Reyes was nowhere to be found. Priscilla Lachaise was, though. She had a Facebook profile and it led Lucky to a page for the shelter in Fresno, with a strangely cutesy "Priscilla's Place" logo that made Lucky angry just looking at it. Who knew what scams Priscilla was running under the guise of reform? Lucky clicked through the photos of the shelter for a while, feeling increasingly skeptical as she did. Priscilla was a con artist through and through. People like that didn't change, in Lucky's experience. She was doing a hell of a job of pretending, though. Lucky had to give her that. She was a master.

And Cary had been her protégé. He was a master, too.

Lucky clicked out of the Priscilla's Place page and typed a different name into the search bar: "Darla Dixon." A private profile came up. Darla was smiling, holding a young child. Lucky squinted at the photo, but it was too small for her to get a good look at. She typed in "Stephanie Dixon," but her page was private, too. However, her "About" information tab led to a business profile. Lucky clicked through. Stephanie Dixon-Carr, Realtor. She lived in Seattle now, not Bellevue.

Lucky remembered that Steph had wanted to be a veterinarian. She didn't know Stephanie, the grown-up version of her old friend. Not at all. This woman in the photos she was looking at was a stranger.

Lucky took out her notepad and made a few notes, then logged off. If Stephanie was a stranger, that was going to make it easier to face her—if that was what she decided to do.

Lucky told Arlene and Benson she was going to be leaving. "Where's that you're going, then?" Benson asked, looking a little sad. "To see that friend in Bellevue you mentioned the other day?"

"Yeah," Lucky said. "She's in Seattle now. I'm going to go look her up."

"Oh, that's nice," Arlene said. "Benson and I were worrying about where you'd get off to next—but if you're going to see a friend, that's a good thing. You keep in touch, please. And you come straight back here if it doesn't work out with the friend."

At the end of her last day, Arlene pressed an extra hundred-dollar bill into Lucky's hand and whispered for her to take care of herself. Lucky almost handed the money back—but she needed it too badly.

She asked for their mailing address and wrote it down carefully on her list of people to pay back.

"You'll be hearing from me," she promised. "One day, when everything is different. I promise."

Then she went outside to wait for the bus.

When Lucky got to Seattle, almost six hours later, it was late afternoon. She found a consignment shop and chose her outfit carefully: black trousers; soft, subtly metallic leather flats; and a little clutch to replace her belt pack. She also found a costume shop that sold colored contacts. She chose blue. Her eyes were still distinctive, but in a different way now.

She hid her backpack in a bush down the street from the house she was going to. The lottery ticket was taped inside her shirt. She had put her small collection of IDs and what little money she had left into her pockets, bra, and purse. If the backpack was taken, so be it. But she hoped not.

She approached the house and stood in front of it for a moment. What if Steph recognized her right away, saw through her potential home-buyer facade? Lucky blinked several times against the gritty feeling of the contact lenses. She climbed the stairs and walked through the front door.

Several couples, small children in tow, were trailing out the door. Lucky started to take off her shoes.

"It's all right, leave your shoes on."

Lucky looked up at a woman with a sleek brown bob and a welcoming smile. She was holding out a hand for Lucky to take. "I'm Stephanie, the real estate agent."

"Hi, Stephanie," Lucky said. "Nice to meet you. This is a lovely house." She turned away from her quickly, her heart pounding fast and hard.

"It is," Stephanie said, behind her. "Take your time walking through. I need to tidy up a bit."

"Thanks." Lucky wandered the main floor, thinking that this house reminded her of an updated version of Steph's house from when they were kids. Grown-up Stephanie went into the kitchen, her flats—similar to the ones Lucky wore—making soft sounds on the porcelain wood-look tile floors (heated, according to the property description in the flyer she now held in her hand) while Lucky moved forward to stand at the window, heart still racing.

In the other room, she heard a cell phone ring, and then Stephanie's voice. "Hi, Mom. Is he really? Adorable. Yes, half hour or so. Just one last person here."

Lucky stood rooted to the floor.

Footsteps behind her. Lucky turned and forced a smile.

"Would you like me to give you a proper tour of the upstairs?"

"Sure," Lucky said. "That would be great."

On the second floor, they stood in the doorway of a bedroom.

"Isn't it sweet? Reminds me of the room I had as a little girl," Stephanie said.

"Yes," Lucky said. She cleared her throat. "I mean, I could see that. Any little girl would love this room." She wondered if this bed was a trundle, too, with a mattress that could be pulled in and out for a friend who was almost like a sister to sleep on. She moved toward it and ran her hand along the smooth wood, searching for a handle until she found one. "My daughter would adore it," Lucky said, straightening up and moving away from her memories. She crossed the room and stood by the window, pretending to check out the view of the yard.

"How many children do you have?"

"Two. A girl and a boy. Four and five." At this lie, Lucky's voice wobbled—and her hand rose instinctively to her stomach, the way it often had during the two-month period in Boise when she had been pregnant with Cary's baby. She tried not to think of this time, of the loss. But in pretending to be a mother now, she had opened that wound. She fought to smile again.

"How lovely. A million-dollar family. I have a son, but we're hoping for another child."

"Yes, well." Lucky turned away from the window, composed herself. "I'm thinking of having a third, but my mom would probably move out on me if I did, and I sort of count on her for help with the kids."

"Oh, that would be *amazing*," Stephanie said. "My mom still works, so she can't help with my son during the day—but she does babysit for me when my husband is working, like tonight."

Lucky wished she could ask why Darla was still working. They'd had so much money, before. But as she remembered the house, the car, from days gone by, she realized it wasn't enough to sustain anyone for a lifetime. Especially after some con made a serious dent in your bank account on his way out of town.

Lucky cleared her throat. "How many bedrooms did you say there were?"

"Three, plus an office. Here, let me show you." Stephanie led Lucky down the hall to a bedroom painted a dark blue with electric-green accents and football pennants on the walls.

"My son would *love* this," Lucky said, the pain from earlier now receded, her focus back on the story she was weaving about herself. "He's a huge Seahawks fan."

In Stephanie's grin, Lucky saw the girl she had known. "I tried to convince the owners to paint out this dark color, but they wouldn't do it. They said it would just be a matter of finding the right buyer."

"Can I see the master?"

As Stephanie walked ahead, she talked about the brand-new Berber carpeting, the hardwood in the bedrooms, the wall sconces. Lucky could tell she was getting excited, thinking she had found the perfect buyer for this house. Enough was enough. Lucky had nothing for her—not yet.

"Listen," Lucky said. "This is a great house—but I just realized, I have to go. It's getting late, and I have to pick the kids up from a friend's place because my mom is at swim class. I got so sidetracked, seeing this house, the sign saying it was for sale when I'd always admired it. It's perfect for my family. You're right, it feels like kismet. And I want to see it again, but right now . . . I can't stay."

"Kismet?" Stephanie cocked her head. "I don't remember using that word."

Lucky was backing out of the room. "I'll call you. I'll bring my husband and the kids to look at it. I'll see you again soon, thank you for your time, bye."

T he year Lucky turned seventeen, her father won a "house-boat" in a New Year's Eve poker game in Palm Springs. When Lucky and her father arrived in Sausalito, where the boat was docked, they learned it was a decades-old thirty-five-foot Catalina live-aboard sailboat and not much of a prize: it wasn't seaworthy.

"But at least it's a roof over our heads," John said, climbing down the steps and putting his rucksack on the kitchen table belowdecks in the tiny living space. There was a bench on one side of the table and behind it was a shelf. A lantern-like chandelier hung above the table; a rusted icebox was tucked beneath the bench. There was a tiny sink, but it didn't work. There were a hot plate and a kettle, too. The bedroom consisted of a cabin belowdecks with leaky porthole windows and two long cushioned benches; mildew crept up from the cushion seams.

Lucky's heart sank a little as she looked around. It wasn't just that it was dingy. There was no privacy here, and as she inched closer to adulthood, she was craving it.

"Did you leave the corkscrew at home?" she heard someone shout a few boats over.

Home. Her father went out to the deck; she opened her backpack and began lining the shelf in the kitchen with her books. She put the last one on the shelf and reached deeper into the bag. Her father poked his head in the door and she zipped the backpack shut, fast. "Sun's setting," he said. "It's really pretty. A little chilly, though. Grab a sweater."

"I'll be there in a minute." She put the backpack on one of the beds but didn't unpack anything else.

When she stepped outside, he turned to her. "Hey, kiddo? You can have the room to yourself. I'll just sleep on the kitchen bench, or out on deck when it gets warmer. You're a young woman. I know you need a little privacy."

"It's okay," Lucky said.

"No, it isn't. Let me do this for you."

"Dad, it's *okay*."

He said nothing more, just looked out at the San Francisco Bay. "Maybe this could be it," he eventually said. The water was silver now, the sky above it a moody blue, streaked with garish pink. Houseboats lined the bay, hulking together in colorful clusters. Lucky looked down into the waves lapping against the side of the boat and thought she saw a sea lion swim by, grinning at her for a slip of a moment before diving down. She smelled grilled meat, and heard quiet laughter a few boats down. *Maybe this could be it . . .*

"It's not exactly the dream house I always promised you. But it's nice, isn't it?"

"It's very nice, Dad."

A sailboat edged past them and docked. She heard a child call out, "Mom!"

Why are my eyes so green, and why is my hair so red? Who is my mother? Where is my mother? Lucky asked herself these questions all the time, but she never voiced them aloud anymore because her father didn't answer her. Lucky would see mothers and daughters out in the world and understand that not always, but sometimes and really quite often, a mother was a soft, safe, beautiful thing. She didn't have that. And she ached for it.

She thought of the stolen items in the bottom of her backpack: a Discman, a trendy watch, some dangly earrings. Why had she hidden them from her father? He knew she stole; he didn't care. But these things felt like they were only hers. She didn't want him to see who she really wanted to be.

She was hiding something else from him, too. But it was time to reveal it.

"'I know I haven't been in school for years, since we were living with . . . when we were in Bellevue," Lucky began. "But I've been studying. I've kept up. I want to find out if it's been good enough. So I want to take my high school equivalency—and then, if I do well, I want to take the SAT. And then . . . I want to apply to college."

Her father nodded slowly. He didn't seem surprised. "You've really thought this through."

"It's all I think about these days."

"And I guess what you're hiding in your backpack is more books."

"Yes," she lied.

"You didn't need to hide this from me. I understand. And it's fine. I'll take care of things. You focus on studying."

"I could still set up a tarot table, down at the wharf. Do that one day a week?"

"Nah, nah. That's small potatoes. If you're going to be attending college, I'm going to need some real money. But don't you worry about it. Like I said, I'll figure it out."

She couldn't believe it had been this easy. She had been sure he would say no, get upset and tell her she couldn't just resign as his partner. But he didn't seem bothered. And now she was going to start taking steps, on her own, to be a regular person with a regular life. That meant studying; that meant school. Diplomas and jobs.

Her father turned in a small circle on the tiny deck. "This place feels like it's full of possibility," he said.

And for once, Lucky had to agree.

John got a job at a seafood restaurant called the Sandbar, an iconic spot perched over an area of the beach littered with oyster shells glittering like broken and discarded treasure. He said his name was Johnny Starr, that he had wanted to be an actor, once—easy to believe, with his good looks, which never frayed at the edges the way his clothes did. He and his daughter, Alaina, had moved here from L.A. for a quieter life after a favorite uncle died and left him the boat.

It was still the low season, but the restaurant had a steady clientele of executives and local politicians. There was money to be made, John told Lucky, and as far as Lucky could tell all he meant was tips. He was working at a real job. She would sit on the deck of their boat, layered in sweaters, and study, and he'd go off to work. Maybe he had been right. Maybe this *was* it. Their home.

When she looked back on this time later, it was as one of the happiest in her life.

Her father would come home at night with bags of leftover food from the restaurant—mostly sandwiches, omelets, fries, and salads, but sometimes a prawn, a crab cake, a pile of steamed Manila clams hidden beneath a leaf of butter lettuce, or a decadent pan-seared scallop atop a tangle of pasta. He'd count his tips while they ate, then hide the money in a lockbox he kept in the berth of the boat. She knew it wasn't going to be enough to pay for college tuition, though.

"Maybe I'll get a scholarship," she mused.

"You just worry about passing those tests first, and I'll take care of the rest."

"I want to help out, Dad. It's bothering me. I can't study twenty-four/seven. Maybe I could work a few days at the restaurant. Do they need a hostess?" The weather was getting warmer and the restaurant was busier. John agreed that a little extra money might help. He talked to his boss and got Lucky two shifts a week seating guests at tables and helping the bussers to clear them after.

One afternoon when Lucky and her father were both working at the restaurant, a striking, elegantly dressed woman with black hair pulled back in a severe French twist came in for lunch. She had a girl with her about Lucky's age who looked sullen and shy, shoving her hands in her pockets and toeing the welcome mat with scuffed combat boots.

"I want table eight," the woman said to Lucky. "That one. By the window." Lucky felt irritated, but the owner of the restaurant said the customer was always right—and table eight was empty. It was in her father's section. Lucky rolled her eyes at him after she seated the two guests, and he shrugged and smiled.

Hours later, long after the lunch rush was over, they were still there. The girl was looking out the window, apparently bored. The woman was laughing as John stood by their table, talking animatedly.

"Got myself another job," her father told her later as he counted his tips and Lucky sat on the boat's deck, munching on slightly soggy fried clams from a takeout container.

"That awful woman who came in today?"

"What was so awful about her?"

Lucky shrugged. "I dunno. Thought she was kind of rude."

"Her name is Priscilla Lachaise. She was with her associate, Marisol Reyes."

"Associate? I thought it was her daughter."

"Nah, they work together."

"Doing what?"

"Some sort of call center. Sounds like a good business, a lot of opportunity for growth."

"Is it legit?"

He didn't answer the question. "They need a manager. Good money, too. High commission."

Weeks passed, and her father started spending a great deal of time with Priscilla and Marisol—whom he called Reyes and treated like a kid sister, or a second daughter. He didn't like to talk about whatever it was Priscilla had him doing at a rented office that he would only tell her vaguely was "downtown." Once Lucky and her dad had been partners. Now it often felt like they were strangers. She spent her days alone on the boat studying, or sitting on the beach, her nose buried in her books.

One day in early March, John returned home with papers for her: a birth certificate, a passport, and a social security card, all under the name of Alaina Cadence.

"This is really you now, kiddo. Alaina Cadence. Nice, right? You can use these to sign up for your high school equivalency, to take your SAT—*and* to apply to college. What do you think?"

"How did you get these?"

"Priscilla. She's a real gem."

Lucky examined the birth certificate and thumbed through the passport. The possibilities dizzied her: not just school, not just college—but travel. She could go anywhere, do anything, with these papers. "Dad, I . . . don't know what to say."

"Ah, just start with thank you."

"Thank you," she said. But she also wanted to ask questions. *What do you do for her, over there at the "call center"? Why do you tell me I need to make myself scarce when she comes here for your "meetings"? Why won't Reyes ever look me in the eye?*

She never asked any of this. And one day, she would come to regret it.

Lucky passed the high school equivalency test, and then started studying for the SAT. It was getting warmer, which to Lucky meant her time was running out: she had to take the test and apply to colleges within a month. She pilfered a bikini from a stall near their boat, and often brought her books and a towel onto the sand with her. Her skin turned golden in the California sunshine; her red hair turned paler, kissed with streaks. It tumbled down her back, almost to her waist.

"Reyes says you're getting a lot of attention out there on the beach," her father said to her one night.

"What, is Reyes spying on me?"

"I asked her to keep an eye out for you. She's street smart, knows what to look out for around here. Lucky, you should be nicer to her. Pay her a little bit of attention."

"Pay her attention *when*? I never see her. You're either working with her, and you don't want me around, or having your meetings with her and Priscilla, and you don't want me around. Do you even work at the restaurant anymore?"

"I do two shifts a week."

"I barely know you anymore, Dad. Reyes probably knows you better than I do."

Her father sighed. "Don't be jealous."

"Why would I be *jealous*?"

"She's not a bad kid. She's just had a rough life. You and Reyes would be great friends, I think, if you'd just give her a chance."

Lucky had never had a true friend—not since Steph, and that hadn't been real. She told herself she was waiting for college. Alaina Cadence was going to have tons of friends in college.

"I need to go, kiddo. Back to work for me. How's the studying?"

"Going great," Lucky said, staring down at her book.

Lucky got a perfect 1600 on her SAT. She finished her college applications just in time. "With that score, you can go to college wherever you want," her father said—but he sounded nervous now. There was money in the lockbox, but not enough, not yet. "Where do you want to go?"

LUCKY 113

"We should probably stay here, live here," Lucky said. "It's more practical." She looked away from her father's obvious relief and tried not to think of all the colleges she wanted to apply to. "The University of San Francisco is only half an hour away by bus, and they have an accounting program in the management school. That's what I want to do."

"An *accountant*? But you love books, you love reading, you could do anything you wanted, anything in the world. That, really? It's such a . . ." He trailed off.

"Boring job? Boring life path? Has it ever occurred to you that boring and safe is exactly what I want? Also, I love numbers. I love their . . . predictability."

"I didn't know this about you."

"We don't talk much, lately."

Doing these normal things—applying to college, getting accepted, making the preparations to go there—gave Lucky a deep and calming sense of satisfaction she had never experienced before. She began to see a map laid out before her, much like the one they had consulted throughout her childhood, trying to decide which town to hit up next. But now, it felt like a path she was controlling herself. College, the certificates she needed to become an accountant, her own business or a job at a large firm—she had a plan, and for once, it didn't include cheating.

It was June. Lucky put on her bikini, took out her Discman and popped her earbuds in her ears. Bikini Kill started screaming about liars. She shoved a twenty-dollar bill in the pocket of her denim shorts, grabbed a book, left the boat, and walked down to the pier. This was becoming her daily routine on the days she wasn't hostessing at the restaurant. She didn't have to study anymore and had nothing else to do.

Today, as she sat reading, a group of teens caught her eye. There were many small crowds of friends who frequented the pier, and some of them were growing familiar to her. One group in particular always drew her eye. She tried not to feel jealous of their expensive-looking clothes and the gadgets and accessories they seemed to take for granted.

There was a cute boy in the group with a good tan and brown hair streaked with California blond. She had walked by him and his crew of six, sometimes seven, a mix of boys and girls, almost every day that early summer. He was the only one who ever looked her way. When he watched her, she understood what it meant to say your heart had skipped a beat.

Today, he smiled at her and she felt shy; she ducked her face back behind the collection of Lucia Berlin short stories she was reading, and she regretted her shyness immediately. What would it be like to be one of those girls in his group?

But she *wasn't*. For one thing, they were all petite, and she was tall. They were blond; her hair was sun-bleached now but still red, and too curly. They were pert-faced and smiling; she almost never smiled. The only feature she liked were her emerald-green eyes, a color she had never seen on anyone else. Everything else about her felt too big. Nose too prominent, lips too wide, too tall in general, feet too large and awkward.

The girls in his group wore white, pastel, or fluorescent tank tops; neatly trimmed denim shorts and Keds with no socks, all in the same varying colors as their tops. Lucky wore ripped cutoffs made from old pairs of jeans over her bathing suit, and thrift shop T-shirts.

There was something about the boy that was different, too. She couldn't put her finger on it. He probably lived in some beautiful home in The Hill with a perfect family, a mom and dad and plenty of siblings. But still, she felt a strange kinship with him.

Later, she walked past him and his group again on her way back from the restrooms. He was holding an ice cream cone now. Lucky watched from behind her sunglasses, now ambling slowly, as one of the girls took a swipe at it with her tongue and he pulled it away, laughing. Lucky averted her eyes and kept walking by, but at the last second, she veered right into the ice cream shop because, for once, Lappert's didn't have a line.

Inside, she puzzled over the flavors: Hawaiian Sea Salt Caramel, Hana Road, Manila Mango. The clerk behind the counter asked what she wanted.

"Um . . ."

Then the boy was standing beside her. He was smiling. She found herself saying, "Just an iced coffee, please."

"Iced coffee? Really?" he asked. "I see you walk by here every day, but you never go in, even though you want to, I can tell. And then you finally come in here and you get iced coffee?"

"Well, I don't really—"

"Kauai Pie," he said to the clerk. "That's the one she wants."

"I don't like coconut," Lucky said.

"The Kona Mocha Chip, then. It's got coffee in it?" He ordered another cone for himself, too, and paid for both of them. Then he held the cones aloft, leading her outside.

The smile on the face of the girl who had swiped at his ice cream cone disappeared when she saw him leading Lucky out, but the rest of the group watched her with interest.

"Thank you," Lucky mumbled as he handed her the cone.

"You're most welcome . . ." He trailed off, expectant. She realized she was supposed to say her name.

"Lu—" She stopped herself. "Alaina," she finished lamely, embarrassed.

"You're most welcome, Lu-alaina," the boy said, grinning a lopsided grin and taking a bite of his ice cream. "I'm Alex."

"You finally talked to her," said a boy with a navy cap pulled low over his face, and Lucky started to blush.

"Just Alaina," she said, her cheeks now officially flaming.

"What are you doing tonight, Alaina?"

Lucky saw the dismay on the girl's face deepen. She looked away from her and back at the handsome boy who had just bought her an ice cream, wiped her fingers with a napkin, shrugged as casually as she could.

"Not sure," she said.

"There's a bonfire down at the cliffs. Meet us there later?"

Lucky wasn't sure what time she was meant to go to the bonfire. She didn't want to be too early, so she read until after nine and then scrawled a note for her father, who was working at the restaurant that night, saying she'd made some friends and was meeting them on the beach.

She headed back the way she had come earlier that day. In the darkness, she could hear the sound of someone strumming a guitar, and a soft voice singing a song about how everything was made to be broken. The fire came into focus, and the cliffs behind it loomed large in the light. Lucky stepped into the area of sand and surf lit up by the bonfire's flames, and Alex jumped up from where he had been sitting on a low rock wall. He had been the one strumming the guitar and singing.

He leaned his guitar against the wall and came forward to greet her. He had a red cup in his hand. "Hey. You came." His smile lit up the night more than any bonfire could. "Here, try some of this. Catch up to the rest of us." The group from earlier that day was there; they smiled and nodded but kept their distance.

"What is it?"

He shrugged. "No clue." He looked older in the darkness. She wondered how old he was, and if he was going to think seventeen was too young. She took the cup from him and had a sip, trying not to sputter and cough. It tasted like paint thinner smelled. There was grape juice mixed in, but it didn't help. They sat in silence, staring at the bonfire for a while. When they had passed the cup back and forth between them so many times it was empty, Alex asked her if she wanted to go for a walk on the beach.

"Sure," she said, but when she stood she felt light-headed, while he didn't seem affected by the alcohol in the cup. She'd never been drunk, or even close to buzzed. Most teens her age had had many experiences like this one, but this was her first party. She often felt out of place, but tonight the sensation was even more acute. Everyone else was dancing to the same beat, and she was out of step.

Alex didn't seem to notice, though. "Are you here on vacation?" he asked her. "I always see you on the beach, but never with anyone. And you seem to have been here for a while."

Had he been watching her? She felt flattered, and nervous. "Oh. Um. Yeah. I'm here with my dad. We live on a sailboat in the bay."

He glanced at her sidelong. "Oh, yeah? Cool. Do you like it?"

"It's different."

"Different from . . ."

"Anywhere else I've lived."

"Where else have you lived?"

"A bunch of places," she said. "My dad . . . worked in sales. We're staying here awhile. I'll be going to SFU in the fall."

"Cool! That's a great school."

"Do you go to college?"

"Taking some time off right now."

His hand reached for hers in the darkness as they walked. His palm was warm and dry, and she was afraid that her nervousness had caused hers to become hot and damp. "What program are you going into at SFU?" he asked.

"Business management. Accounting," she said, suddenly self-conscious of how vanilla that sounded.

But he squeezed her hand and said, "I love numbers."

She found herself squeezing back. "You can always count on numbers," she said, then laughed. "God, I sound like such a nerd."

"Maybe I like nerds," he said. "Especially beautiful, mysterious nerds. I like numbers a lot, Alaina. I like how predictable they are—when so many things in life aren't."

She felt seen for the first time, and the pleasure of it made her feel like she was floating. They moved forward, hand in hand. The emotional intensity in the simple act of linking hands with another person, of becoming one in such an easy, wordless way, surprised her. He'd probably held hands with dozens of girls, but all of this was a revelation for her.

Soon they were approaching the bay, and the restaurant. The warm, happy feeling dissipated. Lucky tugged on Alex's hand to stop him walking. She didn't want to run into her father. This was her moment and hers alone—and her dad would ask her so many questions she wouldn't be able to answer and didn't want to. *Who is he, where does he come from, how do you know you can trust him?*

"Maybe we should go back," she said. Alex was looking down at her, an unreadable expression on his face.

"Maybe," he said, pulling her off the path and into the shadows, staring into her eyes, lifting a hand to cradle her cheek like her face was a precious, delicate thing. He leaned closer and closer until the only thing to do was—

Their lips met in the darkness and it didn't matter anymore that she had never had a friend to talk to about what a first kiss was like, what to do, how to tilt your head. After the first few seconds, none of it mattered. It felt like something she had been doing her whole life. There were things about him she didn't know, but she would learn them all. She felt like a character in one of her books. He was her John Thornton, he was her Henry Tilney, he was her Gabriel Oak. And her life was about to change.

CHAPTER TEN

Lucky stood in a pay phone booth just outside the Seattle Greyhound station. Her hair was blond now; she had bleached it in a bathroom and cut it even shorter. She called directory assistance and asked for the phone number for Devereaux Camp in New York. She wrote it down on her hand, then fed quarters into the telephone and dialed the number, adrenaline coursing through her body. After several rings, a gravelly-voiced man answered. "Devereaux Camp, help ya?"

Lucky didn't speak.

"Hello? Hello?"

"Is Gloria available?" she managed.

"Just a sec."

The phone was put down and there was some muffled talking, some fumbling, and then the man shouted, "Gloria! Phone's for you!"

It had started to rain. The world outside was like a painting in varying shades of gray, with only the odd flash of color: the purple and gold of the Seattle city buses, the green of a tree, the navy trench coat on a woman rushing by, the red of her umbrella.

"Hello? What can I do for you?"

Lucky couldn't speak.

"Helloooo?"

Lucky had the receiver pressed against her ear so hard it hurt—so when Gloria slammed down the phone, that hurt, too. Lucky winced, then replaced the receiver on its cradle and left the phone booth. She stood in the rain, waiting for inspiration to strike. If she wasn't ready to talk to her mother yet, what next, where now?

She walked for a while, then ducked into a coffee shop. Two police officers were sitting at a table in the corner, near the window. One of them caught her eye as she walked in and she forced a quick smile, rather than a guilty look away that could draw attention.

She got in line, bought a small coffee, and left the café. The officers didn't look up as she exited, and her panic receded. She was getting used to living in a constant state of fear. Outside, as she walked, she could feel the lottery ticket against her body, taped to the inside of her rain-damp sweatshirt. The ticket helped. It anchored her to an alternate future. She stopped again when she saw a sign for a used book store, ducked in the door on impulse—and as soon as she did, the familiar aroma of dusty endpapers and shelves filled with books hit her. The volumes she saw felt like companions she had lost along the way.

In the fiction section, she traced a finger along familiar spines, then moved along to French Literature. She swept her eyes along the spines: Camus. Colette. Duras. Hugo—*Les Misérables*. She eased it off the shelf. She had started reading it as a child, then left it behind when she and her dad had moved in with Steph and Darla. This one was a hardcover, and it cost ten dollars, which was more than she could really afford. And she could have tucked it under her sweater: the proprietor of the store was in another aisle, shelving books. But she didn't steal it. She walked up to the cash register, she rang the little bell, and she paid for it. She cradled it against her body, under her sweater, as she walked back to the bus station.

"Ticket to Fresno, please," she said to the cashier at the counter, having finally come to a decision—mostly based on the fact that she had no options. When she was on the bus, she pulled out her book and began to read. She understood Valjean, the way he absorbed the personas he inhabited. She knew he wasn't real, but she still felt less alone, less of a stranger to herself and to everyone she met, as she read.

Hours later, she looked out the window. The bus was approaching the California border now: she saw it on the sign as the bus sped by. She stared at her reflection in the bus window and slowly began to change her posture. Her name was Jean, she decided. She'd been living in Los Angeles, trying to make a living as a screenwriter, but a bad situation with a friend had caused the bottom to fall out of her finances and her dreams. Slowly, over the course of the past year, she had lost it all, and eventually ended up on the streets. She had never imagined something like this would happen to her. She had been sleeping on the beach in Santa Monica for a while, but it didn't feel safe. A transient woman she had met—she couldn't remember her name now—had told her about Priscilla's Place, so she had panhandled enough for a bus ticket and here she was, looking for somewhere to stay. She was not going to tell Priscilla who she really was. She had her colored contacts, her short, bleached hair. She would change her voice, change her posture, do everything in her power to become unrecognizable. It might not work—her father might have called and said to expect her. But she had to try. She couldn't just walk in there and say who she was.

It was getting dark, and she was hungry and stiff. But she had nothing to sustain her, food-wise. She ran her thumb along the lottery ticket inside her shirt and considered the importance of this small slip of paper—how much it could sustain her, and for how long, if she managed to find a way to cash it without having to go to prison. It was too important to walk into Priscilla's with, she realized. They would probably search her, looking for drugs or other contraband before she was allowed to stay at the shelter. She drew her hand away from the ticket. It was just a piece of paper—but it was everything to her, now. She needed to keep it safe. And she had an idea.

"I'd like to book a five-by-five," Lucky said to the young man sitting behind the counter and glass at the storage facility. She slid the two Sarah Armstrong IDs toward him; he barely glanced at them, then slid the license and social security card back to her, as well as a clipboard and some forms in return.

"I saw your deal in the paper," she said. She didn't know about any deal but assumed there was one. There was *always* a deal of some sort, and her dad had taught her you were a fool not to ask.

"Right. It's twenty-one dollars for your first month, plus a ten-dollar service fee."

"Sounds fine to me. I only need the one month. And the locker has a code, not a key?"

"That's correct."

"And I can access it twenty-four/seven after today, with the code?"

"Also correct."

"Okay, great. Just moving out of my boyfriend's place and need to store a bit of stuff until my next place comes through." When she had arrived, Lucky had walked around the back of the building and pulled some boxes out of the dumpster, filled with discarded items: books, clothes, papers, broken dishes, a set of encyclopedias. They sat outside the door now.

The young man just nodded, not at all interested in her story.

"Cash or credit?" he asked.

"Cash," she said, sliding two twenties under the glass and waiting for the change. She was officially broke. She filled out a form, and pocketed the pen while the young man was entering her data into his computer. Then he slid a sheet bearing the locker code under the glass. "It's locker number forty-four, second floor," he said. "You use that same code to get in the door when we're closed."

"Got it, thanks."

She carried the first box and then the second up to the locker, opened it with the code, and went inside. She stood still, looking around. A millipede darted out from behind one of the boxes and startled her. Her eyes swept the empty room, up and down. There: above her head was the fire alarm. The smoke detector was covered by a metal cage, but she was able to stand on one of the boxes and slide her fingers inside, loosen the plastic cover, and insert the folded-up lottery ticket. She got down, took out the pen she had stolen from the counter, and wrote down the locker code on an old receipt, just in case. She encrypted it, made it look like a shopping list. 16234170 turned into:

16 mushrooms
2 pounds of spinach
3/4 pound white beans
170 oz. rice

She had the tape in her backpack, and an X-acto knife She cut open the paper on the inside cover of *Les Misérables*, then slid the receipt inside and taped it there before taping the paper shut. She left the knife in the storage room, in one of the boxes.

She put the book in her backpack, locked the storage room, and went back to the front of the building, where there was a pay phone and a phone book. When she had found the address for Priscilla's Place, she started to walk.

August 1999
SAUSALITO, CALIFORNIA

═══

"Y ou're always there for me when I need you," Lucky said to Alex. They were lying on a towel in the secluded area of the beach that had become their meeting place.

"Where else would I be, and what else do I have to do, except wait around to spend time with you, and come the second you call?" He kissed her, then gazed into her eyes. He had this way of looking at her that was so focused, so interested—as if every time he saw her, he was seeing her for the first time. "Where else would I want to be, except with the woman I'm falling in love with?" he murmured.

Woman. Falling in love. He made her feel like a grown-up. But she pulled away. "We barely know each other," she forced herself to say, hearing her father's voice—as little as she wanted to—telling her to be careful about whom she trusted. "How can we be falling in love?"

His smile widened. "Does that mean you're falling in love with me, too?"

"Alex. I just think it's a bit soon to know . . ."

He laughed. His ego clearly wasn't wounded. He was so easygoing, so simple to be around. So *sure* about them. "Okay, okay. We need to get to know each other better, then. Less kissing, more talking, right? So, what do you want to know?"

"Maybe we can kiss *and* talk," she said with a smile. "Where were you born?"

"Here."

"Do your parents still live here?"

A shadow passed over his face.

"My parents died," he said.

"Oh, I'm sorry, I shouldn't have—"

"No, no, it's okay. It's just . . . still hard to talk about. Maybe it always will be."

He reached up and traced her jaw with his finger, then kissed it.

"What were they like?"

"They were great parents. Real adventurers. My dad had a little Cessna he kept up at our cabin, out near Muir Woods. We used to spend our summers there, go out there on weekends whenever we could."

"What happened?" she whispered, her heart aching for him. Imagine having everything—a loving family, *two* parents—and losing that.

"Engine failure. They crashed. I wasn't feeling well that day, and I was only eight, so I stayed home, with a babysitter. And I . . . survived."

"Oh, Alex. I'm so sorry."

"I still remember what it felt like, to fly with them." His voice was faraway now. "How small the world looked to me, from way up there. How big it made me feel. How important, how special—to be up there, looking down. I've always wanted to do that again."

"We'll get a plane one day," she said automatically, desperate to make him happy.

He was laughing again, the sadness lifted fast. "Oh, *will* we?" he said. "But we've only known each other for a few weeks, so how could we be falling in love, planning to buy small planes together . . ."

He didn't finish. They were kissing again. Finally, she came up for air and nestled against his chest.

"What happened after that?" she asked.

"After my parents . . . ?"

"Yeah."

"Well, it wasn't great. I was mostly raised in foster homes. And now that I'm over eighteen, I'm on my own. I have a shitty apartment, as you know, which is too messy for you to see. But I have big plans for the future."

"I'm really sorry about your parents," she said.

"Don't be. I'm fine. So, come on. Keep going. What else do you want to know?"

They sat up and faced each other. Favorite novel? His was *The Great Gatsby*. Hers was a tough choice between *A Tree Grows in Brooklyn*, *Beloved*, or *Play It As It Lays*. "But I'm really into short stories right now," she said, suddenly worried. "Do I have to choose between short stories and novels?"

He laughed. "Don't panic. You don't have to choose between anything with me."

They both liked old movies. His favorite was *The Asphalt Jungle*. Hers was *Topkapi* but she had a soft spot for *My Fair Lady*. They both liked ice cream better than chips, dogs better than cats. "We should get a dog *and* a plane," he said.

"Yes," Lucky said. "A rescue, right?"

"Rescue plane?"

"Dog, you goof. A big one. The biggest rescue dog we can find."

"A German shepherd."

"A husky. We'd need a big yard for that, maybe a house in the country . . ."

The sun was starting to set, and Lucky smiled up at the dimming sky; she barely knew where the time had gone. Her dad had been asking her lately where she was always off to, and she had lied and said she had met a friend named Alexa and that they hung out on the beach together most days. *Who is she, where does she come from, can you trust her, how do you know that, why don't you bring her back here so I can meet her?* Lucky was so sick of her dad's paranoia. She wanted to keep her burgeoning relationship to herself—so she was dismayed when she looked away from the sky and saw Reyes walking down the boardwalk toward them.

"Oh, shit," she said.

"Who's that?"

"She works with my dad. She's weird. Not my favorite person."

Reyes had seen them now. And Lucky had the sense it wasn't a good thing that she had—that letting anyone else into their insular little world was going to spell trouble for her and Alex.

The next evening Lucky returned to the boat after a day spent with Alex to find Priscilla on the deck, as she often was these days. Her father was inside, fixing a pitcher of the sweet tea Priscilla apparently enjoyed—so now, suddenly, they always had lemons and white sugar and tea bags on hand, when before they had never been the kind of people to have *anything* on hand. Lucky dumped her beach bag on the table and said, "I just got home. I'm *not* going out again. So please don't ask me to leave so you can have your meeting."

"No, no," her father said. "No need. This is a social visit. Priscilla was hoping to chat with you, actually. Get to know you a little more."

"Why?" she asked.

"Good bosses take the time to get to know their employees."

"I'm not her employee."

"Lucky. Don't let me down. Come outside, have some iced tea, be polite."

There was something in his tone that told her he was intimidated by Priscilla, maybe even scared. She took the tray of iced tea and mismatched glasses from her father and said, "Let me serve."

"Ah, the famous *Alaina*," Priscilla said when Lucky emerged.

"It's Lucky, actually."

"Right. Alaina is just what it says on the IDs I got you. For your school stuff. All that is going well?"

"Yes," she said. "I'll be going to SFU in the fall."

Lucky poured the teas and sat. It still made her uncomfortable that Priscilla had been the one to get her the ID, that she was beholden to her for anything. Lucky's father nudged her, and she knew he expected her to say thank you to Priscilla, but she couldn't bring herself to do it.

The sky was black now, and clouds had rolled in; there were no stars. The small talk continued, with mostly Priscilla asking questions, and her father being overly garrulous. Lucky felt more uncomfortable by the minute. Finally, she stood. "You know what, I forgot, I'm supposed to meet my friend for dinner," she said, putting down her glass and standing. "She'll be waiting for me. I really have to run."

Priscilla leaned forward, smiling sweetly. "That's nice you've made a friend, Lucky. What's his name?"

"Her. Alexa," Lucky lied, feeling a sense of foreboding as she did. She grabbed her backpack. "Anyway, nice to see you, bye." She took off before her father could stop her, and started walking down the dock, thinking she would head to the pay phones outside the marina and call Alex, see what he was up to and if he did indeed feel like dinner, even though they had just parted ways less than an hour ago. He always said yes to her, always seemed to be waiting for her to call.

She was walking so fast she nearly ran straight into Reyes. "God! You scared me! What are you doing here?"

"Waiting for Priscilla," Reyes said.

"Why didn't you just go to the boat with her? Why are you lurking here in the dark?"

"Why are you so rude to me all the time? Why do you look at me like I'm a cockroach?"

Lucky couldn't think of anything to say to that. Because Reyes spent so much more time with her dad than Lucky did these days? Because she seemed so secretive?

Reyes shoved her hands deeper into her pockets, the way she always did. "Whatever. I don't care. I didn't really feel like sitting around drinking iced tea tonight, but why should I have to explain that to you?"

"Okay, then, your choice." Lucky started to walk again.

"Wait," Reyes said. Lucky turned.

"What?"

"You need to know something. That's Priscilla's son, the guy you've been hanging around with. I was going to tell your dad—he asked me to keep an eye out for you. But you might as well know now, too."

"What the hell are you talking about? Alex is Priscilla's son?"

"That's not his name. His name is Cary Matheson and yes, he's Priscilla's son, and he's lying to you."

"Fuck you!"

"Why do you think Priscilla has taken a sudden interest in you? What do you think is *really* going on here, Lucky? Have you been to his place? Do you even know where he lives? You don't have all the facts."

"And you do? You know Alex better than I do?"

"Cary," Reyes said in a quiet voice. "His name is Cary. And yes, I do. I've known him for seven years. And he's bad news. I don't know what he wants with you, but now Priscilla knows about you two— and trust me, these are not the kind of people you want to get tangled up with."

"*You're* tangled up with them! You work for her!" But as Lucky spoke, she realized she was the one who was tangled up. She didn't want to believe Reyes, but she already knew it was probably true.

Reyes's eyes were troubled. "I wish I didn't work for her. I wish your dad didn't. But we're in it now. There's nothing we can do. It's not too late for you, though. You can walk away."

"I don't believe you. You just want us apart."

"What reason would I have for wanting you and Cary apart?"

"I don't know. Maybe you want him for yourself."

Reyes laughed softly. "Not a chance in hell."

Lucky turned away from her and ran through the darkness, toward the pay phones. Alex—or Cary, or whoever he was—answered right away. There was music in the background, but he turned it down. "Hey, babe. What's up?"

"Is your name really Alex? Or is your name Cary Matheson and is Priscilla your mother? Where are you, right now? Where do you actually live?"

"Whoa, whoa, slow down, what is this about?"

"Answer my questions."

He was silent. It lasted so long Lucky knew it was all true, and that realization made her heartsick.

"Who told you? Reyes? I should have known. That girl is such a bitch. And she's totally nuts. Weird, like you said."

Lucky closed her eyes and leaned against the wall. She had fallen for it. She was a mark. "Why did you lie to me?"

"Just stay where you are and I'll come to you and explain everything. You're at the pay phones?"

"No. I don't want to see you."

"I care about you so much; I have since the moment I laid eyes on you. I was afraid if you knew who my mother was, you wouldn't want anything to do with me."

"I barely even know your mother—or I didn't then, so why would I have cared?"

"I'm not wrong, admit it. You found out who my mother is, and now you don't want to see me."

This was a familiar sensation, the slow turning of the tables on her. She had been through this too many times with her father. She wasn't going to let him—Alex, Cary, this stranger to her—do it. "So, everything you've told me is a lie. Your parents, the plane crash? All lies?"

"Just let me explain myself."

"You aren't who I thought you were. What is there to explain?"

"Correction. I'm not who you *wanted* me to be. What if I'm something better, Alaina? Did you ever think of that?"

"Yeah, but the difference is, I don't care if your name is Alaina, or Luciana, or Lucky, or whatever. We've both been hiding stuff. But it doesn't bother me. Why should it bother you?"

It felt like a gut punch. "You know my name isn't really Alaina. If Priscilla is your mother, you know that. So don't call me that."

"Because. I don't want to be with someone like . . ."

"Say it. Someone like you? Someone like your dad? You want to find someone you can pretend with, is that it? Someone who isn't smart enough to see through you?"

"I don't want to see you again. Ever."

She hung up.

　　　　　　———

Reyes was waiting for her father outside the boat when Lucky left the boat the next morning. "I broke up with him, all right? Are you happy?" Lucky snarled.

Reyes looked startled. "Of course I'm not happy about this."

"Well, it's what you wanted, right?"

Reyes kicked at a splinter on the dock with her scuffed combat boots, which she wore even on the hottest of days. "I told you. Your dad asked me to look out for you. You were spending time with someone who wasn't being honest with you. Priscilla found out, and that could be an issue. It's what a friend does—"

"You're not my friend—"

"I didn't say I was *your* friend. I'm his friend. Your dad's. And that's why I did it. I don't take any pleasure in this."

Lucky's eyes were swimming with tears. She turned away from Reyes, not wanting her to see them. She started to walk away, but then stopped and turned back. "Now that you've ruined my life, you owe me one. Tell me what it is."

"What *what is?*"

"What you and my dad do for Priscilla. Tell me. I deserve to know."

Reyes lowered her eyes back to the splinter. A long moment passed while she loosened it from the board completely. "It's a charity," she finally said.

"A charity?"

She looked up again. "For foster children. I'm the poster child."

"Are you *in* the foster program?"

"Technically, no. I'm nineteen now. But I lived with Priscilla as a foster when I was a teen, and that's how she came up with the idea."

"So . . . the call center is . . . ?"

"We get donations. But the foundation isn't real." Reyes glanced behind her. "And do you want to know something else? If we're being honest? I'm getting scared. It's turning into big money. And I know if we get caught, Priscilla will find a way to pin it all on us. I feel like we're about to—"

A noise behind them. John had come out of the boat. "Oh, hey, you two! Glad to see you getting more acquainted." But then his expression changed. "Everything okay here?"

"Oh, yeah. We're all good. Come on, let's go, John, the fifty-seven bus leaves in five."

Lucky watched them go. Her plan had been to go to the beach and read all day, but she suddenly realized she didn't want to go there, didn't want to run into Alex, or Cary, or whoever the hell he was. And also that after her unsettling conversation with Reyes, she needed more answers.

She walked down the dock. There was a bike locked to a fence and she saw it had the kind of cheap lock you could crack by listening for the clicks; her father had taught her that ages ago. She looked around, but no one was nearby. It took her a few minutes, but she got the bike unlocked, jumped on, and headed for the bus stop, waiting at a distance while she watched her father and Reyes board.

Then she rode along behind. Traffic was heavy, so she could mostly keep up. She observed from afar as Reyes and her father got off at Chestnut and Windermere. They crossed the street and entered a low-rise office building. She waited a few minutes, then crossed the street, too. The directory inside listed doctors' offices and other businesses—and, there: San Fran Foster Kids Association, at the bottom.

She crossed the street again, found a café, watched, and waited. A couple of hours later, Reyes emerged from the building and walked down the street. Lucky followed and caught up.

"What are you doing here?"

"I followed you to work. I'm worried about my dad."

"I shouldn't have told you," Reyes said. "There's nothing you can do. A few more months, that's all, and then we're going to shut it down. The best thing for you to do is to just stay out of the way. Go home."

Lucky hated doing what Reyes told her to, but she couldn't think of an alternative, so she got back on the bike and returned to the marina.

Later, she would come to wish she had done something more. But she didn't. She just sat on the deck of the boat alone day after day, because she no longer went to the beach for fear of running into Alex. She tried to think of a plan to get her father out of this messy business he was embroiled in. But no ideas came to her—except the idea of taking off. And if they took off, she would have to let go of her dream of attending college.

The day it happened began like any other. Lucky was on the deck, reading a book, when the cell phone her father sometimes left with her when he went to work rang. "Lucky, listen to me. I think we're in trouble here." Her father sounded panicked; he was talking fast. "You know where the lockbox is. The code is under my mattress. Find it, open it, I've left you an— Oh, shit, I have to go." The line went dead.

Lucky stared down at the phone in her hand, then jumped off the boat and ran down the pier, heading for the spot where she had hidden the stolen bike. She rode so fast she was soon gasping for air. But she kept going, until she reached the office building where her father had been working. She pulled her bike to the side of the road just as three police cars roared down the street, sirens blaring, and stopped in front of the doors.

All Lucky could do was watch from afar as first Reyes and then her father were led from the building in handcuffs. No sign of Priscilla. Lucky got off the bike and wheeled it across the street, desperate to get closer. Her father, who was being led toward a police car, spotted her. He shook his head no. *Go get the lockbox,* he mouthed. *Run.* He ducked his head and got in the back of the police car. She couldn't see him anymore.

Lucky felt numb as she rode back the way she had come. It wasn't sinking in yet; she half hoped her dad would be there waiting when she returned, telling her he had managed to talk his way out of trouble again. But he wasn't. The boat was dark and empty. She felt around under his mattress until she found the code for the lockbox, disguised as a recipe. *John's Famous Cajun Rub,* the paper said: *3 teaspoons cayenne, 1 teaspoon salt, 2 teaspoons dried thyme, 3 teaspoons garlic powder.* Her eyes were blurred by tears so she could barely read it. If only he had ever been the kind of dad to have "famous" recipes he made for her, family dinners where she always knew what to expect. She finally managed to get the lockbox open. There was a letter on top of a stack of money.

Dear Lucky,

If you're reading this, I've been arrested. I'm sorry. Take this money, go to a motel for now, then find a cheap apartment. There's enough in here to at least pay for your first tuition installment, and I'm afraid I can't say what you should do about the rest—but here's hoping I'll be around to help you again soon. Sometimes charges don't stick. Whatever you do, do not tell anyone you are my daughter. Don't try to help me. You're better off on your own.

I love you, kid. We'll see each other again soon.

Promise.

Dad

Lucky read the letter over and over, trying to find the part where he told her exactly what to do, and exactly why and how it was going to be okay—but it wasn't there. There was no magic formula.

She was on her own.

She locked the box again and put it in her backpack. She packed clothes, as many books as she could fit, and that was it. Time to run. Alone.

When she stepped off the boat, Cary was waiting on the dock. He had a puppy in his arms, brown and black, furry and wriggling, so skinny you could see her ribs.

"This is Betty," he said, putting her down. "I just picked her up from the ASPCA. The exact kind of dog we dreamed about. Remember? Shepherd, husky, a little of both."

"Go away. You're the last person I want to see." The puppy tumbled over the tops of Lucky's feet.

"My mom got arrested, too."

"Really? Because I was there, and I didn't see her in handcuffs."

"They came to my house. They got her first, and then she told them where your dad and Reyes were."

"Of course she did."

"I'm sorry this is happening. I mean, I'm not sorry my mother is in jail, or Reyes, either—but I know how upset you must be about your dad. I'm so sorry."

"I don't want to hear it."

"You think I'm a liar, but here's the truth, okay? All of it. Months ago, my mom started talking about the guy who was working for her, how he had a daughter named Lucky and he was working to put her through school. I got curious about the fabulous, smart, apparently quite beautiful Lucky. I came down to the beach, and I found you—and I just, I swear, it was love at first sight. I didn't want to tell you who I was; I thought that would weird you out. I also figured you didn't like my mom much, because no one does. So I lied. It went too far, it became too late to come clean. But my feelings have always been real—which is why I kept lying. I was afraid to lose you."

Betty was weaving through Lucky's legs, poking her skinny little nose all over her feet until she almost fell over.

"She likes you. And she's yours."

"You can't buy me with a puppy."

"Well, I couldn't afford a plane, so . . ." He smiled that lopsided smile she hadn't seen in weeks, and she felt herself softening against her will. "We're supposed to be together. Don't you see that? We don't have to be like our parents, we can just be us. Accept it. It's destiny."

Lucky straightened up and tried to ignore the puppy. "I was supposed to be with a guy named Alex, but he doesn't exist."

"Do you really want to be alone?" He stepped forward, looked down at her in that intense way of his. "Because your dad is gone, Lucky. He's not getting out anytime soon."

"You don't know that for sure."

Betty yapped, and Lucky leaned down to pat her head. Cary

crouched in front of her. "Come on, just look at this puppy. Betty needs you. Could you look at me?" he pleaded. "I want you to forgive me for lying to you when we were first together. And I want you to know that I swear on my life, on Betty's life, that I will never lie to you again about anything, ever, not as long as I live. I need you, Lucky—and you need me. Supporting yourself through school is going to be next to impossible. I know how much you want it. And I want it for you. I love you. You love me, too. Admit it. You do."

"It's not a good way to start a relationship, not knowing anything real about the other person."

"Why can't we just make it up as we go along? Blank slate."

"I've been too many people now to ever have a blank slate."

"Are you sure about that? We can start fresh, whenever we want. And I'll love all versions of you. I'll love you no matter what you do, no matter what you say, no matter who you are, always. And I'll take care of you. You won't have to be alone."

"I'm fine on my own," she said. But she had never been alone in her life.

"You know we can do anything, if we stay together." Betty was wagging her tail, hard. "See? She agrees. And she's a smart dog."

Cary put a finger under her chin, lifted her face to his. "I know all your dreams," he said. "I know those were real, when you told them to me. And I want to help make them come true. Let me take care of you. Don't walk away alone."

She stood. He handed her Betty's leash, and together they walked away from the boat and toward The Hill, where there was an empty mansion waiting, and a brand-new life, too.

Later that summer, the arraignment for the "Foster Kid Fakers," as Priscilla, John, and Reyes had been dubbed by the media, was reported in the papers. All the details about the fake charity they had been running were there. And Priscilla Lachaise was negotiating a plea bargain, the article explained. She had information on another case.

"I'm worried," Lucky said to Cary as she sat at the kitchen island in Priscilla's mansion and pored over the article. "When she gets out, Priscilla is not going to be happy you used her bail money for my tuition."

Cary was making dinner. He tasted it, then turned to face her. "I didn't think she'd do this. Didn't think she had the guts. But she's ratting out all my dad's old drug and Mob associates in exchange for a lighter sentence. Which is crazy, because they'll kill her the minute she gets out of jail. She knows that. She's got a plan. I wish I knew what it was."

Lucky kept reading. "Reyes is a first-time offender, so she could go to prison for up to five years. And my dad . . ." Her chest tightened. "My dad could serve twenty-five years to life because he has two priors. I didn't know that."

"Those are the rules in California," Cary said, opening a cupboard and hunting around for spices. His tone was light. It grated at Lucky. Didn't he care about her father at all?

"I love my dad, and I miss him. It's not like with you and your mom. He doesn't deserve this!"

"You think everyone always gets what they deserve?" Cary wiped his hands on a dish towel, then came around behind her. He started massaging her neck, but she held her body rigid. "Twenty-five years is a long time," he said. "And that's just the minimum. A huge chunk of his life. You'll be a different person when he gets out, and so will he."

He was silent now, his hands no longer moving on her neck and shoulders. Lucky knew he was thinking about his own father. "You should forget about your dad," he went on. "It's the best thing to do. It'll protect you from the pain. I'm telling you this because I love you."

She reached up and took one of his hands. "I know," she said. "I love you, too."

He kissed the top of her head. "Now put that paper away and focus on your lecture notes, would you? You told me you got the hardest prof in business accounting. I'm making dinner so you can focus. And this new recipe is going to blow your mind." Cary had taken an interest in cooking lately, and often when she came home he would proudly present her with some new dish or other. "And later, when we're eating, I want to tell you about my plan to get ourselves out from under my mother's roof by the time she gets out of jail so you don't have to think about her anymore. It starts with me pretending to be a student at Stanford . . ." A grin, and that familiar sparkle in his eye. Lucky pushed the paper away and tried to forget about her worries. But when he talked this way, he reminded her of her father. Her worries were all around her.

CHAPTER ELEVEN

Priscilla's Place was on a dead-end street in Fresno, a big yellow clapboard house surrounded by a high black gate. Lucky could see pod shelters in the back of the lot: they looked like little sheds, all painted the same cheery yellow as the house. There was a BEWARE OF DOG sign on the gate, and Lucky could see a massive doghouse, almost as big as one of the pods. But when she reached up and pressed the intercom, she didn't hear barking. Maybe it was just meant to be a deterrent.

The intercom buzzed. "Name, please?"

"Jean."

"Come in the gate, check in with security, then come on through the front door to the waiting area."

Lucky was startled by a large man with a shaved head, dark sunglasses, and a leather Lakers jacket. "Name, please?" he said.

"Jean."

"Last name?"

"Fantine."

"ID?"

"Don't have any."

He studied her face and her heart rate accelerated, but then he said, "Go ahead."

Lucky did as she was told, and found herself inside a small

reception area that smelled vaguely of dog. There was a reception window protected by thick glass; a woman sat behind it, her hair coiled in tight braids around her head. She glanced at Lucky, typed something, then stood and slid the window open.

"Hello. Welcome to Priscilla's Place. What can I do for you?"

"I'm looking for somewhere to stay," Lucky said.

"You're currently experiencing homelessness?"

Lucky nodded.

"How long?"

"A month."

"Name?"

"Jean Fantine."

"I'm Sharon. Do you have any identification, Jean?"

"No."

"Are you able to read and write?"

"Yes."

"Okay. I'm going to give you these intake forms to fill out. Then I'll process them and get you inside."

Lucky nodded again, then took the clipboard and pen and sat down. She looked around. There were two security cameras in the room, and a photo of Priscilla standing in front of the house, cutting a ribbon and grinning.

After the intake process was complete, Sharon led Lucky through the house—which was divided into a large kitchen and eating area, and a living area and recreation room—and out into the yard.

"You're in unit twelve," Sharon said, handing Lucky a key. "It's a single. Get yourself settled in, okay? And dinner is at five, which is soon. Tomorrow, a few appointments are required. Counseling with me, and Priscilla likes to meet all the new intakes, if her schedule allows it. But that might be at dinner. She's out walking her dog right now, but she's around tonight and planning to make an appearance."

Lucky's stomach dropped, but she maintained her smile. "Thank you," she said. "See you later."

"See you later, Jean."

Lucky stared at her food: butternut squash soup, salad, and fresh bread. It looked good, and she hadn't had a proper meal in days—but she couldn't eat a thing. She kept waiting for Priscilla to walk in. Her colored contacts made her eyes feel like they had sand in them.

"I'm Janet," said the woman sitting beside her. She had short hair, turned orange from bleach, and saucer-like blue eyes. One of her hands was shaking, but she still managed to spoon soup into her mouth.

"Jean," Lucky said, smiling once before looking back down, hoping her message was clear: *I don't really want to talk to anyone.*

"Cool. We have similar names."

Lucky didn't respond.

"It gets easier, I swear. This is a safe place."

"Thanks." Lucky forced herself to eat a tomato from her salad. She spooned a little soup into her mouth. Janet looked satisfied with this. Then the conversations in the room paused for a moment, as if a vacuum had been turned on. She raised her eyes and saw Priscilla entering. Her dark hair was shorter now, not swept back severely the way she had worn it years before but feathered around her face. She had on jeans and a cable-knit and homey-looking sweater. She turned in a slow circle, smiling at everyone in the room, meeting their eyes, nodding encouragingly at the shy ones. *You are Jean Fantine. She doesn't know you. You have to believe that.* A dog barked outside in the yard.

Lucky realized she was gripping her spoon so tight her knuckles were white.

"You okay?" Janet asked.

Lucky put down the spoon. "Sure. Totally fine."

"I see a few new faces," Priscilla said, addressing the diners. "Welcome to Priscilla's Place. As some of you know, this is a safe haven for women experiencing homelessness in Fresno and the surrounding areas. Every woman here is treated with kindness and respect. And, of course, we ask that you do the same with each other. Understand, this is a family." Priscilla continued to speak, walking slowly among the tables. "The theme of tonight's talk is dignity," she was saying. "And what it means to you."

"She does a speech every night?" Lucky whispered to Janet.

"Not really a speech. More like . . . a sermon?"

"A sermon? Seriously?"

"She's great," Janet said. "Just listen."

"The dictionary definition of the word 'dignity,'" Priscilla was saying, "is 'the quality or state of deserving honor and respect.' I make no secret of the fact that I wasn't always the kind of person who deserved any honor at all, let alone respect—do I, ladies?" Some laughs and murmurs.

You can say that again, Lucky thought.

Janet leaned forward and whispered, "Did you see the documentary about her transformation?"

Lucky shook her head, gritting her teeth.

Priscilla continued, "There's a second part to the meaning of 'dignity.' It's about taking pride in yourself, respecting *yourself*. And that's a hard thing to do when you don't have a means to provide yourself with even the most basic of necessities. Shelter, especially. Food, of course. But, ladies, there is no shame in that, okay?" Her voice was rising, evangelist-style. "I'm here to tell you there is no shame in asking for help." She was standing near Lucky's table now, and Lucky could smell her perfume, the same scent she remembered from years gone by: Poison.

"She's *so fantastic*," Janet whispered. "Truly an incredible person."

"Yeah," Lucky whispered back, thinking about the dictionary definition of *incredible*: "difficult to believe."

After a bit more fire and brimstone, Priscilla's sermon was over. She then moved from table to table, chatting with everyone.

"I'm *really* tired," Lucky said to Janet. "Think I'm just going to turn in early." She smiled, apologetic, and stood.

"You'll miss meeting Priscilla," Janet said.

"Not tonight," Lucky said. "I'm just . . . not up for it." Lucky bused her plate and headed for the back door. She could hear the front door of the house opening and Sharon crooning, to Priscilla's dog, she presumed. Just before she made it outside, someone touched her arm.

"We haven't formally met yet. Do you have to rush off, or could you come up to my apartment for a cup of tea?"

Lucky turned and forced herself to meet Priscilla's penetrating gaze, her deep-brown eyes. "Oh," she said. "Well, of course, that would be—"

She didn't get to finish her sentence. A large bundle of brown and white fur streaked into the room, Sharon following close behind, shouting. The dog jumped up on Lucky, barking joyfully and wagging her tail.

"Down, girl," Lucky said, and the dog obeyed. Of course she did. She was Lucky's dog.

I n late September, Lucky returned from school to Priscilla's mansion—a place she was having trouble considering home—to find Cary waiting in the entryway, holding a short electric-blue cocktail dress on a hanger. The place was immaculate, the pool cleaned and glimmering, the backyard pergola strung with fairy lights. There were buckets of champagne on the countertops.

"They're coming over. We're having a party. For your birthday. You need to go change."

"But it's not my—"

He planted a kiss on her lips and took her book bag from her arms, dropping it to the floor. "Yes, it is. You're turning nineteen. In Canada, where I'm from, remember—my name is Jonas Weston, and you're still Alaina, but Parkes—you'd be of legal drinking age. And you're a real party girl." He shook the dress. "So, we're celebrating with my new friends from school. You're going to love them." He laughed. "Okay, fine, you're going to barely tolerate them, the way I do. They're okay—a little boring and repetitive, but extremely generous and incredibly careless. And that's important for us."

"Remind me of the details?" This game was familiar to Lucky, but she still felt nervous.

"I'm a softwood lumber heir, but I've had a tiff with my parents. They don't like that I've taken off to Cali to go to school for something other than business—I'm taking liberal arts, of course—and live with my girlfriend. *Your* parents are dead. Plane crash." He cleared his throat and looked away, fiddling with a champagne bottle.

"I'm sorry about that," he said. "I know I've used that one on you. But it's a good one."

Betty came running into the kitchen and jumped up on Lucky, barking her greeting, wagging her tail. She was no longer the scrawny, malnourished pup Cary had presented her with on the dock: her glossy brown coat was now shot through with white hairs, which made her fur look reddish. She was growing fast, turning lithe, wolf-like. She was a good-natured dog for the most part, but was protective of Lucky—even barking and snarling at Cary on the rare occasions when they argued. Now she had a blue bow tied to her collar. It matched Lucky's dress, and Betty's eyes.

"Come on, go put the dress on," Cary said. "This is going to be fun."

Upstairs, Lucky changed and put her hair up—but it was already falling down her back by the time she descended the stairs. Their first guests had arrived: Aaron and Magnolia, a couple who double-air-kissed as they came through the door, followed by two more guests, Hugh and Will. Will had a box of cigars in hand. "For later, my friend," he said to Cary with a wink—while Lucky marveled at how quickly her boyfriend had managed to insinuate himself into an inner circle. "Unless your lady likes to partake."

Lucky smiled. "Cigars aren't my thing. Champagne, however—" There was a bottle waiting on the side table. She grabbed it and popped it open, grateful Cary had shown her how a few days before. She had never opened champagne, had never pretended to be the kind of person she was pretending to be now.

"I *like* her," Hugh said as they trooped into the kitchen.

"She's the best," Cary said, putting his hand on the small of her back and propelling her forward, kissing her ear, and whispering, "*Good job.*"

"Ah, the famous Alaina," Magnolia cooed. "Jonas talks about you endlessly. Says you're a *genius*." She had raven-black hair and bright blue eyes, and was wearing a butter-hued silk dress that draped effortlessly over her perfect body. Lucky's hair was too frizzy and her dress felt cheap—even though she had left the tags on, afraid to take them off because of the price; now they were scratching at her side—but, "You are absolutely gorgeous," Magnolia said, grabbing her hand once they each had a glass of champagne. "Come on, show me the pool. And is this your dog? *Adorable*. She must be a shepsky, right? I have a cousin who breeds those on a farm in the Black Forest."

"Exactly. We got her directly from a breeder in Germany."

Later, by the pool, when everyone was gone and the sun was peeking over the horizon, Cary was jubilant rather than tired. "You did it, babe. You were the perfect sidekick. They thought you were a blast. You're so *good* at this. Didn't you have fun?"

She leaned her head into his chest so she wouldn't have to look at him. He had always said they could lie to other people, but never to each other. Still, she said, "Yes, it was a great time."

"That could be us, you know. It's *going* to be us. One day, we won't be pretending."

Lucky's first year of college drew to a close, and they flew to Madrid to spend the summer with Magnolia and Aaron; Aaron's parents had a house there.

At dinner the first night, in a yard lined with olive trees and hung with lanterns, Cary planted the first seed with their friends: the mansion they lived in was going to be repossessed (this *was* true, actually) because Alaina's parents had had some bad debts before they died. It was easy. By summer's end, Cary and Lucky had a new place to live: a coach house on Hugh's family's property in Alamo. They promised to pay rent—Cary even went as far as to write checks Lucky knew would bounce, but they were never cashed, always ripped up or tossed aside.

"Aren't you afraid they'll find out?" Lucky whispered to him one night in bed.

"Find out what?"

"Who we really are."

"Isn't this who we really are?"

Lucky found she didn't know anymore. She pretended to be one person at school—and she had to be careful never to get too close to anyone, no matter how much she longed for real friends, and no matter how often she was asked to meet for drinks or join others to study. She was someone else with Cary's Stanford crowd, and someone else still once a month when she went to visit her father at San Quentin, where he had been sentenced to twenty-five years. Cary didn't know she went to the prison at all, didn't know about the fake ID she had bought with money stolen out of their safe so she could pretend to be Sarah Armstrong, John's niece, and still see her dad.

"You want this—don't you, Lucky? To leave who we were behind and become great?"

"Of course I do," she said. But she actually wanted to ask him what he meant by great—if great meant rich at any cost; if great meant morally bankrupt. But she didn't, because she had her own plan. She needed to stay the course, that was all. He would understand eventually that there was a better way to build a life, one that didn't involve cheating and lying.

Time passed, and Cary pretended to drop out of school. He told their friends that he had to because they could only afford one tuition. "And Alaina is the genius, so of course it has to be her school we pay for."

Their rich friends offered loans so he could keep going to college, but he refused, said he didn't want handouts. He wanted to work for any money he received. And school wasn't his thing, anyway. What Jonas, Cary's alter ego, really wanted was to open a club.

"Dude, you throw the best parties. Doesn't Jonas throw the best parties?" Aaron said. They were at Hugh's; it was his birthday, and Cary had organized the whole thing: a *Matrix*-themed rave. Everyone was dressed in black leather and sunglasses; techno was blaring; the caterers had made "really good noodles" and "chicken tastes like everything" kebabs; there was a laser tag zone inside the house. "Guys, we have to make this happen," Aaron said. "Jonas wants to open a club. We need financial backers!"

All their friends invested in the venture, which Cary said had to be taken slowly. First, he had to find the perfect location—which took ages, and got Lucky to the start of her final year of school. Then "Jonas" had to travel the globe looking for the right furniture, had to visit vineyards and distilleries all around Europe. Soon, everyone in San Francisco was talking about Jonas Weston's new club—he'd decided to name it Lucky. But Cary was using hardly any of the investment money for the actual club, instead using some to pay for Lucky's tuition and squirrelling the rest of it away.

"What do they care who I really am?" Cary said when Lucky continued to voice her fears. "They're having the time of their lives. And the worst thing that's going to happen? We're going to disappear the day after you graduate, and there will be no club. They'll realize they've been duped, and they'll get over it in about five minutes. What they're investing in this is chump change, not even enough for their parents to notice. This is just fun for them. You need to have some fun with it, too."

The night Lucky graduated from SFU, in June 2003, Cary was sitting in the front row, holding a massive bouquet of red roses. There was an empty seat beside him at the beginning of the ceremony, but when Lucky moved across the stage to collect her diploma, Priscilla was sitting in it. Lucky faltered halfway but forced herself to keep moving.

"What is she doing here?" she hissed after the ceremony. Priscilla was off getting them drinks.

"I'm sorry, I didn't know," Cary said, and he really did appear to be agitated. "I was so distracted by everything we've been doing, I stopped keeping track of her—but she's out of prison and she just showed up at our house—and you were already gone, getting your cap and gown. I don't know how she figured out where we were living."

"Who did you tell Hugh she was?"

"No one was home. They're all at the Stanford graduation. I didn't have to tell anyone anything. But she told *me* a lot."

"Like what?"

"Shhh. Here she comes."

Priscilla handed around plastic cups of cheap sparkling wine. "Oh, please. Don't shush each other, there's nothing you can say I don't already know. To answer the question you probably just asked about how I found you so fast, I had associates keeping an eye on you two while I was in prison. I'm impressed. One phone call, though, and I could blow your con to bits, tell all your friends you've been stealing from them before you get the chance to take off later tonight. Why did you wait, by the way?"

"Lucky wanted to get her diploma," Cary said. "We weren't going to be able to leave a forwarding address for it."

"I suppose not. Well, anyway. Congratulations." She tapped her plastic glass against Lucky's. "You've done it. A business degree."

Priscilla made it sound so small, this thing Lucky had been working toward for four years. But, she told herself, this piece of paper she now held in her hands was hers. It was her path to legitimacy—and Cary's, too. He'd had some fun, but it was risky—and it was fake. With her, Cary was going to build a life that was actually sustainable. Alaina Cadence had no prior record with anyone. And she had a degree.

Priscilla drained her glass. "I'm here as a stand-in for your father," she said to Lucky. "I promised him I'd share a toast. And he wanted me to give you a hug, although I doubt you'd allow that."

"Why is my father even speaking to you?"

"I'm a rehabilitated woman. And part of my penance is apologizing to the people I've hurt. I'm trying to make it up to your father— and the only thing he wants is to know that you're happy. Are you happy, Lucky?"

Lucky had been, about an hour earlier. She had been full of excitement about what the future held, but Priscilla's presence was like a pin in her balloon.

Cary pulled her close. "Of course she's happy," he said. "We both are."

Priscilla tossed her plastic cup in a nearby trash can. "Let's go somewhere we can get a decent drink, at least. And have a proper talk."

Cary sighed. "Don't drag Lucky into this, Mother."

"'Mother.' Now, that's a first." But she was smiling.

He turned to Lucky. "You just head home and keep packing. I'll have a drink and a talk with Mother here, and be there in a few hours." As he kissed her cheek, he whispered in her ear, "I'll pick up the rental car on my way home. We'll leave as soon as I get back."

Lucky took a taxi to the coach house, packed, and waited nervously for Cary to return. Betty was at her feet, watching the door anxiously, too. He didn't pick up his cell phone when she called—and when he did finally return, around two o'clock in the morning, he was drunk, and Lucky was upset.

"Where's the car?" Lucky asked him. "Aren't we going?"

"Do I look like I'm in any state to drive?" He stumbled, landed on the love seat. "We can't leave, okay? We have to stay around for the summer. I have to actually open that fucking club. Mother says so.

There are some things I need to take care of for her, or—" It was dark, but she could see it in his eyes: fear. Then he closed them, leaned his head back against the cushions. "I have no choice. I'm sorry." Soon, he was asleep. Lucky sat staring into the darkness, until Betty nudged her with her snout, reminding her she wasn't alone.

It was Christmas Eve, and the club was empty except for Lucky and Cary. Lucky sat on a corner couch, wearing one of the short, tight dresses Cary had bought her so she would fit the role she was supposed to play while beside him at the club. She was helping him count the night's cash.

"A great night," he said, locking the cashbox and putting it in a bag. "And not just because we made some good money. It's time for your Christmas present." He pulled a card from behind his back.

"But Christmas isn't until tomorrow," Lucky said. "My gift for you is back at the house."

"We're not going back to the house," he said, smiling. "Open it."

She did. There was a folded piece of paper inside. "A title deed," she said. "For a house . . . in Boise, Idaho?"

Cary pointed at the page. "That's your name, right there. Alaina Cadence. The house belongs to you."

"Well—" she began.

"No, that's you. All your official papers are under that name. You've got a passport and a birth certificate, a business degree, and now, a deed. You always said you wanted a simple, normal life. And Boise, Idaho—that's the place! Our future starts tonight."

"But Priscilla—"

"We're done with her. I did what I promised, I did what I had to so she would eventually let us go. I held up my end of the bargain and now it's her turn. Tonight. She's not going to follow us."

"Where did you get this house?"

"It doesn't matter, okay? The point is, it's yours. Ours. This is where it's all going to begin. A fresh start, finally. The life you've always wanted. I've made you wait long enough."

He stood and picked up the bag with the cash box, looked around the dim room. "I think I'm actually going to miss this place," he said. "Turns out I didn't mind running a club. Even if it was just a front." He held out his hand, and she took it and stood, too. "Car's outside," he said. "You'll have to leave everything behind at the coach house, but I promise, what you need is in the car."

"What about Betty?"

He smiled. "We'd never leave our girl behind. She's in the supply room. Let's go get her and then let's hit the road. Are you with me?"

She smiled, kissed him, allowed the happiness, the hope, to edge in and elbow all the uncertainty and fear out of the way. "Of course I am," she said. "Always."

CHAPTER TWELVE

A s the rest of the Priscilla's Place residents looked on, Priscilla advanced toward Lucky; Betty started barking, and Sharon tried to grab the leash again. "I'm *so* sorry—I don't know what's with her tonight; she's normally so gentle. But she sure seems to like *you*, Jean."

"Easy, girl," Lucky said. Betty immediately calmed and stood beside her, wagging her tail. Lucky longed to greet her dog properly, to kneel down and bury her face in the familiar auburn fur. But she needed to try to keep up the pretense, as weak as it now was, of never having seen this dog before in her life. "Is she a rescue?" she asked Priscilla, trying to keep her voice steady. "I must remind her of a previous owner."

"She belongs to my son," Priscilla said. "He went overseas for work. He needed someone to take care of his dog while he was away. You're a dead ringer for his ex-girlfriend, you know. That must be it. She sees the similarity."

"What a coincidence," Lucky said weakly.

"Shall we head upstairs for that tea and chat, Jean?"

Priscilla's apartment was decorated in rich fabrics and dark colors. In such a small space, it was cloying—and in stark contrast to the utilitarian sparseness downstairs. Priscilla closed and locked the door. Lucky knelt beside Betty and she licked Lucky's face. Lucky looked up at Priscilla. "Why do you have my dog?"

Priscilla, ignoring her, crossed the room and lifted a piece of paper from her desk. "I had Nico, my bodyguard—you would have seen him on your way in—search your pod during dinner. All he could find was this, taped into a book." It was the fake shopping list. Lucky could see the numbers there, and started repeating them in her head so she wouldn't forget them. She should have memorized them before. She hoped it wasn't too late. "Why would something like this be important enough to hide? Is it really a shopping list?"

Lucky recalled what her father had said about how important it was to pretend she had something Priscilla wanted. "Yes. It's our code."

"It has something to do with how you and Cary are supposed to find each other?"

"Yes."

"He told you to use this? You two had a plan? You knew he was going to disappear?"

"Yes."

Priscilla looked at Lucky for a long moment, then back down at the sheet.

"When did you establish this code? When you were in Vegas? Don't look so shocked. I had you followed by the same private investigator for years. There is nothing I don't know about you and my son. Now, how does this code work, exactly?" Priscilla was chipper, businesslike, acting as if she were simply have a collegial conversation about a mutual problem they needed to solve.

Come on, Lucky. Think of something. "Facebook," she said. "I'm supposed to set up a profile under the name Doll Conovan, list my home city as Cincinnati and my interests as screenwriting and bird-watching. I make my profile public, and post a recipe for white bean and spinach rice on my wall."

Priscilla walked over to her desk and opened up a rose-gold-colored laptop. "Doll Conovan. From his favorite movie. Of course. Okay. Come here. You can sit in my chair. There, I've got Facebook all cued up now. Make the profile." Priscilla hovered behind her as she created the profile, and followed the steps she had just outlined. "Now what?"

"Now, I wait for him to add me as a friend and send me a message."

"Yes, but what's *his* profile going to be? How will you know for sure it's him? You thought of that, didn't you?"

Silence. Priscilla reached forward and snapped the laptop shut, put her hand on Lucky's shoulder, and squeezed while Betty growled. "Or perhaps it's time for you to stop this charade. It's been fun watching you wriggle, but I'm getting bored. Come on, let's go sit on the couch and have a proper talk." Lucky closed her eyes for a moment, then walked over to the couch and sat. Betty trotted over and curled up at her feet, but Lucky didn't feel protected by the dog's presence anymore because she knew you were never safe around someone like Priscilla. That she never had been safe, as long as she was within Priscilla's reach.

Priscilla crossed her legs and smiled at Lucky, leaned forward. "Should I ask Sharon to bring us some tea? You're looking a little pale. In your condition, I do want to make sure you're properly taken care of."

"In my . . . condition?"

"Don't try to hide it. I know about the baby."

Lucky felt sick. Priscilla had had them followed, but more than that, she must have had the private investigator go through their garbage, maybe even tap their phones. Lucky struggled to smile, as if the idea of this baby were still the one bright spot in her life. But all she could picture was some stranger pulling a positive pregnancy test out of her garbage bin and bringing it to Priscilla.

"You've been pregnant for . . . almost three months now? You should be starting to show soon."

Lucky let her hands creep down to her flat abdomen, pushed her stomach out slightly. It was painful to pretend the baby was still there, painful to even think about the little dream, the big idea, a golden ticket floating in a sea inside her. But she knew she had to. If Priscilla believed she was still pregnant with Cary's child, Lucky had something she wanted. And that was a powerful thing. Priscilla was a con artist and a criminal, but she couldn't kill her own grandchild. *There is nothing I don't know about you and my son,* Priscilla had said. You could have someone followed by a private investigator and see most things—but not what was going on under the surface. The heartaches and losses that happened when you were alone would never be public knowledge. Blood on a bathroom floor was not something a detective sitting outside your house could easily uncover.

"This must be tough," Priscilla was saying, her voice now dripping with fake empathy. "You have no idea where my son is, and you're on the run, pregnant. Your future is very uncertain."

Lucky pressed her lips together and nodded.

Priscilla reached forward and poured water from a carafe on the coffee table in front of them. "Here. Drink this. You should stay hydrated." Lucky accepted the water but didn't drink.

"To answer your earlier question, he brought me the dog last month. Because I asked him to." She poured herself some water and took a sip. "There, you see? It's not poisoned. You can have some of yours now." She laughed. "Oh, Lucky. The expression on your face. Anyway, the dog was collateral."

"Collateral for?"

"The money he was laundering for me through his restaurant. Oh, come on, you really had no idea?" She laughed again. "You really thought Cary's big dream was to be a restaurateur? He told me you didn't know—but I think until this moment I didn't believe it. It makes sense, though, that you weren't aware of what he was really doing. Because if you did know, you wouldn't be here."

"Why not?"

Priscilla leaned toward Lucky. "The people I work for, the people Cary was in turn working for, are ruthless." Lucky looked closely at her. She couldn't be sure, but she thought Priscilla seemed afraid now. Then her expression cleared and she was cool and confident again. "If you had any idea about that, I'm sure you would have kept yourself hidden. I know you think I'm the height of evil, but I'm not. You can trust me to tell you when you are in danger. And you are. I'm probably the only person in the world you can trust right now—"

"I will never trust you."

"—and the heartbreaking truth is that Cary is probably dead, okay? They probably beat him and left him for dead in the desert, those terrible, terrible people." Her hand fluttered up to her chest, and she blinked, hard and fast. Were those real tears there? Crocodile tears? Lucky tried to process what Priscilla had just said, but it didn't feel real at all. Cary, beaten and dead? Tears gathered behind her eyes, too, but she refused to let them fall in front of Priscilla.

"Are you sure?" she whispered.

"I tried to protect him. It's why I asked him for the dog. When I discovered you were pregnant, I was afraid he was going to do something stupid. Like try to run away with you, start a family somewhere he thought I couldn't find him. I told him to do one last job for me, and that I'd come and take the dog as collateral. He loved Betty. And so did you. Stupidly, I thought it would be enough to keep you two in one place, for a while at least. But he simply took the money he was cleaning for my associates and—well, I'm not sure, exactly. He hid it somewhere, with all the rest of the money you were stealing in your Ponzi scheme. Tell me, where were you two planning to go, exactly?"

"Grenada," Lucky lied, blinking the last of her unshed tears over Cary away. Her heart was starting to pound and her fingers were starting to tingle. She needed to get out of there. But how?

"I see. And that's why you had purchased plane tickets to Dominica?" Her voice was steely now. She was leaning so close Lucky could see the blood vessels in her eyes, smell her breath. "Stop lying to me. It's over. You can't hide anything from me now. We're talking about a lot of money. And I need to find it. Or else. Do you know where it is?"

"I swear to you, I don't."

"Millions of dollars. And he never mentioned it?"

"Never."

"If that money doesn't surface soon, someone else is going to die. And in your case"—she glanced down at Lucky's stomach—"two people will die. I care about this child, but I'm not going to sacrifice myself for it. I don't want anything more than to survive. If you're to survive as well, we need to work together to find the money Cary was hiding. And we need to be completely honest with each other about everything we know." This was so familiar; she could almost hear Cary's voice saying the same thing: *We can lie to other people, but never to each other.*

"I swear, I don't know anything about the money. I was under the impression Cary took everything and ran."

Priscilla picked up the receipt on the table and held it up. "Let's start here. What is this list really? What does it unlock, and what are you hiding?"

"It's a code for a storage locker back in Boise. I couldn't bear to let it all go. I had a feeling something was going to happen—I knew Cary wasn't telling me everything. So I put some items from the house that were of value—a few paintings we had, some jewelry, electronics—into the locker. Just in case I needed to pawn them."

Priscilla looked down at the sheet of paper, silent and thoughtful. "All right, then," she said. "We'll go to Boise together and you can show me, just so I can confirm you're telling the truth." She stood and walked to her desk, picked up a day planner. "On Friday, we'll take a little drive, just the two of us," she said, marking it down. "I'll tell Sharon I'm taking you to stay with some family we've discovered who want to help you." She put down the book. "Meantime, if you change your mind and decide to tell me what this code *really* opens, I'll be all ears. Now, go to bed. And take that disgusting dog with you."

The first year, Lucky worked hard. She took investment courses online, got four different certifications, and started her own small investment and accounting firm—the office of which was located above the garage of their Tudor revival in Boise's North End, near Camel's Back Park. She slowly started managing the accounts for small businesses and building individual clients' investment portfolios. She became known for providing consistent returns, but nothing flashy.

Things were starting to feel secure. Everything was perfect: their new life; their house, with its peaked turret and wraparound porch. While Lucky worked, Cary puttered around the garage, or went for jogs, or rode his mountain bike in the park. He cooked, he cleaned, he insisted he was happy, too. "I'm your househusband," he would tell her with a smile. "I love it, I swear." But she could tell he was bored. Sometimes she would come in at lunch and he would be playing video games or asleep on the couch. They didn't have any friends because not making friends had become a habit. So Cary was on his own most of the time.

"Maybe we should have a baby," Lucky said one night, and the moment the words were out she knew she wanted this badly. She had never imagined arriving at a place where being so settled, where starting a family, would be possible. But she was there, the life she had dreamed of within reach.

"Anytime you want," Cary said with a casual grin. "I'd love to have a family with you."

One night, when she came in after work, there was a real estate brochure on the kitchen table. "What's this?" she said, setting down the leather briefcase Cary had given her for her last birthday—the perfect gift, even if she was just toting papers between the garage and the house.

Cary poured her a glass of wine and handed it to her. "I saw this restaurant on Thirteenth Street closed down and for sale. I just started dreaming, standing out there on the sidewalk. So I went in, and the real estate agent showed me around."

Lucky took a sip of her wine. "Why would you want to look at a restaurant?"

He pulled out a chair and sat. He pushed the flyer across the table. "What do you think? Isn't it perfect?"

"Perfect for what? I didn't realize you wanted to get back into hospitality. Things are just starting to get going with my business. I'm not sure we have the money for a down payment for something like this just yet."

"I get that, babe. I do." He stood to serve the risotto he had prepared, placed a steaming bowl in front of her, and sat again. "But the thing is . . . I need to get back in the game. You know that, because you know me."

"But I thought, maybe a baby . . ."

He didn't seem to hear her. "This would give me something to do. I liked running the club, back in San Fran. I didn't expect to, but I did. I miss it. And—well, you know you could have a down payment on a property pretty easily, if you did things differently."

Lucky frowned. "Differently how?" she asked, even though she knew exactly what he meant. "Listen, I'll go look at the property with you. And then we can see if there's anything we can figure out."

In the end, they bought the restaurant—and went deep into debt starting it up. Over the next several months, Cary grew frustrated and stressed. He was no longer the happy-go-lucky, slightly bored guy he had become when they moved to Boise. He was at the restaurant late almost every night. He had insisted it would make him happy, but it did the opposite. Lucky knew it was probably selfish, but she found herself missing the quiet days when he was always home, waiting for her to come in from her office above the garage. The restaurant, the fact that they were *both* now working so hard, had seemed to drive a wedge between them.

"I need more money. I need to expand the patio so I can compete with the other restaurants on the street."

"We don't have it. We've already poured so much into this venture."

"Venture? This is important to me, don't you see? We could borrow the money from one of your investment accounts," he said. "We'll put it back in, once I earn it back . . . which I will. Come on, you've been telling me how much money some of these new clients of yours have. They aren't going to come to you looking for their investment funds anytime soon. I promise, we won't do it again. Just this once. It'll be so easy."

There was no actual harm being done, Lucky kept telling herself. The dividends would still be paid, people who wanted to take their money out to retire could still have it; there was no shortage of money in the corporate account to cover payouts. No one was suffering. No one was getting hurt.

But it didn't happen just once. It was never going to happen just once. Lucky had been reluctant at first, but stealing felt so natural. She barely thought about it. And Cary was happier. He began to relax. Everything started to fall back into place again—except that, after a year of trying, she still hadn't gotten pregnant.

Lucky and Cary went to a doctor and found out Lucky had endometriosis and blocked fallopian tubes; in vitro fertilization was their only option. But it was expensive: tens of thousands of dollars for the treatments and medications.

And so Lucky borrowed more from the investment accounts. Twice, she and Cary tried in vitro, and twice, the implantation failed. Lucky stopped recognizing herself when she looked in the mirror. She was tired and drawn. The hormone shots made her emotional, crying one moment, elated the next.

"If it's making you miserable, maybe we should stop," Cary implored one night.

"I'm not miserable!" Lucky shouted. "And I can't give up now. I just need to relax and work less." But that was impossible. They were in too much debt.

"I will get pregnant," Lucky said. "We'll try again. And at some point, it will work. I'll make it happen like I make everything else happen."

CHAPTER THIRTEEN

Lucky walked around the side of Priscilla's Place and stood in the shadows, watching the guardhouse, and Nico inside. Just as she had at noon the day before, Sharon came out of the main house and brought Nico a plate of food. He put up his feet, took out his phone, and began to eat the sandwich and salad, his finger moving back and forth across the screen, totally focused on the virtual game of Texas Hold'em he was playing.

Lucky watched a moment longer, then turned and looked up at the window to Priscilla's apartment. She had been observing her habits over the past two days, too: Priscilla fasted in the morning, then wandered the premises, chatting with the residents, sipping green juice. She kept a close eye on Lucky almost all the time—except at lunch, when she went upstairs to break her fast and have a session with her personal trainer, an attractive, muscle-bound woman named Dee. Lucky sensed the time ticking away until their trip to Boise, when it would inevitably be revealed that she had been lying about the storage locker. Coming here had been a mistake, and Lucky didn't want it to turn into a fatal one. If she was going to escape, she had to take a risk. It had to be now.

Lucky backed up, turned, and walked into the yard, where Janet was eating her lunch at one of the picnic tables. "Hey," Lucky said, sitting down beside her. "I keep meaning to tell you, I just love your baseball cap. I'm a huge Angels fan, and someone stole my cap while

I was sleeping on the beach in Santa Monica. I keep looking at yours, and it reminds me of it."

"Aw, really? No way. Well, listen, do you want to borrow it?"

"Would you be interested in a trade? You borrow mine"—Lucky removed her *Fabulous Las Vegas* cap—"and I borrow yours, just for today? It really would make me happy."

"Sure. Of course. I'm glad you're doing so well here, Jean. It was the dog, right? The way she took such a liking to you, that made you feel you could really be at home here? I've noticed a change in you these past few days. And Priscilla hardly leaves your side!"

"Something like that, yeah." Lucky paused. "Hey, you know what? It's really so kind of you to let me borrow your hat. I want to give you my sunglasses as a thank-you."

"*Give* me? Oh, come on. Those are really expensive sunglasses."

"Yeah. They're the only thing I have of any value. But—you've been so kind to me. Here, take them. I insist."

"Well, then, you take mine in return." Janet slid her cheap mirrored aviators back at Lucky.

"Thanks," she said, putting them on. "What do you think?"

"I think you look pretty cool," Janet said. Then she glanced at her watch. "Oh, shoot—I'm late. I'm supposed to walk Betty today."

"Right! I forgot to tell you. We got switched. Sharon decided last night it would be better if I walked her today, and . . . you're on dish duty."

"Ohhhhh," Janet said, laughing. "That's what's with the sunglasses gift. You want to make up for the fact that you stole my cushy job and stuck me on dishes."

"Yeah. Totally," Lucky forced a laugh. "I'm sorry. Still friends?"

"No apologies needed. I don't mind doing the dishes. And Betty really does love you *so* much. She'll be happier with you. Enjoy your walk." Janet reached over to the bench beside her and handed Lucky the leash.

"Thanks," Lucky said. "See you in a bit."

Betty was napping at the front of her doghouse, but stood when she saw Lucky coming with the leash in hand. Lucky put the baseball cap and sunglasses on, clipped the leash on Betty, and walked around to the side of the house. With her head down and Betty at her side, she passed the guardhouse. Nico was still eating his lunch and playing on his phone. He barely looked up when she passed and gave a casual two-finger wave, exactly the way Janet would have. She opened the gate. A moment later, she was out on the sidewalk; the gate clanged shut behind her, as loud as her pounding heart felt. Every part of her wanted to sprint down the sidewalk now that she was out, but she forced herself to walk slowly, allowing Betty to stop and sniff flower beds and fire hydrants until they were out of sight of Priscilla's Place.

She started running when she was around the corner. When she got to the storage facility, she typed in the code she remembered. It didn't work. *"Shit."* She tried again. No. She had a number wrong, she knew it. But if she kept messing it up, the lock would shut down. One more try. She closed her eyes and pictured the coded list. And there it was. She had it. A satisfying beep, and she was in. She closed the door behind her and stacked the boxes she had left inside the locker so she could reach the lottery ticket she'd hidden in the smoke detector.

It was still there. When Lucky had the ticket in her hand she sagged with relief—but just for a moment. She wasn't safe yet. She took out her wallet to put the ticket inside, and Reyes's card fell out. She held it up and read it. *Driver. San Diego Third-Strikers Foundation.*

"If only *you* had a car," she said to Betty, picking up her leash. The dog tilted her head, quizzical. Lucky sighed. "Never mind. I'll be right back." She locked the door and went to the pay phone in the parking lot.

"You said I could call you if I needed help. Where are you right now?"

"I just dropped someone off in Bakersfield."

"Okay, so you're less than two hours away. I need help. I need a ride."

Lucky stared out the window of Reyes's white SUV, silent now after explaining as much as she was able. The scenery sped by. They were outside Fresno now, heading west.

"So . . ." Reyes finally said. "Instead of calling me for help first, you went to Priscilla?"

"I had no one else to call. As if I can trust you more than I can trust her," Lucky muttered. "As if I can trust anyone."

Reyes drummed her fingers against the steering wheel to the beat of the song on the car stereo, then chuckled. "I'm pretty sure you can trust anyone more than you can trust Priscilla Lachaise."

Lucky sighed and turned away from the window. "I just . . . I needed to know if she knew anything. About where Cary went."

"And did she?"

"She said he might be dead."

"I'm not sure how to feel about that."

"Me neither," Lucky said. She closed her eyes for a second, and she could see Cary's familiar face. It hurt to think of him for different reasons now. "I know it probably sounds stupid to you because you always hated him, but he was my—" She couldn't finish the sentence, couldn't say aloud that the man who had betrayed her, lied to her for years, made a complete fool of her, had been the love of her life.

"I get it. You loved the guy and probably still do. Unfortunately the heart doesn't often give a shit what the mind has to say to it," Reyes said.

A few more miles of highway disappeared beneath the tires of the SUV before either of them spoke again.

"So, where am I dropping you off?" Reyes said.

"The bus station is coming up. I'm going to New York State."

"You're planning to take the dog on a bus? They don't allow that."

"*Shit.*" Lucky glanced at Betty in the back seat. She had been so happy to find her dog again. The idea of having to leave her behind simply hadn't occurred to her.

"I'd drive you all the way to New York, but I have a job in two days and have to be in Oakland. I could take the dog, though."

Lucky bit her lip, thinking. But she knew there was no other way for her to get to her mother's fishing camp than by bus. "Thanks," she finally said. "I'd appreciate it." The bus station had come into view. "I'll be in touch when I can come get her. I have your card. A couple of weeks, at most. And—and when I do, everything will be different."

"Sure," Reyes said. "I'll keep her as long as you need me to. As long as she doesn't mind long car rides."

"She's good with anything."

"How can I reach you, if I need to?"

Lucky shook her head. She didn't want anyone to know where she was going, not yet.

"Don't you think I should have a way to get in touch? What if something happens with Betty? What if your dad's hearing goes forward? There's been a lot of movement. These things happen fast, when they start to get going."

"I'll be at Devereaux Camp, near Cooperstown."

Reyes nodded slowly. "Your dad said something once about having an ex-wife living out there. Is that your . . . ?"

"My mom," Lucky said. "I have something I think she might like to see. Something she can help me with, I hope."

"I hope she can help you, too. You sure as hell need it. And I wish I could do more. Do you need money?" Lucky did, but there was no way she was asking for charity from Reyes.

"I'm fine," she said.

Reyes pulled to a stop in the bus station parking lot. Lucky turned back and buried her face in her dog's fur. "I'll see you soon, I promise."

She grabbed her backpack and got out of the car. "I'll pay you back someday," she said after Reyes rolled down her window.

"No payback needed. Good luck to you, with whatever it is you're hoping will happen."

Lucky hitched her backpack over her shoulder, then stood watching as Reyes rolled up her window and drove away, leaving her on her own again.

Lucky and Cary were eating dinner on their porch, basking in the summer-evening warmth after a long day. She was pregnant. Their third attempt at implantation had worked, and she was just over a month along. It felt fragile and unreal. But she had other things on her mind.

"You okay, babe?" Cary asked as she pushed her plate away.

"I'm worried," she admitted. "The markets are bad. More and more of my clients have started asking for their investment money back—and if too many more ask, I won't have anything left to give. I'm afraid we'll never really have everything we want, because I've stolen too much from the accounts. I'm going to have to give it all back, and then we'll be ruined."

"No way. We run first," Cary said simply.

"We can't just run . . ."

"Why not?"

Lucky looked away from him, resting her hands on her stomach, which was still flat. "We're going to lose everything: our house, the restaurant. This life. I could be arrested."

"Right. You could be. Or, we just take what we can and get out of here. We have our family to consider. I've been thinking about it, too, you know. Everyone is talking about the financial crisis getting worse and worse. I think you need to move some of the money to offshore accounts tonight. We need a plan to get out."

"It can't be that easy."

"It *is* that easy. Until you get caught. So don't get caught."

"Where would we move the money? Where would we run?"

"Well, like I said, I've been thinking about it a little already . . ."

It turned out he had been thinking about it a lot. He put the entire plan out there: secret accounts; a Caribbean island called Dominica—which apparently had a lax extradition policy for financial criminals.

They started that night. They went up to her office together and began moving funds. Cary found them plane tickets. As the days passed, Lucky became more and more afraid. Every time someone came to the door or the phone rang, she feared it was the police, wise to their scheme already. She stopped sleeping. She worked almost all the time, often not coming in from her office above the garage until the wee hours of the morning as she made every attempt possible to cover her tracks—even though she knew in the end, the only tracks she needed to cover were the ones leading to the place they would take off to.

Late one night, sharp cramps woke her up. The sheets beneath her were warm and wet. Blood, she realized when she stood and looked down at the linen in the moonlight flowing through their bedroom window. She was alone. Cary was still at the restaurant because he had been working late, too, getting everything ready for their imminent departure, he said.

Lucky didn't call him. She went to the bathroom, sat down on the toilet, and tried not to cry. She waited. She hoped it would stop, but it didn't. Soon, there was no denying it. She had lost the baby. Betty stayed by her side through the worst of it, growling with worry, nudging Lucky at one point to get up off the bathroom floor when she collapsed in pain. Now she followed Lucky into the yard and watched as she buried the tissue-wrapped bundle in the garden. Lucky worried Betty might dig it up, but the dog just stood beside Lucky, looking solemnly at the little mound of fresh earth as if she understood what it was, what it represented.

This was her own fault, Lucky told herself. She had been working so hard—too hard. In the past few weeks, she had hardly been thinking about the baby at all. She wasn't a good mother—because she had never had a mother to show her the way. There was also a part of her that thought somehow the baby knew and didn't want to be born to a bad person like her. So she had made her escape.

She.

Lucky would never know for sure.

She went back inside. She cleaned the bathroom floor and the sheets. When Cary got home, she told him the baby was gone, but she didn't have any tears left. She whispered it, stoic in the darkness of their bedroom—and after, in the silence, wondered what they had been working toward together all these months, these years. What all the money had even been for, why they had needed so much of it. What they had been willing to sacrifice for it.

But money and the heist, they were like addictions. Lucky knew this. There was no going back. Maybe in her new life she would become someone else.

In the morning, Cary suggested she go to a doctor, but she said no. She was up and dressed already.

"I feel fine. Soon we'll be in Dominica. I'll have all the time in the world to take care of myself."

She ignored the voice in her head that whispered, *What was all this for?* She just kept moving forward because that was all she knew how to do.

CHAPTER FOURTEEN

Two days later, filthy and exhausted, Lucky made it to New York State. She walked along the side of a highway toward Devereaux Camp, near Cooperstown. The Mohawk River was by her side, beyond the road and the trees, pine-needle green and flowing slow. Hovering in the distance were the Adirondack Mountains. Finally she came upon a sign, brown with yellow writing, that said WELCOME HOME TO THE DEVEREAUX CAMP. There was a flimsy barrier at the top of a dirt-and-gravel driveway lined with gawky pine trees, a few of them brown and ill-looking, one or two of them deep green and sturdy, all of them bearing PRIVATE PROPERTY: NO TRESPASSING signs nailed straight into the trunks at varying heights.

On one side of the driveway was a weathered shed, perhaps once painted red but now a streaky orange; on the other was a murky pond, then a fence, then a pasture containing three bedraggled horses and a bowlegged pony with a spiky mane. One of the horses trotted over to the fence and nickered at her.

She turned and kept walking up the drive. The camp itself came into view: two outbuildings and a few dozen mobile homes, some of them sided in white, gray, and brown, some of them with awnings and porches and small gardens crowded with ornaments. The closest one had a sign in the window that said WE DON'T CALL 911. Another one, faded blue, bore a sign that said OFFICE. Lucky's heels sank into soft mud as she walked toward it.

"Gloria!" she heard a male voice call. She stopped walking.

"Wha'?" shouted a gruff female voice in return. Lucky followed the sound of it. Up ahead on the wide, dusty path, a woman was driving a golf cart like she was racing in the Indy 500. Lucky paused and watched as the woman hit the brakes in front of a man in a plaid shirt, open to reveal a potbelly so taut it looked painful. Gravel and dust flew up, dirty and devilish, enveloping the man entirely before settling back down.

"Toilet's clogged in the bathhouse again, Gloria," he said. Lucky stood, drinking in her first glimpse of her mother.

"And you can't take care of it because . . . ?"

"Because it's *your* job. I don't do plumbing."

"That's convenient. Apparently, nothing 'round here is your job, Gus. I should fire you."

"You're always threatenin'. Why don't you just go ahead and damn well do it?"

"Fine, then. You're fired. Get the hell outta here."

Gloria hopped out of the golf cart and stood staring him down. She was taller than him, big boned, with messy, dun-colored hair. Finally he turned, walked to the river, and got into a tin fishing boat. After a few fruitless tries with the pull cord, he started the engine and chugged off into the afternoon. Lucky waited a few beats, then began to walk toward the woman.

Gloria spotted her. "Help you?" she said, without much interest. Lucky opened and closed her mouth but her words had turned to dust.

Looking into Gloria's flat brown eyes, at her sallow skin, small nose, and thin lips that bore no resemblance to any of Lucky's features, Lucky began to feel there had to have been some kind of mistake. But what had she expected, for her mother to be an older replica of herself, for there to be something profound in this moment?

Yes. She had expected that.

"Gloria Devereaux?"

"Maybe. Who's asking?" She was peering at Lucky with narrowed eyes.

"I heard in town that you were hiring."

"Who'd ya hear that from?" Gloria put a hand on her hip.

"In the diner," Lucky improvised. "I heard someone say to someone else that Gloria from Devereaux's was always threatening to fire Gus, and that one day she finally would. And I had just arrived in town and I thought to myself, well, maybe today is that day. And it is."

Gloria looked amused now, or at least not quite as angry as she had before. "Ah, hell, I guess people've been expecting me to fire Gus for years. What're your credentials?"

"Er, waitressing, mostly, but I also managed a—"

"You got any references?"

"Well—"

"Résumé?"

"Not exactly."

"You fixing to use this place as a hideout from some maniac ex who's going to show up and cause trouble?"

The lottery ticket was tucked into Lucky's bra; she could feel the smooth paper against her chest. "No. No maniac exes to speak of. It's just me."

Gloria took a step closer. Lucky could smell something fetid, either her breath or the stench of the plunger she held in her hand. "And what's yer name?"

"Sarah Armstrong." She searched for a reaction to the last name Armstrong after she said it, but there wasn't one.

"Sarah, this is a fishing camp and trailer park. It's none too fancy—and those horses aren't any great shakes." Lucky nodded and stayed silent. "And it's no damn fun, working here. No damn fun at all. You got that? In fact, to prove it to ya, if you really want the job, your first task is to unplug the goddamn toilet in the bathhouse. Up for it?" She extended the plunger and Lucky took it.

"If I can unclog it, am I hired?" Lucky asked.

"If you unclog it, you got yourself a deal. Ya get cash payment. Fifty bucks a day, paid weekly. And before you complain about that, lodging is included, which I'm assumin' you need. I've got an empty cabin. Toilet doesn't work, but you can use the bathhouse. Like I said, as long as you manage to unplug it."

"Deal." Lucky took the plunger and stalked toward the bathhouse.

That is my mother, she thought, watching Gloria speed away in the golf cart. *My mother has just asked me to unclog a toilet. She didn't know whether to laugh or not. If you'd never had a mother, how were you supposed to know what to feel?*

After Lucky succeeded at unblocking the toilet—an experience she did not want to relive, let alone repeat—Gloria returned and motioned for her to get in the golf cart. She led her toward a tiny cabin near the water with peeling white paint and green shutters. Then Gloria hit the brakes hard. Lucky's eyes ended up full of grit. She wiped at them, trying to clear her vision.

"You okay?"

Lucky nodded and coughed.

"Well, then. Day starts early. Six thirty a.m., report to the office trailer. There's a sign on it says 'office,' you can't miss it, it's thataway. See you tomorrow." She sped off again almost before Lucky had retrieved her backpack from the back of the cart. Lucky stood and watched her until she was out of sight.

She went inside the cabin. The toilet didn't work in the dingy beige bathroom—everything was beige, including the plastic shower curtain, and everything was stained with mineral rust—but the sink did. She turned on the water and waited for it to turn hot. When it did, she scrubbed her hands with soap all the way up to her elbows, then left the bathroom and took her bag to the bedroom, which was small and faux-wood-paneled, with a tiny window up so high she couldn't see out of it. There was a strange smell, like rot covered up with air freshener.

She began to unpack her meager belongings, tucking her few pairs of underwear and bras into a drawer that protested with a shriek as she opened it. A few wire hangers clung together in the closet, then jangled objections as she hung up a shirt.

She retrieved the lottery ticket from her bra, smoothed it out, and checked it for rips before folding it carefully and putting it in her wallet. It took only a minute to unpack; then she walked from the bedroom into the rest of the cabin, which consisted of a living room–kitchen combo. It was sparsely furnished: a couch upholstered in nubby army-green fabric, a stuffed pike affixed to a board hanging above it. There was a wooden chair next to the window, and a tin-topped table in the kitchen with two mismatched chairs. White-painted cupboards contained a motley gang of cups and dishes. She knew it wasn't much, but it was a roof over her head. Somewhere she could be alone. And her mother was out there. Lucky was going to get to know her—and then she was going to tell her about the lottery ticket. It was all going to come together. This was the start of a new and better life.

There was a corkboard by the back door with a list of rules:

No smoking inside. No candles. No open flames. No moving the furniture. No parties. No loud music after 10 p.m. or the police WILL be called. **Fish gutting**

happens in the gut house ONLY! Not on the back deck. Not in your kitchen!

Lucky's empty stomach groaned, even at the unappetizing thought of gutting fish. She didn't have any tackle to catch anything with, anyway. But frankly, she wished she did. She opened the fridge out of habit. It was empty. She stood in front of it, letting the cool air hit her face and body for a moment before closing it again.

A door in the living room led out to a wood-planked deck. It overlooked the river and was flanked by pine trees. She stepped outside and her toes landed in a wodge of pine sap that had dripped down from the trees. She looked at the slow-moving river for a while, trying to distract herself from her hunger.

After, she went inside and slid her shoes on. She walked back out of the cabin and along the dusty drive. Just before she veered off toward the road, she paused to say hello to the horses, all gathered at the fence. She petted one's soft muzzle, made a mental note to ask Gloria their names tomorrow. Then she followed the main road that led to the nearest town. It didn't take long. The sign said it was called Duvoyage, and had a population of 534. Downtown consisted of a gas station, a shuttered gift shop, a grimy-windowed pizza parlor, and a grocery store.

Inside the grocery store, Lucky took a basket and meandered through the cramped aisles, picking up coffee, peanut butter, some battered and bruised apples that were on sale. She kept the tab under twenty dollars in her mental calculations: a loaf of bread, some boxes of macaroni and cheese, a bagged salad, granola bars, and milk.

"That'll be $19.11," the cashier said, and Lucky handed her a twenty. Then, when the woman opened the register, Lucky pulled her final twenty out of her wallet. "Can you make change for this? In fives?" she said.

"Sure." The cashier counted out four fives, handed them to Lucky, and turned back to the register. Lightning fast, the way her father had taught her, Lucky folded one of the fives up her sleeve. "Oops, sorry. You only gave me fifteen," she said, fanning out the three fives.

"My apologies. I could have sworn I counted out four fives," the cashier said. "But I can't open the register now, so you'll have to wait."

"S'alright, Carla," said another voice. "Here, you take my five, and Carla can square up with me after."

Lucky turned. It was Gloria, and her eyebrows were raised. "Take it," she said, and Lucky did, feeling her cheeks start to burn with shame. Gloria had seen her shortchange the cashier, she knew it.

"Thanks," Lucky said. "See you back at the camp." She picked up her paper bag of groceries in one arm and walked out. But Gloria paid for her own groceries quickly and followed.

"Hey," she said, coming up behind Lucky. "I'll give you a ride." She pointed to a dull red pickup. "There's me."

Lucky climbed in. Gloria turned the truck on and pulled out of the parking lot. "Where'd ya learn to do that?" she asked as she signaled to turn left. "'Cause there's only one person I know who could short-change a person so fast you almost didn't know if you saw it. And his name was Armstrong, too, just like you, John Armstrong. You related? We were married. God help me, we still are, though I haven't seen him in more than a few decades." Gloria pulled a flask out from under the seat, took a sip as she drove, then pointed it at Lucky. "Want some?"

Lucky's heart was beating fast. She took the flask. Whatever it was burned its way down her throat and she tried not to sputter and cough. She had hoped it would give her courage, but she had to take one more gulp before she could say, "Yes, I'm related to John Arm-strong."

"I didn't think he had any people still alive. Lost his family in a car crash when he was little. God, haven't thought about him in years. How is he?"

"In prison."

"Can't say as I'm surprised by that." Gloria tipped the flask her way again, but Lucky shook her head. "You see much of him, ever visit?"

"I'm his daughter."

Gloria hit the brakes and the truck skidded on gravel. She turned down the lane toward the camp. "His *kid?*" She parked the truck in front of her trailer.

Now was the time. She had to do this. Lucky lifted the crucifix out from under her T-shirt, turned to Gloria, and held it up. "I'm your kid, too. The one you left behind, in Queens."

Gloria looked down at the crucifix on the chain around Lucky's neck. "What the hell are you talking about, and what the hell is that?"

"I'm your daughter. This necklace is all I have of you. He said you were—" It sounded so ridiculous now that she had met Gloria, but still she pressed forward. "He said you were very religious. This crucifix was yours. And you left it for me, when you had to leave us. Because you had postpartum depression and couldn't stay. I forgive you, I just want to get to know you."

Gloria let out a barking laugh. "He told you that, hey?" She reached forward and touched the cross on Lucky's chain, holding it in her calloused fingers before letting it drop. "Girl, I am not your mother, or anyone's. Got an infection when I was a teenager and had all my internal lady bits removed. John said he didn't mind—but then he got to hankering for a kid, and one day, he came home with one. You, I guess."

"Me . . . you guess?"

"That's why I took off on him. It was the craziest thing, just picking you up like that off those church steps. He should have called the police."

Lucky stared at her. What was she saying? That John had found her somewhere?

Gloria squinted down at the crucifix. "He came home with you in his arms and was rambling something about finding you on some church steps, telling some nun you were his, and the nun giving him that necklace so he could buy you some baby formula and diapers. He came home with a lot of things that weren't his—but a baby was a goddamn first."

Lucky didn't want this to be true. She reached for the door handle, her cheeks hot with a shame she couldn't trace the source of, tears welling up behind her eyes. Damned if she was going to sit in Gloria's pickup truck and cry over the truth about where she had really come from.

"Wait," Gloria said. "Don't go. You're shocked. I get that. But you wouldn't have come to me unless you had no place else to go. Right? Maybe we can team up."

"Team up?"

Gloria tilted the flask her way; Lucky shook her head, numb. "I'm getting sick of this place, sick of this life, ya know? And—and seeing you, thinking about John, as bad as it was with him, is reminding me of some big dreams I had, once. It just seems there's only one way to make those dreams come true at this stage in my life, and that's the fast track. If you were raised by John Armstrong, then you know what I mean by that."

Lucky clutched the crucifix with her fingers, then pulled on it. She wanted the chain to break, but it held fast.

"The people who live at the camp, most of them are older. Makes me wonder if there's any way to skim a little extra off them without anyone getting suspicious. You know? But without a partner, it's hard to do. Except now, here ya are, John Armstrong's daughter, with a fast hand at shortchanging. I'm sure he taught you a few other things, too. Right?" she pressed.

This time when Gloria passed the flask to Lucky, she took it, and let a big gulp burn and sear its way down her esophagus. "He sure did."

"So whaddya say? Got any ideas on how we can pair up and make some fast cash?"

Lucky hated it, the way that bubbly, excited feeling surfaced against her will and started coursing through her veins again. The way she suddenly felt alive, the way she suddenly believed she had the chance to be something, to be someone. The way even though she knew Gloria was not her mother, she had wanted to be loved by her for so long, she could do nothing but clutch at this chance.

Picked up off some church steps.

She closed her eyes, briefly. She was nothing but trash.

"I've got tons of ideas, Gloria. There's always a brighter future ahead." It was true, wasn't it? There just might be.

A few mornings later old Al Hinch, who lived in trailer number 11, peered at Gloria and Lucky with his rheumy eyes and frowned as they stood on the deck of his trailer. "You're sure?" he said.

"'Fraid so, Al," Gloria said. "Sarah here, my niece, just graduated from architecture school, and I asked her to come have a look at everyone's trailers round here as a favor." Lucky frowned now, too, because that wasn't exactly what they had discussed. Architecture was too vague; Gloria was supposed to say structural engineering but had clearly forgotten. Al didn't seem to notice. He lived alone with a rakish dog named Mutt, and the day before he had smiled and waved hello when Lucky passed his trailer. Now Lucky was grateful she was wearing sunglasses, because she couldn't meet his eyes. But she needed to do this, needed to work with Gloria a little so she could figure out whether she could trust her with the lottery ticket. So if she asked her to go cash it in for her, it wouldn't feel like she was trusting a stranger with the most important thing in her life.

"We're going around and checking out everyone's place. And Sarah and me are going to do the work on our own, so you'll get a deal on materials and labor. Six hundred, flat rate. Pay us cash and we won't charge you no taxes."

A sigh. "All right then. I'll get you the money by the end of the week."

"Sounds good, Al. And we'll get started on fixin' your skirting ventilation right soon."

They moved along to the next trailer, knocked on the door, poked around underneath it, and declared it to be fine—even though it was in the exact same shape as Al's had been. Two more trailers were given the all-clear before they found two more in a row with the same supposed skirt ventilation issue.

It took a few days to get through all the trailers on the property, and only two residents started arguing and said they were going to call in their own professional to take a look. "They won't bother," Gloria told Lucky. "And they'll get worried when they see all their neighbors getting the fix-ups. They'll do it. Trust me, I know these people. Honestly, what a fabulous idea. You're brilliant, girl."

"Thanks," Lucky said, and felt a dull pleasure at the compliment.

"Want to have dinner with me? I'm no chef, but I got a lasagna in the freezer and some beer in the fridge. Maybe even a little vino. Yeah?"

"Oh. That would be nice." Lucky thought of the wilting bag of lettuce in her fridge. "I could bring a salad . . ."

"Nah, no need. Tomato sauce is a vegetable, right? Why don't you just come sit on down here on the porch while I pop it in the oven? We've had a long day, we need refreshments."

Gloria's front deck looked out at the horse pasture. Lucky sat and watched the animals in the fading light. The pony was trotting back and forth on one side of the field while one of the little girls who lived in the trailer park hung on the fence and watched her. The three horses were hunkered around the hay pile.

Lucky heard one of the floorboards creak on the porch. Gloria was back, a bottle of Blue Moon in each hand, an orange slice shoved into the top of each one. "Ya see that, I got fancy for ya. It's not often I have a guest."

Gloria popped the orange slice inside the bottle and took a swig, and Lucky did the same. "Saw them do this at a restaurant once, thought it tasted pretty good when I tried it," Gloria said.

Later, Gloria brought the lasagna out on plastic plates with a floral pattern around the edges, plus paper napkins and knives and forks for them to eat with on their laps. She also had a dusty bottle of wine she said had been a Christmas gift from someone who used to live at the camp. "Been saving it," she said. "But I never have company."

It tasted sour, but Lucky drank it anyway. She was nervous. She kept imagining herself telling Gloria about the ticket, asking for her help. Once it was out, she wouldn't be able to take it back. But who other than Gloria could help her with this?

"Hey, ya know what?" Gloria said a little later. "I got some pictures of John, from back then, when we were together. I know he's not really your dad—but did you want to see them anyway?" She didn't wait for an answer. She went inside and came out with an envelope, opened it to reveal a handful of old snapshots of Gloria and John almost thirty years before. Gloria had been surprisingly attractive, pert-faced and trim, smiling up at John like he was the best thing she had ever seen. He was looking at her the same way—but he could look at every woman like that, if he wanted to. Lucky knew that.

Gloria put down the photographs and sipped her wine. "I sure was in love with him, for a while. He used to tell me there weren't nothing we couldn't do together, that I was all he had."

Lucky drained her wineglass; Gloria refilled it. "He used to say the same thing to me," Lucky said.

"I'm sorry," Gloria said. "It's a shitty deal you got. I wish I could help you out more than I am." She shook the nearly empty bottle. "Want me to go in and get us something stronger, something that'll really take the edge off?"

"Sure, why not?"

A few moments later, she accepted whatever moonshine Gloria

handed her, slugged it back, and held out her glass. "Attagirl," Gloria said. "This will make it all better."

Gloria's lips and teeth were purple from the wine and her hair was even more askew than usual. She settled back in her chair and kept talking. Lucky tried to focus on her, but whatever had been in the glass was strong. Her vision blurred as Gloria spoke. "I told him he needed to take you to a police station, you know, and when he refused, I left him. That was it for us. Never saw him again—though I did sometimes wonder what had happened with all that. Hoped, for once, that he had decided to do the right thing. Figured he'd have a few days of diapers and no sleep and change his mind. Apparently not." She kept on talking and Lucky closed her eyes. Eventually, Gloria's words just became noise, blended with the chorus of crickets and hum of cicadas and trucks speeding past out on the road. At some point, she felt Gloria putting a blanket over her knees, and then it was silent and dark and Lucky was asleep.

"Cary! Where are you?"

Her panicked voice brought Cary downstairs, his footsteps pounding. "Are you okay?"

"Betty is gone! I let her outside a few minutes ago, in the yard. And now she's . . . she's just gone!"

The two of them spent hours walking up and down the streets of their neighborhood, calling Betty's name. They printed signs and taped them to telephone poles. Cary had to go back to the restaurant eventually; Lucky sat at home, waiting by her phone, staring down at the papers she had procured to take Betty to Dominica with them, crying endless tears. Just like the loss of the baby, this was her fault. She had been preoccupied, too focused on the money they were moving offshore. She ignored the voice that told her she hadn't done anything wrong, anything different from what she did every day.

"It's like someone took her," Lucky said to Cary when he got back.

"Like someone stole her. Betty would never run away."

"Maybe she sensed we were about to leave, and she didn't want to go. You have to try not to worry about it, okay? You can't fix this. We have to keep moving."

"How can I not worry about her? She's all I—" She had been about to say, *She's all I have.* But this wasn't true. She had Cary. They had the money. She had to start believing that the things she actually still had in her grasp mattered.

Betty didn't come home. Days passed, and then it was time for them to leave. "What if someone finds Betty, though? Can't we delay our departure? Just a few more days?"

"We can't stay here," Cary said. "We're going to get caught. The stock market has gone even lower. How many clients called you today, asking about their money?"

"Too many," Lucky admitted.

"Babe, it's time. We have to get out of here. We've waited too long already."

But it didn't feel right. It felt like bad luck to leave on this note, like if they left like this, any chance they had of ever having a happy life would be lost. And she was still holding out hope. Someone would call about Betty.

"I have an idea," Lucky said. "What if we go to Las Vegas? What could be more fun than that? And it's safe there; we know how to go incognito." It felt like exactly what they needed to do, all of a sudden. Like the perfect way to hit the reset button on her life, and buy a tiny bit more time. "We've lost so much. We need to do something special—go out in a blaze of glory. Don't you think? Before we leave forever?"

Cary took her in his arms, looked down at her. "Will it make you happy again? Because I hate seeing you sad like this."

"Yes, it will."

"All right," Cary said. "What's one more night in America, I guess? No one will find us in Nevada."

The next day, they got in their silver Audi, and they started to drive.

PART
TWO

Margaret Jean went back to bed the night the baby cried on the steps of St. Monica's cathedral and the man with the shiny shoes stared into her eyes and said, "This is my child." But she couldn't sleep. When dawn broke, she went to the sisters and asked about her aspirancy. They told her they had indeed decided she could join their order, and she felt something unexpected: relief so deep it was almost rapturous. All at once, this was what she wanted. To redeem herself, and to redeem others.

It was weeks later when Sister Margaret Jean—as she was now known—heard there was a young woman in the parish asking about a baby left on the steps.

"You didn't hear anything that night you were on watch, did you?" the sisters asked her.

"No, of course not," Sister Margaret Jean said, and they believed her, because who would lie about such a thing? Poor girl, the nuns all said. Poor thing, she mustn't be in her right mind.

Sister Margaret Jean immediately knew out of her mind, with grief. And, in this new incarnation of herself, as helper, as redeemer, as someone different from the woman she had been before—someone who had bilked people out of their money and then hidden herself away so she wouldn't have to pay for her crimes—she was going to help her.

When she reached the steps, the young woman was at the bottom, walking slowly, shoulders sloped downward, a portrait of dejection. Her hair was red, like a flame, so she was easy to follow. Sister Margaret Jean walked along behind her, trying to think of what to say. Finally she was close enough that she could reach forward and touch the young woman's shoulder.

"Get your hands o—"

"No, no, I don't want to hurt you," said Sister Margaret Jean. "I want to help. Please, come with me."

There was hope in the young woman's eyes—eyes that were an unusual green, like emeralds, or the lime-flavored hard candies Margaret Jean used to buy for pennies as a child.

"Do you know where my baby is?" the girl said.

"Let me buy you breakfast. Let's talk."

They went to a café Sister Margaret Jean remembered from her life before the parish, when she had spent her time befriending people who were sick or old and lived alone. She would work her way into their lives, and then into their wills. It was systematic, and became an addiction. She got more money than she knew what to do with. She had told herself the harm she was doing wasn't real, that she was in fact making people's final days happy. But if there was one thing she had learned at the parish with all that Bible reading, it was that stealing was stealing was stealing.

The young woman was silent, her eyes haunted and wide, so Sister Margaret Jean ordered for both of them: pancakes, eggs, potatoes, fruit, coffee, orange juice. The young woman was obviously famished. Sister Margaret Jean watched her eat, then finally asked her name.

"Valerie Mann."

Sister Margaret Jean noticed that the front of the girl's shirt was wet, and she took off her cardigan and gave it to her to cover the leaking milk. She wanted to ask her who she was, where she came from, and why she had left her child on the steps of the parish—but asking her this would give Sister Margaret Jean away; the girl would know she had seen the baby and allowed her to be carried off by some stranger. She wanted redemption—but she did not want to get caught. So she did something she was good at: she made up a story.

"I . . ." Sister Margaret Jean paused, then began again. "I am known for my holy visions. And I had one about your baby. I saw her in a long and vivid dream. She is a beautiful baby, with hair like yours, and a determined, hearty cry."

Valerie put down her fork. "You saw her," she said, her green eyes now laser intense.

"In my mind," corrected Sister Margaret Jean. "In a dream."

"So you believe me, that I brought my baby to your parish?"

"I do. I know she was there."

"So, what else? Do you know where she is now?"

"She is safe," Sister Margaret Jean said. "She is loved." She closed her eyes, as if seeing the child. The only way to get people to believe the things you said was to really believe in them yourself. "She is with a family. They found her on the steps, and because they had prayed for a baby they thought she was a miracle. So they took her home. You don't need to worry about her. She is safe, and she is taken care of. I know this for a fact."

Valerie sat still, her fork now abandoned. "So someone just took her?"

"A family. She is safe."

"Do they live in a nice home? My parents threw me out when they found out I was pregnant. My boyfriend moved to Texas."

"She is healthy, well, and loved, I promise."

"Could we call the police? Could we try to find them?"

"Is that what you want? To find her?" Sister Margaret Jean watched the girl, watched her look away, afraid.

"Abandoning a child is a crime. If I try to find her, I'll have to admit what I did." One of the young woman's tears plopped down onto the Formica table.

Sister Margaret Jean despised herself. But she was too deep into this now.

"Where do you live, girl?"

Valerie looked up. "I'm living in a shelter," she said, then sighed. "I wanted so much more for myself, you know? I was determined to keep my baby, to do right by her—but then, after she was born, and I was alone, with no one, no money, no nothing at all, I just—snapped. Saw my life and what it was going to look like. Saw all the other women with children living in the shelter and how bleak it was for them. Suddenly I decided my daughter—I called her Julia—should have a chance at something better." She put her face in her hands, and her shoulders shook for a while. Her crying was silent but intense, like an inward scream. It didn't draw attention. "I got so scared. I made a mistake. I thought maybe—I had this idea that I could leave her with someone who would find her a good life, and I could still finish high school and go to college and be someone—that we could both be someone, even if we had to do that separately. I decided that if she stayed with me we would both be no one. That maybe we would even starve. I decided I was making a sacrifice and that it was for her own good. I believed it—but how could I? I woke up this morning and I realized I was never going to be anyone without her. So I came back—and she's gone."

Sister Margaret Jean said, "I'm going to help you." She was thinking fast now, talking fast, too, so she couldn't change her mind. Thinking of the money she had in a bank account she had never told anyone about, the money she should have given to the church but had not. This was even better. "Find an apartment, come back to the parish, bring me to see it, and I'll pay the rent. Finish high school. We'll meet weekly until you do and figure out the plan after that."

Valerie's green eyes were wide. "But why? Why are you helping me?"

"My visions are always a call for me to do something. I'm going to support you. Ensure that in giving up your child you were not sacrificing your own life. That you are indeed going to be someone."

For a moment, Valerie narrowed those brilliant green eyes. Sister Margaret Jean thought she might begin to question her motives, but she didn't. She just nodded and went back to her breakfast.

"What would you most like to be?" Sister Margaret Jean finally asked Valerie.

"I've always wanted to be a lawyer," Valerie answered, her eyes still on her plate. "Maybe even a judge, or a district attorney, or, I don't know. Something big."

"Don't let go of that dream," Sister Margaret Jean said. "See about the apartment. We'll meet back here on the first of every month. Do we have a deal?"

Valerie nodded. "Yes," she said.

And so it began.

CHAPTER FIFTEEN

S omeone was shining a bright light in Lucky's face. She opened her eyes with difficulty. Her head felt like it had been hit with a mallet. The bright light, she realized, was the sun. She had fallen asleep in one of Gloria's deck chairs. She looked down and saw that she had dropped her wallet. Everything had spilled out across the deck. She picked up Reyes's card, the fives from the grocery store cashier, a few of her ID cards. Then she got down on all fours, suddenly panicked, and started scrabbling around. Her lottery ticket. It was gone.

"Gloria?" she called out, standing. She checked inside her bra, turned out her pockets, but the ticket wasn't there.

"Hello?" She knocked on Gloria's door, but there was no answer. She tried the handle; it was unlocked. Inside, all was dim and quiet. It smelled like peach room spray. Gloria's bed was unmade and empty. There were dirty dishes and wineglasses in the sink. A liquor bottle on the counter that said "100 proof" on the label.

Lucky ran to the office trailer, but it was empty, too. She picked up the phone and tried Gloria's cell phone but it went straight to voicemail.

With a shaking hand, she dialed Reyes's number.

"Hello?"

"It's me."

"Hey, I've been trying to call you at the camp! I spoke to Gloria a few times, but she always said you were busy. Did she give you any of my messages?"

"No. She didn't."

"How are things going?"

"Not well," Lucky managed. The room was spinning and she thought she might throw up. She gripped the counter.

"Listen, I'm actually only about two hours away. And I've got your dad with me. They let him out! I'll explain everything soon. See you in a bit."

Betty's barking alerted Lucky to their arrival. She stood and left the office trailer, a little steadier on her feet now after drinking half the contents of Gloria's water cooler.

Reyes got out of the SUV and Betty followed, bounding forward, delighted. Lucky leaned down and greeted her, feeling relief for a moment. But it didn't last.

"Your dad's fallen asleep. We've been on the road for days. He's exhausted. Let's let him rest. You can catch me up on how things are going here."

"Come inside, then. I'm going to make coffee."

Betty stayed by her side. Inside, Lucky found the Folgers tin and spooned coffee into a filter, turned the machine on, kept herself busy in the corner of the office, trying to figure out what to say to Reyes. When the coffee was ready, she poured two cups. "We don't have milk or even sugar. Black okay?"

"Sure."

They went outside and sat in rickety lawn chairs that had been abandoned in front of the office. Betty curled up at Lucky's feet.

"So, tell me how things went with Gloria."

"You tell me first, what happened with John?"

"It was so fast," Reyes said. "I got a call right after I dropped you off. The court date was the next day." Lucky shot a glance at Reyes's SUV, where her father—no, *not* her father, where John Armstrong—was asleep in the front seat, his head tilted to one side, his mouth open. He looked like a very old man. Like a stranger. Which was what he was to her, now. "It was quickly determined he'd done his time for his actual crimes already, and the third-strike clause was waived. So, there he is."

"Great," Lucky said.

"You don't sound all that happy. Are you okay?"

"I found out that he's not my dad," she said.

"*What?*"

The SUV's door opened. Betty barked, John was awake, and had exited the car. He was looking around, bewildered. Reyes stood up. Voice low, she said to Lucky, "I don't know what you're talking about, but it might be best not to tell him what you just said to me right now. He's really slipping, is confused a lot of the time. He needs to see a doctor, but he wanted to see you first."

Reyes turned and jogged toward the car. "Hey, John! It's all right. I'm right here. And look, I brought you to Lucky!"

His face lit up the moment he saw her. All the anger Lucky felt dissipated for a moment. She heard Cary's voice in her mind now, telling her that when John finally did get out of prison he would be a different person, completely lost to her. But in this moment, with his eyes lit up like that, he was the man she remembered.

And then, he wasn't. Because she knew the truth now. He was lost to her. And Gloria was gone, and so was the lottery ticket. She couldn't handle it. She was finally broken. She had to choke back a sob.

Lucky got up from her chair and started to walk, fast, toward the river. Betty followed along.

"Lucky, wait up, it's me, your old dad! They sprung me! You aren't happy to see me? Why're you running away? Are you crying?"

She kept walking until she was at the edge of the riverbank. Betty reached her side first, then John. "Lucky. It is you, right? I haven't been myself lately. It is you? You're acting like we're strangers."

"Do you realize where we are, John? Do you know what this place is?"

He turned in a slow circle, taking in his shabby surroundings. "Not . . . really?"

"Devereaux Camp. You told me about it, when I visited you in jail just a few weeks ago. Remember that?"

"Oh, ah, right, I did." He looked startled. "Reyes said so. She was telling me, reminding me. Shit. You met Gloria. You sought her out. I told you not to, but you did."

"I did. I met Gloria and I made a fool of myself, telling her I was her long-lost daughter when it turns out . . . it turns out you stole me from some fucking church steps?" She had been trying to stay calm, but her voice rose.

"Not stole," he said, shaking his head. "You were abandoned! I saved you—"

"You lied to me my entire life! You aren't my real father. And Gloria was never my mother."

Reyes had started to approach, but now she backed off, gave them their space.

"So you think I'm no good? Just because I tried to hide that one thing from you? What's wrong with you? You think you're so perfect?"

"I'm a criminal," she said, her voice lower now. "You raised me to be one. And the man I thought I loved was a criminal, and now he's—" She almost sobbed, but swallowed it back. "He's probably dead, and I'm going to be held accountable for everything we did, and then some. And my one chance, the only thing I had—Gloria has the lottery ticket now, and she's disappeared."

"That lottery ticket! Where is it, where is Gloria? Get it from her. I can cash it, and I won't take a cent, not a goddamn penny, because you're right, I did you wrong by lying to you, but I swear, if you'll let me make it up to you, I will make things better. I'll go cash it for you. I'll get Reyes to take me right now. All that money, you can do anything! The police will never find you —"

"I just told you, the ticket is gone! Gloria stole it!"

"So? We'll find her."

Lucky just shook her head. "How? How are we going to get to her before she cashes it in?"

He looked out at the river, then back at her. "I loved you the second I saw you, you know. It isn't what you think. I wanted to take care of you. I did take care of you. I said you were my daughter because that's what I've always felt. You are."

"No. You didn't love me: You saw my potential. Saw a way to mold me and use me in your cons. There's nothing you can say to make things better, so don't even try."

"When you were little, for the longest time you didn't even know what a mother was," he said. "You were four . . . or maybe five the first time you asked. I froze. I couldn't think of anything to say. And so I said your mother was Gloria because she was the first woman I could think of. The lie just spiraled from there. I never thought —" He raised his hands, at a loss for words.

"You never thought I'd find her."

"I guess not."

"I don't want to talk to you anymore. I want to be alone. Come on, Betty. Let's go."

She walked away from him, toward her cabin. Before going inside, she turned back and saw her father standing alone. Reyes approached him. She put a hand on his shoulder, and he bowed his head; Lucky could tell her father was weeping. No. Not her father.

Betty whined, and she led her inside. Lucky closed the curtain and sat on the bed, staring down into her empty hands.

It was too late. Nothing about her or her life was ever going to change for the better. The only thing to do now was turn herself in and pay the price for her crimes.

" I still dream of finding her someday," Valerie said. It was the first of the month. She and Sister Margaret Jean were sitting in the luncheonette they had been meeting at for almost thirty years. "It would be a miracle. Wouldn't it?"

"A miracle," Sister Margaret Jean replied. "Yes, it truly would."

Over the years, Sister Margaret Jean had slowly drained the contents of that cursed bank account filled with ill-gotten gains until there was almost nothing left. *Hallelujah*. College for Valerie, law school, a long climb up. She had indeed become a lawyer. And now she was Manhattan's district attorney. Sister Margaret Jean felt proud. It was the greatest joy of her life. She had done it. The world was a better place because of Valerie Mann, and therefore it was a better place because of Sister Margaret Jean. *You are forgiven*, she would tell herself—even though she knew this wasn't true, not really. Only God could forgive her. And Valerie was lonely, unhappy. She had almost everything: an incredible career, money, the good kind of notoriety—and yet, she had no people. She had never married. Sister Margaret Jean didn't know if she had any friends but suspected not really. Her secret probably loomed too large. Valerie didn't speak to her family; she sometimes spoke of a long-dead grandmother she had been close with, but her relationship with her parents had ended long ago, when they had kicked her out for getting pregnant. And

Sister Margaret Jean could see that even after almost thirty years, the weight of abandoning her child still felt heavy to Valerie. It isolated her from everyone.

"I look for her everywhere," Valerie had said, month after month, year after year, during their regular meetings at that same café, one of the few remnants of a city that had changed, and one they doggedly returned to. Sister Margaret Jean wanted to say, *I look for her every-where, too. And I look for him.* But she only smiled and nodded, sympathetic. She kept her thoughts to herself, as always.

"But the thing is, I think I saw her," Valerie said now. "I know it's happened before and I've always been wrong, but I saw this young woman on the news a month ago, and I can't stop thinking about her. She looks so much like me." Valerie slid her phone across the table. She seemed younger when she spoke this way, less like the accomplished woman she had become and more like the scared, sad child she had been when Sister Margaret Jean first met her in this luncheonette.

Sister Margaret Jean looked at the photo of the pretty young woman in the crisp white blouse and navy blazer, leaning toward the camera, a smile in her eyes. She had to admit, she *did* look like Valerie. Same color hair, same curls, same face shape, same mouth—same unusual eyes. She zoomed in on them.

"It's uncanny."

"She's wanted by police," Valerie said. "For embezzlement. I've tried to find out more about her, but it's all dead ends. No parents. No family. I know I shouldn't waste my time. But I can't stop looking at this photo."

Not for the first time, Sister Margaret Jean thought of the man with the shiny shoes, of the kind of life he might have given the baby she had allowed him to walk away with that night. Could the child have been led this far astray? Sure, she could have. Anything was possible. But she hoped not.

"I don't think this could be your daughter," she said to Valerie, sliding the phone back to her.

"Don't you?" Valerie looked down at the image for a long moment, then put the phone away. "I guess there's no way of knowing."

"No," Sister Margaret Jean said, the guilt weighing more heavily. "There isn't."

CHAPTER SIXTEEN

Lucky was still sitting inside her cabin. She had been in there alone for hours, unsure of what to do next. Outside, it had started to rain, and it was getting dark. Lucky rose from her bed and looked out the window again. The white SUV remained; Reyes and John were now inside it, waiting.

Betty was asleep, curled at the bottom of the bed, but she opened one eye when Lucky opened the door.

"It's okay, girl, I'll be right back." Lucky ran across the wet grass toward the office, ignoring Reyes and John, who were watching her. She went inside. First she tried Gloria's cell phone, just in case—but it was still off. It reminded her of Cary's disappearance, that morning in the Vegas hotel room when she had tried to phone him, and the pieces of his betrayal had slowly and sickeningly fallen into place. It was that same feeling of fruitless frustration, fear, and abandonment.

She pushed those memories aside, put the phone down, and looked around the dim, empty office. All she felt were the empty spaces around her and inside her. The space her father had once occupied—now he was no longer her father. The space Gloria had once occupied—now she had no image of a mother to cling to. The space Cary had once occupied—now he was gone, possibly dead, and no longer someone she could ever hope to understand. And the space the lottery ticket had once occupied, that effervescent hope that had lived inside her and kept her going? It was a gaping hole, like a wound. Gloria had told her she was not her mother, but still, Lucky had started to feel like maybe she could come to trust her. She had even started imagining telling her about the ticket, asking her to cash it in. Instead, she had let her guard down, and Gloria had stolen the ticket from her when she was at her most vulnerable. She put her face in her hands.

The door creaked open. It was Reyes.

"Hey, how are you holding up? What's going on?"

Lucky shook her head. "Just go. Please? It's pointless for you to stay here."

But Reyes pulled up a chair. "I had no idea. John never told me, either. We've talked about it now, a little. He has moments of clarity, and for a while there earlier, he seemed to understand what he had done, what you had found out. He really wants to help you."

"I don't want his help. I don't want him here at all."

"But, the thing is . . . Well, he just loves you so much. I used to be jealous of that. I thought that if I could only have someone in my life who cared about me the way he cared about you, if I could maybe have a real dad, I'd be set."

"I didn't have a real dad."

"Better than the one I had. He used to beat the shit out of me. I got yanked out of my house and put in foster care. Which is how I ended up meeting Priscilla, and that nearly ruined my life, so . . ."

The only sound was the pelting of the rain on the roof of the trailer.

"Prison is brutal," Reyes said. "It takes a lot away from you. All you have to do is look at the state your dad's in now to see that. But it does help a person understand the importance of second chances."

"I can never forgive him for lying to me about who I am."

"He's a good man."

Lucky snorted. "You must not have met very many good men in your life."

"He was kind to me when no one else was. He kept working for Priscilla because he wanted to try to keep me safe."

"I thought it was because he was trying to pay for my tuition."

"That was only part of it."

More silence, more dripping rain.

"Your dad told me about the lottery ticket."

Lucky looked up. "Ah," she said. "Now I see why you're being so nice to me."

Reyes laughed. "Really, Lucky? You think I want to help you and be your friend because of some long-shot chance we'll actually find this Gloria woman who stole your ticket and get that ticket back from her?" She shook her head, still laughing. "Do you realize what I stand to lose if I get caught with you, a fugitive? Just being here with you is in direct violation of the terms of my release from prison. Driving you to the bus station the other day—that was a big risk for me, too. Not to mention the fact that Priscilla will probably try to kill me when she finds out. I had no clue about the ticket at that point, did I? You're going to have to learn to just trust people at some point. It'll save you a lot of pain."

"Right. Consider what happened to me the last few times I decided to trust people."

"Maybe you need to let people prove themselves to you first, with actions, not just words."

Lucky wanted to be angry but found she no longer had the strength. She knew she was being harsh, and unfair. "I'm sorry," she said. "You didn't have to come and pick me up, and you did." She sighed. "Thanks for that."

"No problem. People deserve second chances. And third chances. All people do is make mistakes. If we never forgave, we'd all be alone."

"I *am* alone."

The rain stopped and it was silent in the small room. Lucky ran her index fingers underneath her eyes, catching all the tears that had gathered there. She wiped them off on her jeans.

"You're not," Reyes said.

"I think it's time for me to just turn myself in."

"No," she said. "Not yet. I have a friend I met through work who's a private investigator in New York City. She owes me a favor. We can drive there tomorrow morning."

"What for?"

"To see if she can help you track Gloria. And that missing ticket. You can't just give up. It's too soon. Plus—John had the idea that he could take you to the church where you were left. That maybe that would help. Maybe someone there has answers?"

Lucky wasn't sure anything would help. But she still agreed to Reyes's plan.

Slowly, inevitably as they drove, the mountains gave way to rolling hills, then to houses, and big-box stores, trees that were scrubby rather than stately green.

"Mind if I turn on the radio?" John asked Reyes. Lucky hadn't spoken to him yet that morning. She had barely been able to look him in the eye. And he was acting as if nothing had happened, which made Lucky wonder if he had forgotten the entire conversation by the river. Could you be angry with someone for something they'd forgotten they'd done? John's decline was undeniable. He had lucid moments, but his confusion was frequent, and profound.

"Whatever you want," Reyes said.

John dialed through the channels until he found a Yankees game. Lucky lifted her hand and touched the cross at her neck. They were in city traffic when announcer John Sterling crowed, "*Theeeeee*

Yankees win! John pumped his fist and said, "Well, how about that?"

Lucky found herself smiling, a reflex from another time and place.

John grinned at her in the rearview mirror. He was back in time, too.

Lucky looked out the window. They were getting close now, and Reyes was slowing down.

Reyes maneuvered into a parking spot and turned off the car.

"We're here," she said. "I'll wait in the car with the dog."

St. Monica's was a relic tucked in among apartment buildings and high-rises; its spires looked like arms raised up in a holy fervor that no one on the ground below noticed anymore. Betty was in the back seat of the car; she popped her head over the seats and licked Lucky's hand encouragingly.

"I think I remembered her name," John said. "The nun who was there the night I found you. Something Jean. Maybe Mary Jean? We'll go in there and ask for Mary Jean."

They got out of the car. They approached the steps, and John stopped. "Lucky," he said, pointing down. "It was right here. This is where I found you. It was cold, and you were crying, and I thought you were a miracle."

"No. I can't." Lucky moved quickly over the step, trying not to imagine the mother who would just leave her there, in the cold, in the dark, crying and alone.

Inside the church the air was cool. It smelled of wood and dust. Lucky craned her neck to look up at the stained glass and vaulted ceilings. John passed her and walked to the front of the church. Lucky watched as he approached a table full of candles, all lined up in translucent red glass holders. He lit one of the candles and bowed his head. How did he know what to do? It was a side of him she hadn't seen before.

She walked up to the front, uncertain. He gave her his lighter. "Want to light one?" She took the lighter and turned away.

How did a person pray—and why did a person pray, exactly? If you prayed for something, did it come true? Was it like a wish? How long did it take to come true? Was it immediate, like rubbing a genie's bottle? Or did it take time? In the past, Lucky would have asked these questions of John. Now she couldn't. She lit a candle, then another, and another. She looked down at all the tiny flames, tucked down low in their red holders.

"Lucky, people light these candles to remember the people they've lost," John said.

She thought of Cary, and she wished he hadn't suffered, no matter what he had done. She lit a candle.

She thought of the mother who'd left her on the steps of this church. She lit another candle.

She thought of the fact that the man she had believed to be her father was no one to her. She lit another.

The lottery ticket. One final flame.

Then she blew them all out.

"Lucky!" her father hissed. "You can't do that! It's . . . it's . . ."

Movement behind them. A nun was making her way down the aisle toward them.

"Hello?" she was calling. "What are you doing?"

Lucky had thought they were alone, but clearly they weren't.

"I'm so sorry, Sister," John began.

The nun stopped walking. She was just a few feet in front of them.

"Hey," John said. "Mary Jean, is that you?"

Lucky was sure she saw recognition in the nun's face, as though she knew who they were. But when the woman opened her mouth, she said, "I have no idea who you're talking about."

The nun turned and walked down the aisle, fast, then out the front door of the church. She left them standing there, truly alone with all those extinguished flames.

Sister Margaret Jean had recognized them right away. She had been standing near the door, letting the fall breeze blow over her, when through the front entrance they had emerged.

"Lucky." It was the man. She knew this voice.

At this point, Sister Margaret Jean opened her mouth, but no sound came out. She took her cell phone out of the folds of her habit and held it in her hand, pulled up Valerie's number, but didn't dial it, not yet. She couldn't be sure. She watched them approach the candles. The man was so much older. He no longer looked so sure of himself. But his shoes were still shiny. The young woman was beautiful, even with the ragged haircut, the bad dye job.

Sister Margaret Jean watched in silence as they lit candles. All at once, the young woman blew the candles out. Sister Margaret Jean was shaken from her dreamlike state. She ran toward them, calling out, but not sure what she was going to do.

If there had been any doubt in her mind that it was them, it was extinguished the moment she saw the woman up close. Her eyes were green like emeralds, the same as Valerie's.

For almost thirty years, Sister Margaret Jean had held out hope that miracles could really happen in Queens, although she had never seen one—but now, here it was. It had come to pass. They had returned.

Her gaze moved from the familiar green eyes to the necklace that had once been familiar to her, now hanging around the young woman's neck. It hadn't had much meaning when she had owned it, but now that shining gold cross felt like a sign. Everything would break if she did the wrong thing. But what was she supposed to do?

That was when the man called her Mary Jean.

"I have no idea who you're talking about," she replied. She ran out the door of the church, pausing on the steps to write down the license plate number of the SUV she had seen them pull up in. She stepped into the street and hailed a taxi.

The drive lasted fifteen minutes. She got out of the taxi in front of the stately gray office building where Valerie worked. She had walked by it many times, although she had never gone in. They only ever met at the café. But today, for the first time, she pushed open those heavy glass-and-metal doors and walked to the security desk.

"My name is Margaret Jean, and I'm here to see the Manhattan DA, Valerie Mann. Please tell her it's urgent. Please tell her it cannot wait."

CHAPTER SEVENTEEN

"What happened in there?" Reyes asked when Lucky and John came out of the church and got back in the SUV. Lucky squinted in the city sunlight, too bright after the dimness of the church.

"I don't know," Lucky said, still dazed.

"I'm sure that was her," John said. "Mary Jean? Maggie Jean? I can't remember her name. Oh, it was so long ago." He wrung his hands and glanced back at Lucky. "And then she took off. Maybe it wasn't her. I don't know, I just don't know."

"Well, if you're talking about that nun who ran out, she did take down our plate number," Reyes said, starting the engine. "That's probably not a good thing. Anyway, we have to go; we're due to meet my private investigator friend in half an hour." She pulled back out into traffic and eventually the church was far behind them.

Reyes stopped the car again, this time in the parking lot of a low-rise building in the Bronx.

"Best for you to wait here," she said to John and Lucky. "Keep your fingers crossed." She got out of the car, slammed the door.

"I'm sorry," John said in the silence after she had gone. "I hope you can forgive me someday. I hope you can understand."

"I hate you for what you did," Lucky said, and it was the truth.

"But I also miss you." Her voice broke. This was the truth, too. "I have for years. And now you're here and I just—I can't do anything. I can't tell you I don't want you in my life, and I can't forgive you. Not now. I need time."

"I understand that."

They waited for Reyes in silence. She returned half an hour later.

"She traced her credit card easily," Reyes said when she got back in the car. "And it's a bit odd. Apparently she's staying at a DoubleTree not far from the camp—back in Oneonta, only about twenty minutes away from there. So, looks like we have to drive back now if we're going to find her, and figure out what she's doing holed up with that ticket. Okay with you two?"

"We have to do it," Lucky said, but she found herself thinking of the nun, and the possibility the nun knew something about her mother. There was nothing she could do about that right now, though. She could come back once she got the ticket back. If she got the ticket back.

John reached forward and turned off the radio.

"What's our plan?" he said. "We need one, for when we get to the hotel." He sounded like his old self again. Lucky was starting to get emotional whiplash, wondering who he'd be next: a doddering old man, or his calculating, smart old self?

"What if you accused her of stealing it from you, John?" Reyes said. "What if you called the police and said your ex stole your lottery ticket, and then you formally contested the win?"

"But John couldn't have been in Idaho buying a lottery ticket on the date I bought mine," Lucky said. "Because he was in prison."

"We could say it was yours, Reyes," suggested John. "And that Gloria stole it when we arrived at her camp."

"Still no good," Lucky said. "Reyes reports it stolen, there's an investigation, they look at the security camera footage at the store I bought it at and they wouldn't see Reyes, they'd see me."

"So, there's possibly a way to prove *you* bought it?" Reyes said.

"I don't know," Lucky said. "I honestly have no idea how this all works."

"Come on," John said. "Keep thinking. We need a plan."

"Blackmail," Lucky finally said. "If we can find her, I'll tell her I'm going to call the police and tell them about the fake construction jobs. I can make her believe that I recorded her. I'll make her think I'll tell the police unless she gives me the ticket."

Reyes pulled the SUV into the parking lot of the generic-looking hotel. They had found a boarding kennel for Betty. They would pick her up when this was all over, but for now, they needed to keep her out of the way, and definitely safe.

The trio walked inside and stood in the lobby, looking around at the beige walls, beige tiles, burgundy and gray couches and chairs.

"I'm going to get her room number," Lucky said. "Reyes, give me your cell phone." She turned the phone off. "Go stand by the elevator, you two. Once I get the number, I'll meet you there."

"Hi," Lucky said, approaching the concierge with an apologetic smile on her face. "I'm so sorry, but can you help me with something? I'm meeting someone here—Gloria Devereaux? And she texted me her room number, told me to come on up when I got here, except my phone died—she held the phone out in front of her, and pushed the home screen; the screen stayed blank—"so I have no idea what room she's in. Would you mind looking it up for me?"

"I'm sorry, I can't give out that information. But I could call up to her room for you and let her know you're here, Miss . . . ?"

"Shoot. Okay, sure, give her a call." The concierge lifted the receiver to dial—and Lucky caught the numbers he pressed with a quick glance: 513.

"Oh!" she exclaimed. "You know what? She's probably at the

casino. You can hang up, it's okay." He did, but Lucky heard a woman's voice saying hello just before he landed the handset back on the receiver.

She walked toward the elevator, where Reyes and John waited. There was a couple on the elevator with them. They didn't speak until they got to the fifth floor.

"Okay," John said. "Let's go over the plan one last time."

"Maybe Reyes should knock. She could say something like, 'Time for your complimentary turndown,' and then—"

"Gloria will like that. Tell her you have chocolates."

They walked down the hall while Reyes knocked. "Who is it?" came Gloria's voice.

"Housekeeping," Reyes said. "Chocolate turndown service."

"What the hell is that?" Gloria growled.

"You get a special turndown service . . . with chocolate."

"Just leave the chocolate outside the door."

"There are a few different kinds to choose from. Chocolate mints, chocolate strawberries, chocolate-covered orange peels—"

"Go away."

Silence.

"Shit," said Reyes, under her breath.

Lucky stepped forward and knocked on the door now. "Gloria? You know who this is. You have something of mine. But I have something of yours—a recording of you admitting to all those fake repairs and bilking senior citizens. I have witnesses back at the camp who are pretty upset. And I have the police on speed dial."

Still nothing.

John stepped forward. He tapped on the door. "Gloria. It's John Armstrong. Open the damn door."

A moment later, the door flew open. Gloria's hair was sticking out in all directions and her eyes were wild. "Jesus Christ, could you all just shut up?" She looked down the hall, then stood aside. "Come in. Quickly."

When they were all inside, Gloria double-locked the door.

"Who the hell are you?" Gloria asked Reyes.

"A friend," Reyes said.

"I've met the kind of friends she has," Gloria replied, nodding her head toward Lucky. "And they are truly fucked-up people."

"No greeting, Gloria?" John said. "It's been thirty years, and you don't even want to know how I've been?"

Gloria just stared at him. "Do you really think I care about that right now? I know what you're here for, and the ticket is gone."

Lucky had been looking around the room, at the clothes strewn about, the empty take-out containers. A bottle of Blue Moon was open on the dresser.

"What do you mean, gone?" John asked.

Gloria sat down on the bed and put her face in her hands. Then she looked up. "Look, I'm sorry. She got all pissed-drunk on some hundred-proof I gave her, started babbling on about winning the lottery, so after she passed out, I checked her wallet. Looked the ticket up, saw it was a winner, and I just—lost my mind a little. But when I left the camp, I didn't get very far. Some crazy bitch and her body-guard ran me off the road. They asked me what I knew about Lucky. I said, Who the fuck is Lucky?"

"That's her real name," John said. "Luciana, actually."

"Well, I know that now. They knocked me around a bit, until I told them I may not know anyone named Lucky, but I had recently met a young woman named Sarah who fit the description they were giving. And then they made me march toward the river." Gloria's voice was shaking now. "They were going to shoot me and push me in, I heard them talking about it. So, stupidly, I told them I had a winning lottery ticket that was worth a lot of money, and they shouldn't kill me. The big guy got all excited. They took the ticket from me and took off. That was it. I came here. I was too afraid to go back to the camp. I've been hiding out here ever since." Now, she looked at Lucky. "Listen, I'm sorry."

Lucky shook her head. "It doesn't matter," she said. It was over. She wasn't going to be able to get the ticket back from Priscilla. If she went anywhere near Priscilla, Priscilla would just kill her. The odds had always been stacked against Lucky, but now they were insurmountable.

"I'm going to take a walk," Lucky said.

Reyes stepped forward. "Here," she said, holding out her car keys.

"Go sit in the car. It's raining again."

"Okay. I'll be back." The lie felt worse than any of the others she had told.

Lucky walked through the lobby. When she got outside, she stood underneath the car park overhang for a minute, looking out at the rain. She forced herself to focus on the tiny glimmer of hope left, in order to keep herself moving forward. Yes, turning herself in would mean prison, but she could also tell the police everything. She could tell them about the lottery ticket, stolen first by Gloria and then by Priscilla. She could see if they'd be willing to investigate that. If she could manage to prove the ticket and therefore the money was really hers, if she could get someone to look at the footage from the Idaho gas station she had purchased the ticket at, maybe it could be held in trust until she got out of prison.

Lucky stepped forward into the rain. She walked a few steps—and saw that ahead of her in the darkness was a woman. The woman's hair was wet and her face was streaked with dirt. She was sitting on a blanket that was soaked through. She was holding a piece of card-board over her head. The words on the sign in front of her were starting to run, but Lucky could still read it: BROKE, STARVING AND SAD. A HOT COFFEE WOULD MAKE MY DAY.

Lucky reached into her pocket. She still had the bills from when she had shortchanged the cashier at the grocery store. She handed them to the woman. "Thank you," the woman said. "Bless you."

"Hey, is there a police station near here?" Lucky asked.

"Sure," the woman said. "About eight blocks down that way."

As Lucky began to walk away, a car pulled up beside her. When she heard the window roll down, she said, "Please, Reyes, it's over. Pretend this never happened. I'm turning myself in."

But when she looked up, it wasn't the white SUV at all.

"Hello," said a woman in the driver's seat. "I'm not Reyes." The woman had red hair, streaked with gray, pulled back in a low bun. Green eyes. Familiar eyes. This was the woman Lucky had seen on television back in Vegas, when she had been in the midst of conning Jeremy Gibson. It was the Manhattan DA. And her eyes—Lucky saw eyes like this in the mirror every day. All the hairs on her arms stood up.

"My name is Valerie Mann. I'm wondering if you might be willing to speak with me for a few moments."

So this was it. She was being arrested. "It's okay," Lucky said. "You don't need to cuff me. I'll go quietly."

"No." Valerie shook her head. "It's not that. I want to talk to you because . . . I think I might be your mother."

"I was sixteen," Valerie began. "I fell in love. I thought I would die without him. Now I don't even know where he is. Now he doesn't matter at all. But I've thought of you every single day. After I left you on the church steps, thinking it was for the best and you would have a better life without me, I went back to look for you. But you were already gone."

The young woman wrapped her hands around the coffee cup in front of her, but it looked like it had gone cold. She closed her eyes. She bowed her head. Her shoulders shook, and Valerie recognized that; it was the way she cried, too—silently, quickly. It was over, and the young woman looked up. Her daughter. Those eyes. "What's your name?" Valerie asked.

"Luciana," she said. "But people call me Lucky."

Valerie wanted to tell her the name she had given her that night, but it felt too soon. "I've always counted your birthdays," she said instead. "Twenty-six of them so far, right? I think I see you everywhere, and find myself constantly searching for you in the faces of strangers."

"Me too," Lucky said.

"Abandoning you was a terrible, terrible mistake. Can you ever forgive me? I would love to be able to get to know you."

"Then you'll be getting to know a criminal. I'll tell you everything, and then you can call your colleagues to come and arrest me."

"No," Valerie said. "I already know all that. I want to help you. That's not going to change, no matter what."

CHAPTER EIGHTEEN

When the coffee shop closed, they moved to Valerie's car. The windows fogged up as they kept talking, safe in their little cocoon. First, Lucky told Valerie everything about her own journey—including the story of the lottery ticket, and its theft. Then Valerie told her how she had managed to find her.

"When Sister Margaret Jean came to tell me she had seen you, I started to piece it all together," Valerie said. "I traced the license plate number she gave me, found it belonged to a Marisol Reyes, and learned who she was, and that she had just picked up John Armstrong at San Quentin. When I showed Margaret Jean a picture of John, she confirmed he was indeed the man I was looking for—the man who had taken you from the steps all those years ago. But that wasn't all there was to it. I dug deeper, and it was your involvement with David Ferguson—whose real name is Cary Matheson—that I was interested in."

"Cary. Yes. He was my partner."

"Do you know that he was the son of Joshua Matheson and Priscilla Lachaise?"

"I know Priscilla, not Joshua."

"Joshua Matheson was a drug kingpin who was killed years ago by a gang leader in California. But the theory has always been that Priscilla had him killed. She didn't deal drugs, though; she laundered money. Less messy, easier profits. But she was greedy. She started a fake charity to launder the money, but started pulling in large enough sums that someone looked into it. She went to jail, as did John and Reyes. Priscilla came out of jail claiming to be a reformed woman, but I've been investigating her for years. And I'm not the only one. Police departments across the country have been trying and failing to prove that she is still a massive money launderer with deep ties to organized crime in several states. She's been so hard to catch. Apparently she doesn't trust anyone."

"Except family," Lucky said.

"Exactly. Which brings me back to Cary. I checked in to see if there had been any John Does admitted to Nevada hospitals in the past month—and they found someone who fit Cary's description."

"Oh my God." Lucky's hand rose to her mouth, and for a moment she tried to keep her emotions in check.

"He was found badly beaten in an alley near the Bellagio. He's in a rehab facility now, and claiming he has amnesia—but I think we both know that probably isn't true. Are you okay? Here." Valerie reached into the back seat and handed Lucky a bottle of water and a tissue box.

"We know where Priscilla is," Valerie continued. "She's staying at a hotel in Syracuse."

"She stole the lottery ticket from Gloria," Lucky said.

Valerie nodded. "Meaning she's probably holed up, planning to cash it in—but she may be delaying for a few reasons: because she won't be anonymous after, and because all of her contacts will catch up with her and make her pay for her crimes."

"I have crimes I need to pay for, too," Lucky said.

"You haven't had many choices in your life. And what you've done pales in comparison. Plus, you can help us. I'm going to be able to negotiate a plea bargain if you work with us on catching Priscilla."

"I don't want to avoid punishment. It's about time I actually tell the truth and make amends for what I've done. I've wronged people, stolen from them—I've made conscious choices. I need to repay all the money I took. And then I can serve my time. Someday, maybe I can start fresh. Without any black marks to atone for."

Valerie looked at her thoughtfully. "There are different ways to pay for things. Yes, if we can get the ticket, and you can cash it in, those funds could be restitution—which is a big part of redress when it comes to crimes like this. But if you help us put Priscilla behind bars, trust me, you'll have done a lot more good for society than you realize. Are you willing to help my department with that?"

"Of course."

"And you'll help with Cary Matheson, too?"

"Yes. Him too."

Valerie had been looking out the windshield, but now she turned to Lucky. "And then, after that," she began, "we can find a way—" Her voice broke, and she reached for a tissue, but then crumpled it in her hand and swallowed her tears, in a manner Lucky recognized. She did this too. Valerie kept gazing at Lucky steadily. "I'm so sorry," she said.

"I know," Lucky said. "I believe you."

The calls would be recorded. Lucky was surrounded by police officers and FBI agents. She had a wiretap on, ready for the next steps. The phone call to Cary was the first one.

"You found me," he whispered. "Oh my God, Lucky, how did you do it?"

"When your mother told me you might be dead, I started to think, what if you weren't? I called hospitals in Nevada, and I didn't give up until I found you."

"Typical Lucky. Relentless, a survivor. I've been so scared. I'm so sorry."

"What happened?" Lucky said, reading her lines. "I thought you took off on me, but when I went to your mom's place, she let some stuff slip. She said she had done this to you—"

"That *bitch*—"

"That you had been working for her, and that you were trying to take off with some money, a lot of it. Is it true?"

"I don't think we should talk about this on the phone. Where did you say you were?"

"I'm in New York. I'm at a pay phone." One of the officers hit a button on a computer, and the sound of a bus rolling past rose in the room, then other traffic sounds, which rose and faded.

"Can you come here?" he asked. "Get a bus? Meet me here. We'll run, together. I love you so much. I've been lost without you; it's been hell. But I need you to know I would never leave you."

The lines on the page in front of Lucky blurred. Her mouth had gone dry again and she reached for her water. "I've been so worried about you. But—you lied to me. You pretended you were running the restaurant—but you were laundering money for Priscilla, weren't you?"

"Yes. I'm so sorry. I could never get away from her. I tried, but I couldn't. She had me in too deep. When she gave me the house for us in Boise, I thought maybe we could work for us a while, then get away from her somehow. It didn't work out that way, though."

"No. It didn't."

"Will you come?"

"Yes. I'll be there. It'll take me a few days, but I'll get there."

"I'm so glad you found me. Okay, I'll be waiting. I love you."

"I love you too, Cary." It caught in her throat. She *had* loved him once, so it wasn't a lie. It was possible she still did, possible she always would, no matter what her head tried to tell her heart. She didn't know yet. All she knew was that she had to keep moving, keep telling herself he was finally going to get what he deserved. That she was no longer his victim. That she never again had to be who she had been before.

Lucky hung up and sat still, composing herself. Valerie stepped forward and sat down at the table with her.

"You did great. Okay. Next step. We have a phone number," Valerie said to her. "You're clear on what you need to say to Priscilla?"

"I think so." Every time Lucky looked into her mother's eyes, she felt a jolt. It was like looking in a mirror.

"You did a good job there with Cary. What's important is clarity. Nothing can be ambiguous. With Priscilla, you need to get her to admit that she hired a hit man to beat up, or possibly kill, her son. That he was working for her, laundering money, for years. When you were in San Francisco, and then again in Boise. Okay?"

"I can do that," Lucky said. "Bluffing is a skill I have." For once, there was no shame in admitting this. She was good at this, and it turned out it was a skill that didn't always have to be used for cheating.

"Tell her to meet you at this restaurant," Valerie said, sliding a name and address across the table. "Tell her that you know where Cary is, that you went to Vegas to find him after what she told you, that he's hiding in an apartment and you'll only tell her where if she gives you what you want. Tell her that Cary has agreed to meet up with her and let her know where the money is, but say you want to negotiate. Okay?"

"Yes."

"If what we suspect is true, she'll meet you. Her life is on the line. She owes you that money. The proceeds from the lottery ticket are enough to cover it—but she has to come forward to redeem the ticket, and that means coming out of hiding."

Valerie crossed the room to speak to a collection of officers overseeing the setup of the recording devices. "Okay. We're with you."

Lucky sat silent, alone now with her thoughts—and her fears.

"Ready, Lucky? Time to move forward."

Lucky set up the meeting with Priscilla for five o'clock. *I know where Cary is. I know where the money is, too. And I'll tell you where, but we need to talk in person.* Priscilla went for it.

Now, exactly on time, Lucky walked into the restaurant and sat alone. Priscilla was late, by ten minutes, then twenty. Lucky became sure she wasn't going to show up.

But finally, Priscilla walked in. She wasn't alone. Nico, the guard from Priscilla's Place, was with her.

"Hello," Lucky said. "Thank you for coming."

"Fuck the pleasantries, Lucky. Tell me what I want to know."

"Give me back my lottery ticket."

"Tell me everything or I'll have Nico here shoot you in the head."

"We're in public. I don't think Nico is going to shoot me in the middle of a restaurant. Give me back the lottery ticket you stole from me."

"I didn't steal it from you, I stole it from that idiot Gloria."

"Who got it from me. And I want it back. If I give you the information about the money, I'm going to need that ticket. I know where it is, the money Cary owes you. And I know where he is, too. He's not dead."

"Where is the money?"

"That's what you care about? No 'Oh, my son is alive, thank God!' Where did you even get all that money? Why did Cary have it?"

"Are you stupid? He was cleaning it for me. Until he betrayed me. Now, I don't really care what happens to him, but I need that money. Or you're dead, I'm dead, we're all dead."

"Give me my ticket. I won't tell you where he is if you don't. I'll walk out of here."

"And I'll have you killed."

"You would do that? While I'm carrying your grandchild? Would you really do that, for money?"

"It's a lot of money, Lucky. I told you back in Fresno, I care about the child—but my own survival is what matters most to me."

"How much money is it?"

"Tens of millions. It wasn't just the restaurant. Cary was laundering some of it through your business, you just didn't know it."

"Who was it being laundered for?"

"I'm not going to tell you that."

Lucky wished she had a piece of paper in front of her this time, like she'd had on the phone with Cary. She was struggling to remember exactly what she was supposed to say, worrying she wasn't getting it right. "The thing is, Cary lost some of the money."

"What do you mean, *lost* some of it?"

"The money he was laundering for you," Lucky said, heart pounding. This was what they had practiced at the police station. "He had developed a betting habit. He gambled some of it away. Online. He started to get scared. He admitted that to me when I found him. He's in a rehab facility in Vegas. He was badly beaten, but survived."

"This is bullshit! You're making this up!"

"Priscilla, I think we need to start working together. I need to build a life for myself and my child. Your son is a cheat, and a liar. Cary betrayed me, he betrayed you, he betrayed both of us. Give me the lottery ticket, and I'll give you the banking information you need to get the money back, plus I'll wire you the money Cary lost from my funds. And I'll tell you where he is. We need to start trusting each other. You can't possibly know how much I hate Cary. How badly I want him to pay for putting me in this position."

"Oh, I do," Priscilla said. "I understand completely."

"Just give me the ticket you stole."

Priscilla sat still, thinking. And Lucky knew exactly what she was thinking as she reached for the large handbag beside her on the padded bench: Priscilla was thinking she would give Lucky the ticket, yes. And then Lucky would tell her everything she wanted to know. And then Priscilla and Nico would follow her, and shoot her in some alley somewhere, and take the ticket back again.

"Here you go," Priscilla said, removing a mini-safe from her bag, typing in a combination, then taking the lottery ticket out and handing it across the table to Lucky. "Now tell me where the money is. And exactly where Cary is." She slid her phone over. "You can call him from this phone. It's a blocked number. Put him on speaker. I want confirmation that he is indeed alive before you walk out of here."

Lucky looked down at the ticket. It was hers. She recognized it immediately: the numbers, and every little mark, every little rip, all the evidence of the journey she had taken with it. That journey was not over. She slipped the ticket into her pocket.

"So? Where's the money?" Priscilla demanded.

"I have no idea," Lucky said. "Turns out we're exactly alike. Both stone-cold liars who will do anything to get what they want." She stood. "Also, I'm not pregnant. I lost the baby, before we left Boise. And I'm sad about it, of course." This next part was hard, because it wasn't true; she had wanted her baby, and missed it still: the idea, the dream. Like a golden ticket. "But frankly, I'm also relieved I don't have to carry your son's child. Be the mother of the grandchild of a woman like you. You are not the kind of woman who should have progeny."

"You little bitch. You think we're going to let you go? You're dead. No matter where you go, we'll follow you; no matter what you do, we will know what it is. You'll be dead by the end of today."

"Are you threatening me?"

"You bet I am."

It happened quickly: the sudden movements, the loud noises, police rushing through the doors, the shouting, the guns.

Nico had pulled a gun and jumped up, but he didn't get the chance to use it; he was shot by a SWAT officer. He fell to the side and Lucky felt the weight of him, slumped against her. She collapsed to the floor with Nico on top of her, and for a moment she thought she might suffocate. Someone pulled him off her; she could smell the strong metallic tang of blood, reminding her of some of her worst moments. She could hear Priscilla screaming, swearing to God that she would kill Lucky someday, that it was a promise she would die to keep. Someone led her into the parking lot and she didn't have to hear the shouting anymore, the ugliness of Priscilla's words—but she knew she would never forget the things she had said.

Nico's blood was on her shirt. She was shaking.

"Is he dead?" Lucky asked. But no one answered her. She felt so alone.

But not for long. Her mother appeared in front of her. "You did such a good job, you were perfect. I'm so proud of you," Valerie said. She opened her arms, and for the first time, they held each other. Lucky's shoulders shook with the silent weight of her tears. But they were tears of joy; they were together at last.

Valerie drew back and looked into Lucky's eyes. "To answer your question, no, Nico is not dead. They're taking him to the hospital. My team is very grateful to you. Many people are. You brought Priscilla Lachaise down today. You did it. You've made a difference in the world."

Later, when Lucky was sitting in the back of a police van with a blanket around her shoulders and a warm cup of coffee in her hands, Valerie explained the process that was about to begin. Lucky was going to be placed in police custody for the time being. The lottery ticket would be kept safe. Valerie's staff had already contacted the lottery and gaming commission. Once the ticket was verified, the winnings would be held in trust while Lucky testified against Priscilla and Cary in court. Reyes and John would both be protected, that they wouldn't be charged with violating parole.

"Where are they?" Lucky asked as she held the warm coffee in both hands.

"On their way back to the city, under police escort. They're safe, and they have your dog with them. She's beautiful, by the way," Valerie said.

"Thank you. She's family."

"I understand that. But I want to be your family, too. I know you'll have some forgiving to do, and I'll want to be patient. I won't abandon you, ever. Not again. Okay? Everything is going to be fine. Trust me. I will make it all better for you. I can do that. I promise."

Second chances, third, fourth. *If we never forgave, we'd all be alone*, Reyes had said. She was right. "What about Gloria?" Lucky asked.

"That all depends on you. Do you want to press charges against her for stealing the ticket?"

Lucky shook her head. "I don't," she said. "Just let her be."

"All right, whatever you want."

What Lucky wanted was to tell Valerie she was going to change— that she was going to become a daughter Valerie could be proud of. There would be time for that, though. Time to prove who she was with actions rather than words in this brand-new life she was standing at the precipice of.

"There's something I've been wanting to tell you," Valerie said. "About back then." Her green eyes shone with emotion. "I gave you a name after I gave birth to you. I called you Julia—it was my grandmother's name. She was my pole star. To me, it's your real name. But I can't deny it: *you are Lucky*. So you should call yourself whatever you want."

From the van's windows, the city, with its bright lights and dark shadows, loomed in the distance. Her true history was there, too, woven through those streets. And the story belonged to her now. She couldn't decide yet if she felt like a Lucky or a Julia. But for the first time in her life she was sure of two things: she knew who she was, and she knew she was safe.

Acknowledgments

My gratitude begins with my mother, Valerie Clubine. This book would not exist without her, and neither would I. She encouraged me to write even on the hardest days and promised there would be no regrets. She was right. Mom, I believe in myself because you believed in me. I miss you—and I feel lucky that you were ever mine.

I'm also grateful to my steadfast agent and friend Samantha Haywood, who is simply the best; her team at Transatlantic Agency; and my film/TV agent Dana Spector at CAA, who is an absolute hustler.

Thank you to everyone at Simon & Schuster Canada, especially my excellent editor, Nita Pronovost; my delightful publicist, Jillian Levick (puffed sleeves forever!); Karen Silva, Rebecca Snoddon, Adria Iwasutiak, Felicia Quon, David Millar, and Kevin Hanson.

Lucky Armstrong stands alone, but I do not. I'm deeply grateful to my coven of writer friends—Karma Brown, Kerry Clare, Chantel Guertin, Kate Hilton, Jennifer Robson, and Elizabeth Renzetti—for always being there, even if it had to be in witchy spirit for most of this year.

Special thanks to Laurie Petrou for helping me find a patronus in Miss Piggy.

I'm also grateful to Taylor Jenkins-Reid, Colleen Oakley, Samantha Bailey, Lisa Gabriele, Hannah Mary McKinnon, and Catherine

Mackenzie for early reads and generous endorsements of a character so dear to my heart.

And to Sophie Chouinard, Sherri Vanderveen, Alison Gadsby, Kate Henderson, Nance Williams, and my many other dear friends (lucky me) who have offered support and love this year, and beyond. Without Rich Caplan's help, I would never have been able to write a convincing poker scene. (Without Ruth Marshall, I would likely not smile as often as I do.)

Without my readers, I would have very little reason to do what I do. Thank you also to the bookstagrammers and book bloggers who help get the word out and warm my heart with their bookish enthusiasm. And to booksellers far and wide: you are the very best kind of people.

Without my family, I would be lost. Thanks to my dear old dad, Bruce Stapley, for *really* loving Lucky (but refusing to choose a favorite book); my stepdad, Jim Clubine, for believing in me just as much as my mom did; the Ponikowski family; and my brothers (in order of favourites; just kidding, it's age), Shane, Drew, and Griffin Stapley.

Finally, thank you to my beautiful children, Joseph and Maia, the best characters in my life, the luckiest stars in my sky. And to Joe, for being the cheese-stuffed meatball in the spaghetti of my life. I write for many reasons—but one of them is because you make it possible with your love, support, faith, and willingness to dream with me.

About the Author

Photo by Eugene Choi

Marissa Stapley is the bestselling author of *Mating for Life*, *Things to Do When It's Raining*, and *The Last Resort*, which was shortlisted for an Arthur Ellis Award. Her journalism has appeared in newspapers and magazines across North America. She lives in Toronto with her family. Visit her at MarissaStapley.com or follow her on Twitter and Instagram @MarissaStapley.